"Author Jodie Leigh Murray will have you glued to the pages from the very start with amazing sensory stimulation. The characters are relatable and likable and are described with great visuals. With an exceptional plot and a great pace, expect some well-planned twists in The Gangster's Mistake."

Ronél Steyn for Readers' Favorite

"Author Jodie Leigh Murray has crafted a compelling tale of redemption, second chances, and the power of love amidst adversity, with a central pair that will no doubt keep romance readers engaged from start to finish. The narrative flow is filled with slick, witty moments and great characterization to show-case the attitudes and power dynamics of the game at play, and the well-developed cast of ensemble characters populates Riley's world with realism and charm."

K.C. Finn for Readers' Favorite

"By capturing the deepening of Riley and Ty's relationship, the romance is both electrifying and profoundly moving. It feels genuine and relatable and readers will find themselves rooting for their happily ever after. The author offers a poignant exploration of forgiveness and transformative love with the intricacies of human relationships, which are hard-won but worth fighting for."

Manik Chaturmutha for Readers' Favorite

The Gangster series is best enjoyed in order:

The Gangster's Daughter
The Gangster's Mistake
The Gangster's Game

The Gangster's Mistake

The Gangster's Mistake

Jodie Leigh Murray

Jodie Leigh Murray Books

Copyright notice: All rights reserved. No part of this book may be reproduced or transmitted in any form or by any means, electronic or mechanical, including photocopying and recording, or by any information storage and retrieval system, without permission in writing from the publisher.

This book is a work of fiction. Names, places, characters, and incidents are either the product of the author's imagination or are used fictitiously, and any resemblance to any actual persons, living or dead, organizations, events, or locales is entirely coincidental.

Copyright @ 2024 Jodie Leigh Murray
Cover design by Diren Yardimli

Book design by Jodie Leigh Murray

Published in the United States by Jodie Leigh Murray Books
Printed in the United States

Paperback ISBN: 978-1-968598-02-0
eBook ISBN: 978-1-968598-03-7

First edition: April 2024

Second Edition: June 2025

www.jodieleighmurray.com

Content Warning: This book contains strong language, sexual situations, stalking and harassment, drug/alcohol abuse and addiction, and mental health issues. Readers who may be sensitive to these, please take note.

For my mom:
For all the times you tell me to take a break,
And I tell you I am
. . . I'm really not.

"A writer never has a vacation. For a writer, life consists of either writing or thinking about writing."
Eugene Ionesco, Romanian-French Playwright

Chapter One

As I looked at the two-story De Luca family home, I thought of all the people here today who could easily find their wallets missing. I couldn't help it. Being a thief for so long, thoughts like these defined me, etched in my memory like a part of my DNA. Thievery was bound to me for life. These guests would go a long time before they noticed anything was missing, all of them sidetracked by the festivities happening on this joyous day.

I've been a thief since I was eight years old. Stealing at such a young age was a way of survival. My mother cared more about her next fix than she cared about me. If she couldn't get her hands on drugs, alcohol was the next best thing. There was never enough money for food, clothing, necessities, and definitely not toys or books. Stealing was a way to make sure I got fed and the lights usually stayed on, not that I decided where the money was spent. Not once.

The past was something I preferred to keep well hidden, but when my limousine pulled up through the eight-foot tall black iron gates of Regan De Luca's family's estate just north of Los Angeles, I couldn't help but to think of how out of place I felt. My life was very different now, at twenty-four, than it was when I was eight. I wasn't poor, but I wasn't wealthy. A highly skilled thief, such as myself, could easily target this house, if it weren't for the security guards.

Shit, I thought, looking around the perimeter of the front lawn. *No one's going to get past this security. Not today.* The driveway was long, under thick shady trees where cars lined the perfectly manicured lawn, attesting to the importance of the day. There were at least ten guards at the gates, and several trying not to be noticed. But I noticed. I learned at a young age to watch for the men who stood in the shadows, the way they held their hands loose and ready, and the way their heads tracked your movement even if you couldn't see their eyes under dark glasses.

Growing up in one of the poorest parts of Las Vegas, I couldn't remember ever being invited to a house of this size. I'd never owned a house, and given my history and my current job, I wouldn't. And I was fine with that.

But even an invitation to this house, on this day, was something to be coveted. Besides, robbing houses wasn't my thing. Stealing from people was. When I was younger, I could have targeted houses, but I was good at slipping through crowds. Because of my petite stature, it was easy. Why change what I was good at? That, and I could never go stealing on my own.

My life changed the second I met Cameron Moretti.

Cameron was the sole reason for me being here. He was my oldest friend—oldest being five years older than me. I had known him for just over ten years, which also made his friendship the longest lasting.

Now, he was getting married. I couldn't wrap my head around it. Eight months ago, he wasn't considering settling down. When he told me his father arranged a marriage with the daughter of an old friend, I almost peed myself laughing. Cameron hadn't been ecstatic about it, either. Until he met Regan.

Tearing my eyes away from the intimidating house, I looked down at my dress and pressed my lips together. Cassie, my roommate, therapist and best friend, all wrapped in one, insisted that I look my best for this occasion. It was something I wouldn't ordinarily do. She knew me well and knew I wouldn't put forth the effort. She prohibited dark clothing of any kind. Instead, I wore a white V-neck mini-dress with pale blue and purple flowers. Finished off with strappy wedge sandals, I felt more girly than I ever had, and it wasn't bothering me as much as I thought it would. Having Cassie in my life, I had to admit, was a blessing. She was my second oldest friend, having met her while I was in high school.

"Miss?"

I whirled at the manly voice behind me, surprised that the limousine driver was still there. It must have been several minutes since I had been staring up at the house. *Shit*, I muttered under my breath and opened my purse.

"No, no," he said quickly, watching me pull out a twenty. "Mr. Moretti instructed me to bring your luggage to Miss De Luca's house in Malibu."

"You *don't* want a tip?"

"They paid the drivers extra for our services to the guests today."

Oh. I was wondering what to do with my bags since I had just come from the airport. Hating to admit that it took me longer to decide whether to come, I had gotten on a flight just in time. I hope Cameron wouldn't notice just how late I was.

"Thank you."

"You're welcome, Miss Parker."

Paid extra indeed, I thought. *The driver knows my name. I doubt there's another person here other than Cameron who knows who I am.* And I was getting dangerously close to missing the wedding entirely if I didn't move. As I approached the doors, I half expected them to open automatically for me but they didn't. The open foyer was empty, and I stepped in with wide eyes at the gentle curve of the staircase leading to the second floor, splitting into two directions at the top.

I didn't have time to look around and hurried past an enormous living room and into a spacious ballroom where open doors led to the backyard. Walking across the shining floor, I almost wished I had on stilettos just to hear the click of them.

Gavriel De Luca had made this ballroom specifically for Regan when she was younger. Envy ran rampant through my veins. To have grown up with this much money, I couldn't even imagine. Or any money.

The day was beautiful, the sun glowing in the vast sky, void of clouds except for a few stray wisps. I could hear the hum of the crowd followed by a fading quiet, and I knew I was on the verge of missing the wedding. Despite my petite figure, my legs were long, and they carried me quickly out the doors to the poolside. The wedding was set up beyond the pool.

Hundreds of people already sat watching the couple at the altar, separated by the aisle with a blinding white runner, just as I expected. I walked down to the hedges separating the pool from the back lawn, stopping when I saw Cameron suddenly grab Regan and kiss her. *Shit, I'm too late.*

But then the gasps from the crowd started, murmurs sweeping from one side of the guests to the other. People were looking at each other, some chuckling, others in confusion. *What the hell is happening?* Swallowing a deep breath, I hurried toward the white chairs set up in perfect rows. And the people. If I walked down, every eye would be on me—the latecomer—instead of the couple. I stopped, hanging back by the hedges as Cameron pulled away from Regan and the ceremony continued.

I shook my head. Whatever had happened, Cameron never played by the rules. I stayed by the hedges and settled for watching the ceremony from here instead of drawing attention to myself by searching for an empty seat, convinced there wasn't one to begin with.

From this distance, I could hardly hear anything, but I could see clearly enough. I envied the two people at the altar, Cameron with his dark hair and black tuxedo and Regan, although I hadn't met her yet, with her pale golden hair styled perfectly and hanging down her back. From what I could see, her gown was exquisite. Jealousy hit me with ferociousness. Marriage was something I was positive would never happen for me. I had too many issues with men. And trusting them. But that didn't mean I couldn't dream that someday it would happen.

Only in my dreams would I live in a house like this, in a neighborhood like this, and associate with people like this. These were wealthy people. I would never be part of this crowd. How I fit into Cameron's life was something I had never quite understood, but after I tried to rob him, he caught me and wouldn't let go. He never told me why.

It was my belief that it was because I was only thirteen. He was eighteen, on the cusp of adulthood and living his life to the fullest, in downtown Vegas on a business errand for Reno. When he suddenly snatched my wrist and saw the fear in my eyes, something that had only happened once before, I think he knew I needed his help.

Instead of calling the cops, he gave me his phone number and told me to call him whenever I needed help, or whenever I needed something. I was so scared that my mother's adopted son would find the number; I memorized it and swallowed the paper like a piece of gum. I hadn't needed to contact Cameron until my grandmother took me and my little sister, Ivy, out of my mother's care five months later, and that was only to tell him I had moved away from Las Vegas.

Clapping roused me from my memories. Cameron and Regan were walking up the aisle toward me. I scrambled to the shadows next to the pool while they walked to the reception area. Tents covered the other half of the lawn, providing shade for tables set with sparkling glasses and impeccable China. A DJ booth and a large, makeshift dance floor sat beyond tables. I wasn't sure I had ever seen a party this big before. Patiently, I waited while swarms of people moved from the ceremony to the reception before I swallowed deep breaths and finally moved.

I was comfortable sliding through crowds, but these people were daunting. They *looked* rich and there were way too many of them. I waited for the crowds to reach the reception area before slipping in behind the last of them.

My eyes scanned the crowd for Cameron. *Stupid. He's busy with his guests. He doesn't have time to soothe my nerves right now.* I would need to make do on my own and hopefully strike up a conversation with someone at my dinner table.

"Excuse me."

Without moving my head, my eyes snapped over to a curly, blonde-haired woman on the arm of a guy almost a head taller than her. There was a bounce in her step, causing my lips to twitch at the urge to smile.

"You're Riley," she announced. "Riley Parker."

The declaration stunned me for a moment. How could she possibly know who I was without ever speaking to me before now? I couldn't imagine. I didn't recognize either of them. Did I look obvious? Did I look like I didn't belong here? Suddenly self-conscious, I glanced at the guy on her arm. He gave me an apologetic smile.

"How do you know that?" I asked slowly.

As they stopped in front of me, she extracted herself from him and thrust out her hand. "I'm Tatum. This is Alex."

I looked at him again, wondering if he could be one of those boyfriends who allowed his girlfriend to speak on his behalf. From what Cameron had told me of the pair, they met around the same time he had met Regan. It seemed they were about as evenly matched.

Alex smiled, holding out his hand and meeting my gaze as though he were looking deep into my soul. "Please tell me she's right, and you're Riley."

A nervous laugh escaped from me. "She's right. I'm not sure I want to know how she knew it, but she's right."

So it begins. It took me a moment to stare at his outstretched hand before I slipped my hand into his. I couldn't escape people today. Normally, I wasn't shy around people. I wasn't a shy person.

I was a *guarded* person. Especially around men. This many rich people, all at once, intimidated me.

"Tate is always right."

A grunt escaped from him as she gave him a slight elbow to the side on her way to linking her arm with mine, wasting no time in pulling me toward the tents.

I can do this, I reminded myself.

"You're staying with us. Get to know us," she casually said, leading me down across the cushy lawn. She glanced down at my wrist, slightly turned toward me but visible.

"Interesting tattoo."

"A gift to myself when I was eighteen."

"What's it mean?"

My eyes lifted to meet hers. At that moment, I couldn't recall ever having met someone like Tatum. Her energy was stunning. "It's a reminder that my story is not over yet. Life will continue despite my struggles."

She said nothing else about my tattoo, no comments or questions following. For that, I was relieved. The tattoo hadn't been a mark to draw questions about my past. It was truly as I explained. It served as a reminder. *My* reminder.

Guests stood in groups talking with others, not paying attention to Tatum and me walking in with Alex trailing behind us. This was much better than walking into the wedding ceremony late and having all eyes on me.

"It will be nice to meet Cameron's family. Finally. And Regan."

Alex's voice drifted from behind us. "Stay away from Stefan. Peter and his wife are around somewhere. And Zoey is probably steering clear of family."

As we came closer to the party, I counted to maintain my breathing. The crowd looked more intimidating the closer I was. Tatum must have sensed my distress. She pulled me slightly closer as we strolled. *One, two, three ...*

"Okay?"

"Fine," I whispered when Cameron came into view. "Just one of my struggles."

Closer this time, he made a dashing figure in his black tuxedo. As soon as he spotted me, his mouth curled into a devilish grin. Even from this far, I could see the happiness etched on his face.

With his hand cupping Regan's elbow, he cut off whomever they were speaking to and met us at the edge of the tent.

"Riley."

I hadn't seen him since before last summer when he traipsed off to his house on Cape Haven, an island off the coast of South Carolina. In the years I had known him, I'd never seen a light like this in his eyes. Abruptly, Cameron pulled me away from Tatum and hugged me tightly. I felt the tension ease away as soon as he had his thick arms around me. I felt safe. In so many ways, Cameron was almost like a brother to me.

When he stepped back, his arms slipped back around his new wife. Regan was even more stunning up close with her bluish-green eyes. Brides were supposed to be beautiful. She was more than beautiful. And the light in her eyes matched Cameron's perfectly.

"Riley, this is Regan. Regan—"

She pulled me into her arms so fast the breath whooshed out of my lungs. I had never met two people more suited for each other than Cameron and Regan. She was as strong as he was, but I knew that already by the way she had taken matters into her own hands over the phone yesterday when Cameron found out I hadn't confirmed my invitation or booked a flight yet. When she pulled away, I could see the sparkle of a tear in her eye.

"It means so much to us you're here. We are so happy you'll be staying with us for a few days."

"I'm surprised you aren't taking a honeymoon."

"We were married in January," Cameron said. "In secret because I couldn't wait. And because she was in danger. This is just to satisfy Gavriel's girlfriend, and everyone who was planning on attending."

I laughed. "Shit, Cameron."

He shrugged. "Anyway, we're happy to spend some time with you."

"Only a few days. I have to get back to work."

"You have to tell me all about it," Regan said. "When Cameron told me you steal back stolen dogs, I couldn't believe it. I almost didn't. I have so many questions to ask you."

"Yes!" Tatum shouted, even though she stood right next to us. "Tell us what it's like. It sounds fascinating."

A nervous laugh escaped. "I've rescued dogs when the need is there. That's not all I do." But Regan was right. I was stealing back stolen dogs, all the same. On the side.

"If you need anything, you tell us. We've got your back," Regan said.

During our interchange, Cameron was whispering to Alex. I couldn't help but wonder what the secrecy was until I noticed another guy join our group. He looked like a younger version   of Cameron. He was slightly shorter, just slightly, and had a lighter shade of brown hair.

The way he looked at me, studied me, was unnerving. He extended his hand.

"Stefan Moretti."

Behind him, I saw Alex roll his eyes dramatically when Stefan took my hand in a hearty handshake. Stefan's eyes remained on me, and I couldn't help but get an odd feeling that the warning Alex had provided would be easily something I could do. The feeling I got from the way he looked at me gave me the creeps.

"Riley," I said.

He tilted his head. "Has anyone told you that you have a striking resemblance to our-"

"Stefan, leave it alone," Cameron snapped.

While Cameron faced off with his brother, I couldn't help but notice the animosity between them. He pointed his finger into

Stefan's chest with a snarl. "Stay away from Riley. She's not for you."

Stefan only laughed, strolling away with the sound wafting behind him.

What the hell. Shivers danced on my skin. *His laugh is almost like . . . No, I won't think about that today.* Cameron offered me an apologetic smile, curling his arm around Regan's waist.

Tatum leaned toward me. "We're going to get drinks. We'll see you later, Riley."

"I'm truly envious of you," I said, shaking off the interchange. Cameron had nothing to worry about. I'd steer clear of Stefan. "You both look so happy."

"We are, and I'm sure you'll find someone who can make you just as happy."

As much as I wanted to believe Cameron, I wasn't looking for someone here. This wasn't somewhere I fit in. I didn't want to fit in here. Still, I offered him a small smile. It wouldn't kill me to mingle for a while and get a ride back to Regan's condo.

He leaned toward me. "Not him, though."

I nodded. After hearing Stefan's laugh, I was safe from falling prey to his charms.

"Cameron, are you going to introduce me?"

The deep voice strolling up behind Cameron and Regan belonged to a man slightly taller than Cameron with the same shade of dark hair, graying at his temples. Instead of Cameron's translucent blue eyes, his eyes were brown. Both of them were extremely handsome in their tuxedos. Next to him was a mousy woman, who smiled at those wandering about around us until she finally centered her attention on me.

I watched her eyes widened and her smile falter. Her arm withdrew from the man and she took a step back. *What an odd way to greet someone*, I thought. It almost seemed like someone had slapped her in the face.

"I must excuse myself," she said with an air of superiority in her whimsical voice. "I see an old friend I must greet."

While she removed herself from our circle, I looked at Cameron while he exchanged a look with the man. I wondered what that was all about. Then I thought maybe this was normal with them. I didn't need my private investigative skills to tell me about Cameron's family and their black market dealings.

"My father Reno," Cameron finally said. "And that was my mother, Orianna."

Reno stared at me as though he were studying every detail of my face, much like Stefan had done. His mouth was slightly open, as though he was at a loss for words. It was my fervent hope he wasn't recognizing me from my sleazy past. He snapped his mouth closed and extended his hand.

I slid my hand into his, gripping his hand just as hard. "Riley Parker."

"Good to meet you, Miss Parker. Are you from here?"

"No, no . . . I live in Seattle. And you can call me Riley."

I looked curiously at Reno. As Cameron's father, I knew it would be easy to be around him. He seemed like a good-natured man. Like Cameron, one probably didn't want to be on his bad side. Being around people of wealth and power, Cameron aside, caused me higher anxiety than I wanted to admit.

"It was good of you to come," Reno said. "Cameron tells me you rescue dogs. Could I interest you in a drink?"

"Steer clear of Stefan," Cameron added, leaning into me and causing me to laugh.

Cameron and Regan strolled away to greet other guests, leaving me alone with Reno.

When Reno picked up my hand and tucked it in the crook of his elbow, I was stunned for a moment. The men in Cameron's family were very formal and highly protective, I noted. He led me toward one of the ten bars situated around the area. Whoever planned this wedding was not about to allow guests to wait long for a drink.

"I am inclined to agree with Cameron," he said, stopping us at the end of the bar and catching the attention of the bartender with a mere wave of his fingers. "I love all of my children, but Stefan is what you would call a . . ."

"Womanizer?"

He smiled. "If she walks and talks, she's for him."

I smiled.

Reno laughed. "What can I get you to drink?"

"Tea, please."

"Long island?"

"Iced tea, or sweet tea. I don't drink."

With an incline of his head, Reno gave his order to the bartender. The lull gave me the chance to look around the classy reception. Although the number of guests was overwhelming, most of them were still speaking in groups and I could relax. Servers dressed formally laid out salads to begin the dinner service.

A jolt shot through me, causing my body to jerk, when I swore I saw a server across the tent that looked exactly like David. My mother's adopted son, even though the adoption had never been legalized. The breath caught in my throat, my hand flying to my throat. He was supposed to be in prison. The last time I checked, he was.

"What is it? Are you okay?"

I waved my hand in front of my face. "I . . ."

It must be a hallucination. The possibility of David being out of prison and working as a server at a highly guarded event such as this was virtually impossible. It's unlikely that they would hire a felon to be a server at this wedding. Not by the Moretti and De Luca families. With the heightened security at the event, they would have heavily scrutinized anyone working here today. David was serving a prison sentence for possession of drugs with intent to distribute. It was impossible for them to have released him yet.

Abandoning our drink order, Reno guided me over to the

closest empty chair and eased me down while he looked around. He looked panicked. I centered all my thoughts on breathing steadily while I stared at the edge of the tent where I could have sworn I had seen David, convinced my eyes had played a trick on me. I could see no sign of the server now.

"What brought that on, if you don't mind my asking?" Reno asked.

"I think it's how many people are here."

Reno wasn't buying my lie. I couldn't blame him. He didn't know me, but I'd never been very good at lying. No one had to know about David. Not even Cameron.

"You can tell me, you know."

My eyes snapped to his, then softened. "It's all good."

"You'll sit at my table for dinner." He waved over a woman server, giving him orders to move around some place settings. "Cameron told me about two boxers you rescued in Fresno. Is it true one of them refused to move?"

His kindness at changing the subject, averting my sudden panic, was admirable. Even the way he effortlessly changed seating arrangements to make room for me was kind.

"Boxers," I said with a shaky laugh. "They look so mean and scary, but they're huge babies. I appreciate you offering a seat at your table, Reno, but your table is for family. I can find another place to sit."

He smiled. "You'll sit at my table, and I'll not hear another word otherwise. It seems you're good at what you do. Besides, Cameron thinks very highly of you."

Like Cameron, you couldn't argue with Reno. *Must run in the family*, I noted. After he retrieved our drinks, he handed me my tea and guided me by my arm again to one of the two family tables. Since there was no wedding party, there was no head table.

"Miss Riley Parker, this is one of my closest and oldest friends, Gavriel De Luca."

I offered my hand to the distinguished-looking man. With a

liberal sprinkling of gray, his dark hair was complemented by a dapper little mustache. Now, I wasn't innocent enough to know that I wasn't in the company of notorious gangsters. Gavriel had quite the reputation in California, while Reno had his in Nevada. They kept their family names out of the mouths of the legal system, but they were not innocent of a lot of criminal activities. I wasn't one to talk, though. Thievery was only one of my criminal activities, much to my shame.

"Very nice to meet you, Mr. De Luca."

"Gavriel," he said. "It's a pleasure to meet you. And this is my wife, Isabel."

This ordinarily would have been the reason for panicking, meeting these people all at once, but they charmed me almost instantly. Regan was almost the spitting image of her mother, except Isabel had a deep tan and blonde hair swept up beautifully.

"It is so nice to meet a friend of Cameron and Regan's. I've heard you'll be staying with them for a few days," she said.

"Yes, just a few days before I have to get back to work."

"And what is it you do, Miss Parker?" Gavriel asked, pulling out a chair for Isabel to sit.

Being truthful to a known gangster had me biting my tongue between my teeth. No way would I admit I was a junior private investigator with a degree in criminal justice. If Cameron hadn't told them, I wouldn't offer it. "I rescue dogs. Dogs stolen either for resale or for dog fighting rings."

"Ooooh!" Isabel shrieked. "That's amazing! It must be so exciting."

Reno pulled out a chair for me and as soon as I sat down, it appeared the rest of the table had already filled. It wasn't a large table, and I had a feeling the sudden change in seating arrangement had misplaced someone. The table next to it contained the rest of Cameron's siblings.

At the same time I slid a glance toward Zoey, her eyes met and locked with mine. My lips parted. Her perfect straight, shoulder-length jet black hair added to her exquisite beauty.

There was no further sign of David, as I originally thought, but I was watching. Carefully. After a few days, I would be home. But in the meantime, I needed to do some digging to make sure David was still in prison. If he had gotten out, I would need to be extra vigilant. Prison was the only thing keeping him away from me.

Chapter Two

I pulled my stuffed dog closer to me, burrowing further into the threadbare blankets. I was grateful we didn't live in one of the colder states. Southern Nevada was usually warm enough, although in the winter months the nights could get chilly. Absently, I rubbed the worn fabric of Bobo against my nose. It was my most prized possession, even at thirteen years old. My grandmother bought it for me when I was a toddler. Naomi was choosy about what she bought for me, knowing that everything usually disappeared. Rubbing it against my nose was something I did to comfort myself, but as I slowly opened my eyes, I wondered why I was doing it now.

My small corner of the room was dark, but there was light coming from the hallway. I rubbed my eyes, shifting until I faced the door to see why there was a light. And then I saw him, and ice ran frigid through my veins. He didn't look at me like he had when I was a kid.

David. Most of my life, I believed he was my brother until Naomi told me he was not my mother's son. He was a boy that one of Simone's boyfriends had abandoned before she had gotten pregnant with me. It was a relief to know, but now I wasn't sure it was a good thing, the way he was looking at me.

Pulling the blanket up to my chin, I shrank back into the lumpy mattress while he leaned against the doorjamb. My little sister, Ivy, slumbered without disruption beside me while David continued to gaze at me with his steely blue-gray eyes. Dread washed over me, knowing I'd need to get up even though it hadn't been but a few days since we'd gone out. For once, I wanted to sleep and not need to worry.

Fear had its way of knifing through me whenever he came to the room, waking me up to go out and steal. Anxiety about when I would get caught again, or when a misstep would make him angry. And what was worse was the fact that I was growing up.

The way he was looking at me was far more frightening than when he was angry with me. Abruptly, he pushed away from the door and walked into the room, glancing around before his eyes came back to rest on me.

He stopped when he was hovering over my makeshift bed on the floor, looking down at me. I knew I was changing. I was getting older. My body was developing even though I didn't want it to. There was nothing I could do to stop David when he wanted something. He would make me do things by threatening something I cared about, or just threatening me.

"Get up," he said. "We're going out."

He turned and left before I could say anything. He knew I wouldn't say a word in dispute. When I sat up, I looked down at my stuffed dog. This one was my favorite because I couldn't have a real dog. It was missing its eyes because David had pulled them out when he was angry at me the first time I refused to go. I picked it up; the head lolling to the side because David had ripped the head off the first time I got caught stealing. I never got caught after that. I had to steal the sewing kit to sew Bobo's head back on. It was the one and only time I had stolen something other than someone's wallet.

I tucked Bobo in with Ivy. At only six, I often shared Bobo with her. Naomi had long since been forbidden from seeing me and Ivy after she had a vicious argument with my mom, which meant we didn't get any new clothes or things like toys. We had barely anything. I had no watch or clock to see what time it was.

We lived in squalor because my mother would get fired from any job she could get. She didn't have to steal like David and I did, but I knew she did bad things to get money. Things that made Ivy and I have to sleep in the living room sometimes, on a couch with many cigarette burns in it. I didn't need to get dressed, learning to sleep in my clothes most of the time. I couldn't trust anyone in this house. Only Ivy.

I darted a glance at Simone's bed, where she laid haphazardly on her stomach with one leg hanging off the side of the bed. She slept where she fell, oblivious to anything that was going on around her. Her latest loser boyfriend must be out for the night. I left the room, closing the door and tiptoeing down the hallway. I scoffed at my stupidity. Simone never heard us sneaking out.

David was waiting for me in the tiny living room that joined the equally tiny dining room. The lower-level townhouse we lived in was not in the best neighborhood, but it kept us sheltered. He jerked his chin toward the door and we stepped outside into the warmth of the Vegas night without a word.

I felt his hand at the small of my back, guiding me down the street. "You know what happens if you get caught."

"I know, David."

There was bitterness in my voice. I couldn't help it. I was tired. All I wanted was to be asleep in my bed, since it was a rare night when Simone didn't have a man in our room. I didn't want to be out in the streets looking for people to lift money from. Getting caught and the threat of being arrested had scared me more than anything in my life. It wasn't something I cared to repeat, but David wouldn't let me stop. I was his minion. Without me, he would go nowhere in life. I was small enough to sneak my way in, blending in nicely with crowds because of my petite size, and no one would notice.

I would have no way of knowing that night would be such a pivotal night for me. It was the night I tried to pick-pocket

Cameron Moretti. And got caught.

◆

The sunrise from Regan's deck in Malibu rivaled the sunrise in Seattle from Cassie's deck. Regan and Cameron's in California was on the beach while Cassie's front deck faced the bay and the back deck faced Mount Rainier. Gorgeous views all around.

It was mornings like these I took the time to appreciate my life and how far I've come. I glanced down at my wrist tattoo. There was nothing I would change, except the possibility of sharing these mornings with someone. Out of the few guys I'd dated, none of them worked out to be anything close to a relationship. My invisible wall was high and thick. That, and I never knew when I would need to pick up and leave if David found me.

The door to the deck opened, but I kept my eyes on the horizon and my hands around my mug of coffee. It was chilly outside, but not so much that I needed a jacket like I would this time of year at home. Steam rose from my coffee, and I would have smelled the deep aroma if I wasn't already enjoying the smell of the salty tang of ocean in the air mixed with the earthy scent of the beach.

"Did you have a good time last night?"

Cameron slid into the chair across from me, setting his mug down on the table. I was sure that we hadn't slept for more than a few hours. Much to my surprise, I had stayed at the wedding reception until after midnight and hitched a ride back to Regan's with Cameron, Regan, and my two new friends, Alex and Tatum.

A yawn escaped. "I did. I'm surprised you're up already."

"I'm an early riser no matter what time I get to bed." He

picked up his mug and took a tentative sip before setting it down again. "I don't like to bother Regan. She needs the sleep. Why are you up so early?"

"I'd still be in bed, but I love sunrises."

He stared at me. Was it strange that I loved sunrises? I loved sunsets just as much, but there was something about sunrises that captivated me. The way he was looking at me was strange, like he wanted to say something. I raised my eyebrows.

"Regan's pregnant."

It was a good thing I wasn't still holding my coffee. The revelation momentarily stunned me. A lot had happened in their relationship in the last eight months since they'd met. As a daughter and only child of a gangster, Regan had been in danger the entire time.

Cameron looked like he couldn't possibly be happier. Jealousy struck me again. My little sister was the closest I would get to having a child of my own.

"Are you happy?"

The grin that curled his lips was enough of an answer. "She told me yesterday during the ceremony. Guess she couldn't wait. And I'm glad she didn't."

"That's what was going on!" I wondered how many other people knew why Cameron had kissed Regan in the middle of their wedding ceremony because she had spilled the news of their impending parenthood to him. "And how far along is she?"

"Three months. She's extra tired lately, but I'm not sure if that's from her recent ordeal or the pregnancy. Either way, I don't want to disturb her." He shook his head, looking out at the ocean as though he was deep in thought.

I could tell by the light in his eyes what he was thinking. You didn't know someone for as long as I had known him without knowing what was going on behind his light blue eyes.

"You're done for," I whispered.

He looked at me. "What do you mean?"

"She's wrecked you, my friend. There isn't anything in this world you wouldn't do for her. Anything you wouldn't give her. You love her that much."

"Fuck yes, I do," he muttered. "I almost lost her . . ." His voice broke. "That bastard had a gun right at her, and it didn't faze her."

"And you?"

"I couldn't have done anything. There were too many of them and too many of us. It would have been a bloodbath had anyone pulled the trigger."

"What are you going to do now?"

He shrugged, picking up his coffee again and cradling it in his hands. "We're going to head to Cape Haven for a while. Regan loves it there, and after all this stress, she needs the relaxation. We'll be gone for a while. A month, maybe more."

"You deserve it, Cam. She deserves it." I leaned over, cupping my hands over his. "I'm happy for you. And I adore her. You're a lucky man."

"You know, I have this friend."

"No! Nope. Don't want to know any friends, brothers, or anything. I'm good."

"You can't be alone forever."

"Just because you're happily married doesn't mean I need to be."

Cameron sat back with a laugh. "Someday, Riles, you're going to get caught. I didn't think for a minute I would fall in love. I couldn't have stopped it if I wanted to. It'll happen to you."

I wouldn't have believed it if I didn't know him so well. A year ago, Cameron wouldn't have considered settling down with one woman. I didn't think any of the women he had dated deserved him. He must have known it, too, because he was never with any of them longer than six months. Prior to Regan, he'd been single for several months after his last model girlfriend—

who was shallower than a parking lot puddle.

"Do you have to go back to work so soon? Can't you stay longer?"

A sigh slipped from my lips. "Unavoidable. I wish I could tell you I'd stay longer, but you have an island to escape to."

"You know damn well we'd wait. Both of us would much rather spend more time with you before you head home."

"If we weren't short on people, you know I would. Two more days is my limit, Cam."

His lower lip stuck out like a petulant child. "You never take time for yourself."

True. I'd never taken more than a few days for myself. Never in my life had I taken a full week's vacation other than traveling for side jobs. My career wasn't high paying, and I was barely skating by on what I had. An actual vacation wasn't in my plans for a long time.

I was only here because I could afford the plane ticket. I didn't have to pay for a hotel, food, or rides. The money I earned from my job was enough, and I would never resort to being a pickpocket again.

"You'll come out to the island to visit sometime, right?"

Guilt for not fessing up to him since I didn't have that kind of money gnawed at me. A plane ticket to South Carolina was probably more than I could afford, not to mention a ferry ride to the island. It might take a while of saving, but I would figure it out. Picking up an extra job wasn't an option. Being a junior private investigator had me doing the dull tasks like reviewing cases and writing reports. Not to mention shadowing senior private investigators like my boss, Maria, and performing my own smaller undercover investigations. And sometimes it took weeks. Not accommodating for a part-time job.

It was bad enough I needed to take time off when someone called me to track down a stolen or missing dog, which had happened. What Maria didn't know and could get me fired was I'd used company equipment and programs to help track down those dogs. There were only a few occasions, the first time having been for an old friend missing her two boxers, but word got around and damn if I hadn't been called to do it again after that.

"Visiting an island where I can lie on the beach for hours? I can't wait. It won't be soon, I hope you know. You and Regan need your time with no one hanging around."

"Regan and I are making Cape Haven our permanent home."

That brightened my mood. From what Cameron had told me about the island, it was a slice of heaven on earth.

"That's wonderful! Maybe I will come for a visit."

He looked me in the eye. "I'm counting on it, Riles."

There wasn't a day that didn't go by since that night I found my tiny wrist seized in the large hand of Cameron Moretti that I wasn't grateful he had caught me. Sometimes I think back to that night and surmise it must have been fate that brought us together. There were few people in my life I could count on to save me from trouble. Cameron was one of them. He'd never hesitated to put someone in their place for me if he had to.

If only the younger me had known that. I would have called him the night I stabbed my mother's boyfriend instead of relying on David. David not only had me in his pocket, he had stalked me for years after Naomi took us away from Simone. At least he's behind bars now, and we've securely hidden ourselves where he won't be able to locate us.

Chapter Three

My mistake, while walking through the parking garage at Sea-Tac airport, was paying more attention to my phone than my surroundings. It wasn't a good thing to do when walking alone, even in broad daylight. I knew better, even when I heard the car pass me and stop. I was too interested in the debriefing email from the agency about the biggest case we had undoubtedly received to date. Someone tipped off that a popstar's missing dog, worth over ten thousand dollars, was spotted here in town.

Approaching my old Jeep, I slipped my phone back into my pocket and stopped dead in my tracks at the steak knife sticking out of the front tire. The black handle stared back at me while terror struck me down like a bolt of lightning. My legs lost feeling, and I stumbled, crashing against the cold metal. My bag slipped from my shoulder, landing with a thump behind my Jeep while I pressed my body close to the car. A white piece of paper fluttered in the breeze under the driver's side windshield wiper.

Reading what was on that piece of paper had my heart thundering like mad in my chest as I reached for it, but I needed to see . . . needed to know. My hand shook as I slipped it out, ripping the corner while I did so. I couldn't breathe, unfolding it to see the black ink scrawled across it. "Nice try, *Alexis*. Looks like you aren't the only one who can put a steak knife to good use."

Crumpling the piece of paper in my fist, I fought for air. *David.* He found me. He found us. My body slid to the cold, hard cement on my hands and knees. While my heart thundered in my chest, I wondered with fear if he was watching me while I read the note. If he knows I'm here, does he know where we live?

Through the buzzing in my ears, I heard a car rolling slowly by, followed by the screech of brakes. Even after I heard the slam of a car door and footsteps coming closer, I was paralyzed and unable to get up, still struggling to catch a full breath.

"Miss?" I heard behind me. "Miss, are you okay?"

I held up my hand, still on my knees, trying to gain control of my panic attack. If airport security was here, I was safe. For now. He kneeled beside me, a man dressed like security with a thick midsection. My focus remained on the tag on his shirt, stating he was security while I counted, regaining control of my breathing and my heartbeat.

"Miss?"

I crawled back until I sat on my haunches, taking a few deep breaths. "Someone put a knife in my tire," I said. "Can you help me change it?"

Worry marred his bushy brown eyebrows while he squatted next to me, but he nodded and stood. I waited for him to go to his cruiser before I stood up, keeping my back pressed to the driver's side door.

"Who would put a knife in your tire?" he asked, coming back with a car jack. He set it down next to the tire and looked at the tire. "A steak knife? What the-"

"Can you help me or not?"

"Sure, sure." He started jacking up the car while I went around the back, kicking aside my bag to get the spare tire. "Looks like someone wanted to make a statement. Are you sure you're okay?"

"I'm fine," I said, yanking off the tire and rolling it to him. "I work for a small PI firm. This is probably someone who we helped bust. Not a big deal."

Playing it off like nothing happened helped keep my breathing normal while helping him change the tire maintained my focus on something other than being watched, even if in the back of my mind it was there. The need to get home hastened my movements.

Once the tire was changed and the man graciously took the steak knife to dispose of, I slid into the driver's seat and locked the door. I drew my hands up onto the steering wheel and pressed my forehead to my wrists while I gathered my thoughts. After a minute I lifted my head and looked out at the drizzling rain.

Alexis . . . No one called me that except Simone and David. When Naomi took me and Ivy out of Simone's house, she called us Riley and Hannah Parker. Parker was her name before she married my grandpa Gus, who passed away before we could meet him. From that day forward, she never referred to us as Alexis and Ivy. I didn't understand why until David found me the first time. She helped me officially change it after I turned eighteen, from Alexis Monroe to Riley Parker. No one else knew me by that name, and no one else would.

Ivy would need to wait another year to become Hannah officially.

I glanced down at my wrist, my fingers tracing the curves of the black ink. Setting my jaw, I threw the shifter of my Jeep into gear and left the parking garage behind me, uncertain when David would find me again. And uncertain what I would do now.

◆

"Tell us everything" were the words that greeted me before I got through the back door.

Gus and Gatsby greeted me with wagging tails and bumps against my legs, their way of getting my attention without jumping on me. Hannah wasn't home from school yet, but it wouldn't be long before she was.

We moved to Seattle seven years ago when I was a junior in high school, after David found me the last time. The house we lived in belonged to Cassie's dad, Lex Edwards, who was a drummer in a rock band. We didn't always live here, though.

When Cassie's mother, an actress, had overdosed when she was fifteen, no one was there to care for her. Lex was in the middle of a tour, unable to make it back for his daughter. My uncle Ricky had been friends with Lex for most of their lives, so when Cassie's mom died, Lex called Naomi to ask for her to take in Cassie. We moved from Fresno to Los Angeles at the insistence of Lex to live in his empty house.

Rarely did Lex Edwards come here to his Seattle residence, gladly providing a permanent residence for his only daughter and the woman who had saved his ass by taking her in when he needed her the most. I grew up with no father, never knowing who my father was, while Cassie grew up with an absentee father. We were only a couple of years apart in age. It didn't take us long to become friends.

Gus and Gatsby followed on my heels into the open concept kitchen and living room. The focal point of the living room, aside from the giant windows facing the bay, was the enormous fireplace with rocks embedded from floor to ceiling.

Cassie eyed me over the back of the ivory sectional. Her dark blonde hair was thrown up in a messy bun, yet always looked like every wisp was exactly where it should be. We couldn't be more opposite.

It didn't matter how many times she tried to get me to care about how I looked. I preferred a pair of leggings and a t-shirt that was three times too big, cut off at the neckline so it was always half-way falling off one shoulder. My dark hair was always tossed in a ponytail, but it never looked as good as Cassie's messy bun. I wore Doc Marten boots almost every day, sometimes I was in such a hurry I forgot to put on socks. My dress for the wedding was about as far from my daily ensemble as it could be.

My oversized bag slid off my shoulder, landing on the floor, tugging my bulky shirt half-way down my arm when I crouched down to talk to the boys again. They still eagerly danced around my legs. They were all our dogs as much as they were mine, but they were mine mostly because they helped with my anxiety. All four of us took care of them, Cassie and Naomi taking the brunt of it when I was working for an extended amount of time, and while Hannah was at school.

Despite my inability to lie, I wished I could tell her I had a horrible time at the wedding and days following. But I had a wonderful time with Cameron and Regan, along with Tatum and Alex. It was as though I had a newfound family in California.

Regan, Tatum and Alex had made me feel like they had known me for years, like Cameron had when we first met. I escaped my problems for a few days. Something that I could rarely do. Not with David lurking.

"Come on, Riles," Naomi said, her whimsical voice matching her hippie-like persona. "Don't leave us hanging here."

I laughed. "The boys haven't seen me for days. Let me give them some love first."

Once my face was satisfactorily wet with dog kisses, I finished my journey to the living room with the boys right behind me. Naomi, with her bright multi-colored peasant shirt and a pair of bright red baggy pants, sat on one end of the sectional with her legs tucked up against her to the side.

I bent down to kiss her cheek before plopping down on the couch beside her. Cassie sat curled up across from us, in her classic skinny jeans and a baggy white sweater. A mug of steaming tea held firmly between her hands. I rolled my eyes. Cassie always took the healthy way. She gave up on trying to convince me to do the same.

"I don't have long," I said. "Maria called and wants me to come into the office as soon as I can. I'd like to see Hannah when she gets home first, though."

Naomi's eyebrows cinched together, adding more wrinkles to her already wrinkled face. Smoking for years had aged her. That, and she loved to garden and didn't care for sunscreen. Both had taken its toll on her skin.

"They can't be serious! You just got back!" she said.

"I'm pretty sure she wouldn't have asked if it wasn't important. It's not a big deal. Maybe she has an assignment for me."

Cassie tentatively sipped her tea. "You heard about Ellie Varro's dog, Queenie."

"That was a few days ago. I'm sure they have someone already working on it." *Which is good for me, so it buys me some time to figure out this issue with David, and how to get out of it,* I added silently.

"But you're the best at finding dogs," Cassie said, earning her my fiery look.

"Maria doesn't know I've been doing that," I reminded her. "And she won't know if I can help it."

I hadn't been with the private investigation agency long, having only graduated last year with my degree in criminal justice, which is why I was only a junior investigator and never assigned big cases. This was a big case. I doubted Maria would let me in on it.

"They'd be idiots if they didn't assign you to it," Naomi murmured.

"How did she lose her dog?" I wondered.

"Someone broke into her dressing room while she was doing a show," came Hannah's musical voice from the hallway a second before the backdoor clicked shut.

Gus and Gatsby made a mad dash for Hannah, nails clicking on the hardwood floors as they ran toward her. A minute later, her angelic face appeared around the corner. Her hair was much lighter and shorter than mine was. We had the same mother but practically none of the same physical features.

"You're back!" she said, coming into the living room and plopping down on the couch next to me. "How was it?"

"It was fun," I said, not wanting to delve into details. "Now tell me about Ellie Varro's dog."

If a thief wanted a dog, a thief was going to get it. Usually, the owner never stood a chance, but there were things an owner could do to make it much harder to steal. Microchips made it easier to track dogs down, but it was more effective in the cases of lost dogs more than stolen. The police were never much help, either. Even in states where there were laws against stolen dogs, they still helped very little. That's why I worked on the side sometimes.

This was what all the years of stealing I did were for. I would do anything to recover a stolen dog. Even if it meant risking my life. Dogs meant everything to me. All animals, really. But dogs meant the most. It was what I clung to in the darkest days of my childhood. Pretending Bobo was a real dog. It was why I had Gus and Gatsby. I tugged Gatsby close to me and kissed the top of his smooth black head. He kissed me back with a lap to my chin.

"My good boy," I murmured, scratching behind his ear before turning my attention to Gus and giving him equal attention.

Cassie set her tea down on the glass coffee table. "Apparently, this Löwchen is worth over ten thousand. Queenie is her emotional support dog. I don't think she wanted that to get out. She relies on this dog to calm her. Ellie Varro, popstar extraordinaire, is autistic even if higher on the spectrum."

"There are many people on the spectrum," Naomi reminded her. "Too many."

Cassie smiled. "Naturally, I know that since I treat a good number of them."

I shook my head, reserving judgment. I could relate to needing a dog for emotional support. I glanced down at Gus and Gatsby. In my case, I needed two of them. It would take nothing to scoop up a small dog like a Löwchen and hurry away. Not like stealing a Mastiff or a German Shepherd, both highly sought after, along with several other purebreds. But to break into her dressing room? She had to have a lot of security. She was a pretty big star. That would take a highly skilled thief.

"I'm sure whoever they assigned will get the dog back, working with the cops, of course. You know there's only so much the agency can do except help them locate." I wasn't sure who they assigned, but I hoped for the sake of the agency that it was true. "As long as states don't have strict laws protecting dogs from being stolen, this is going to continue to happen."

Naomi sighed. "I admire your resourcefulness, but please be careful."

"You always say that."

"Always mean it."

"We're going to worry about you," Cassie said, picking her tea back up. "Nothing you say will convince us otherwise."

"I know."

"So tell us about the wedding." I was glad Hannah changed the subject. "Was it as beautiful as you expected?"

"It was stunning. And hard not to be jealous of Regan. Her family estate is where dreams come from. I can't imagine what it was like growing up in such a house." I absently patted Gatsby's head. Hannah knew what I was talking about. Although she was only six, almost seven, when Naomi took custody of us, she still had vague memories of how we had lived. "I had a good time, though. Everyone was nice. Nothing at all like I expected."

Cassie's grin wasn't hard to miss. "I knew it! And Cameron?"

"Hard to describe how happy he is. They complement each other like no one I've ever known. I envy their relationship. He'll do anything for her, and she'll do anything for him."

"Glad you had a good time," Cassie said. "You didn't meet any charming men? Anyone to convince you there's a better way of life?"

"No," I said, rising from the couch along with the dogs. "I've gotta get to the office. I'll be back before dinner."

"Naomi is cooking tonight," Hannah said.

Thank God, I almost said out loud. Naomi, Cassie and I took turns cooking when I wasn't on assignment. Cassie, although she tried, wasn't the best cook, but then again, neither was I. We both breathed a sigh of release when Naomi cooked, but we never took her for granted, which was why we took turns. We decided Hannah should focus on finishing school rather than on what to make for dinner.

After a quick shower and a change of clothes, I was back in my crappy Jeep, headed toward the city. The agency office was on the outskirts of the city, but on the south end, so it took some time to wind down the freeway. I parked across from the five-story brick building and sprinted across the street.

The first floor had medical and dental offices, the second floor had several businesses in technology and staffing, and the third office was my place of salary, even though it wasn't much. I was comfortable enough, thanks to Lex's generous living arrangement. There wasn't much else that I needed, although Naomi and I made sure Hannah had everything she needed. We wanted her to focus on school and not a part-time job, mainly because David could find her just as easily as he could find me.

And apparently he did find me, I thought as a chill swept through me. Hannah didn't need to know that, though.

I strode through the front door, greeting the front desk receptionist whose name I could never remember. Going to the office was something I avoided at all costs. Only when getting a new co-assignment, or coming in for check-ins, I stayed away. A hallway forked behind the front desk, both paths leading to offices and conference rooms on each side and cubicles in the center.

A line of windows at the back of the office overlooked the bay. The view was unhindered by taller buildings. I could almost see the boardwalk from Maria's office, which was one of the two offices at the back that had windows.

When I heard voices from her open door, I slowed my pace. Dread crept up my spine, recognizing the smooth and sultry voice of Maria. A whimsical, highly emotional voice followed it. I turned the corner, seeing none other than Ellie Varro facing the wall of windows while Maria, all business in her pants-suit and swept up dark red hair, sat calmly behind her desk.

Ellie whirled, as though sensing my appearance. Mascara and tears streaked her cheeks, and her full, pouty lips quivered. I slipped into the room, stopping just inside the door and leaning against the wall. A huge map of the city and surrounding suburbs covered most of the wall across from the door. A perk to being a senior investigator.

"Close the door, Riley. Please," Maria said as she rose.

The look in Ellie's eyes was a mixture of surprise and doubt. Being a scrawny kid, I grew up to be a petite woman. I certainly didn't look that impressive. I was hoping to come to the office to use some resources to look into David's sudden presence and hoping to find him still behind bars. It was possible he sent someone to scare me.

"You?" she scoffed. "They're sending you after my Queenie?"

I felt the invisible slap. "Excuse me?"

"Riley, I need you to take over this case."

"What? Why?"

Maria gave me a look that begged me, calmly, to not give her a hard time about this. "Mandy backed out."

Mandy was good. I was good. Mandy was better. I couldn't imagine her reasoning for backing out of a case. In the years I'd been here, I couldn't recall *anyone* backing out of a case. Sure, we lost some, but we always gave it a go.

"Why would she do that?" I asked, aware that Miss Varro was looking between us like a tennis match.

"We received a tip that one of the city's most notorious and dangerous gangs *might* have taken Queenie. This gang has a reputation for dealing in arms and even dabbling in drugs. We don't know why they would want a dog. Mandy could get some information, but not a location; however, I have some leads."

I looked at Ellie. The sadness behind her deep brown eyes was clear. I could relate, not wanting either Gus or Gatsby to go missing. Not only would it break my heart, I needed them for my support. When I looked into her eyes, I could feel her emotions. I couldn't promise her I would recover Queenie, but I would do my damndest.

"I'll do whatever I can, Miss Varro."

The side of her mouth quirked up. "You?"

My anger flared. "Do you want your dog back?"

"Riley is the best," Maria interrupted.

"I need Queenie back before my tour starts," Ellie said, her voice sounding small, as though burdened with fright. "I *need* her."

"How did your dog get here? Don't you live in LA?"

"I was doing a concert in Vegas when she was stolen out of my dressing room. Worthless security guards weren't paying attention, apparently."

Vegas, I said silently. *I can never get far enough away from that place.*

Offering a manila folder, Maria left me with no option but to enter the office completely. Ellie Varro, although famous, would not be a treat to work with. I hoped it was because she was emotional. I understood too well how stressful it could be to lose a beloved pet.

Bypassing the empty chair next to Ellie, I went to the small table in the office's corner to review the contents of the folder. There was a picture of a man. Rough-looking and covered with tattoos. This would be interesting.

"Miss Varro, you may wait outside while Riley and I go through the details."

I kept my eyes on the file, waiting for the door to open and close before saying a single word about the contents of the file. It was safer for her to not know anything we knew. Especially in such a high-profile case.

"Now, Riley. I've traced one of the gang members to the coffee shop down the street. We also received an anonymous tip that whoever took the dog could wait until the publicity dies down. You need to stake out the coffee shop immediately."

"Grady Allen," I said, looking at the picture of a man with a partially shaved head with dark blond hair flopping over to the side and jaw, chin and upper lip covered with raspy hair. He had the most piercing, mean green eyes I had ever seen in my life. Cleary, he was a person someone would think twice to mess with. Formidable came to mind.

"Try not to tangle with him," Maria said, sitting down next to me. "We think he's part of the gang. Hopefully, you can find something out at the coffee shop."

I scoffed. "No known residence or current job."

"But there's a list of possible previous jobs."

"Did Mandy discover anything else?"

"Afraid not." Maria laid her hand on the folder before I could close it, her eyes serious when they met mine. "They are dangerous, Riley."

"Usually are."

"I don't think you should underestimate them. Drug dealers, arms dealers . . . there are a lot of rumors about these guys if you stop to listen. People who had tangled with them, people who had gone *missing*."

"Aw." I grinned. "You caring about me, Maria?"

"Get the hell out of here."

I almost laughed, but the fact was Mandy didn't give me much to go on at all. Almost like starting at the beginning, and already a few days had passed. That would mean I would need to get started immediately. There was still time to head over to the coffee shop to hang out for a while and be back before dinner.

"Are you sure you want me to do this?" I stood up. As much as

I cared about my job, she was putting me on a big assignment. I wouldn't be shadowing anyone this time. This was all mine.

"Yes," came her answer, without looking at me. "Try not to get hurt. You'd be hard to replace."

I left the office without another word, not bothering to look at Ellie again on my way out. The look on her face when I handed Queenie back to her was what I wanted to see, not the look in her eyes right now.

"I want weekly updates on your progress," Maria called after me. "At least by phone!"

I was already on my way down the hallway, but I heard her. Phone call check-ins were much preferred to coming to the office, especially if I found the location. I would be too busy watching and waiting for the precise moment to run in and grab the dog. We were supposed to get the police involved, but I wouldn't. If I had a chance to grab Queenie myself, I would do it.

Chapter Four

Based on Maria's information about the coffee shop, I strolled into the shop down the block by late afternoon. I didn't have enough time in the office to stop at my disorganized desk to boot up my computer and look into anything related to David. Maria was watching, and I didn't dare make her doubt my ability to take on this case.

I didn't need to drive since it wasn't far from the office, but I did anyway so I could watch for a while to see who was coming and going. Any strange activity and I would notice immediately with my trained eye for detail. This was huge for my career, and I needed to come up with something for Maria. Only then I could become a full private investigator with the salary to prove it.

As luck would have it, as soon as I parked I had the urge to pee, so I hurried in. On my way out, I ran smack into a guy that looked like he worked in construction, his muscular arms bare despite the lack of sun and the chilly temperature. His blue eyes caught me off-guard when his hands came up to my arms, making sure I didn't topple over from the contact.

"Sorry," I mumbled, pulling away quickly.

"No problem," came his smooth, deep-voiced reply.

Not wanting to be suspicious, I moved away from him toward my car. I couldn't help but to cast a glance over my shoulder to see him watching me walk away. The look in his eyes was unmistakable. I had caught him watching my ass. I yanked open my car door and slid in, dropping my head against the headrest.

I took in a few deep breaths, then continued to watch the entrance as though it was normal to do. It was a couple minutes later; I got momentarily distracted when the construction worker emerged with a cup of coffee. Damn, but he was sexy.

When my phone rang, I noticed I had been sitting here for a while and I had seen no one looking remotely close to Grady Allen.

"Riley!" Hannah said. "Are you coming home? Where the heck are you?"

"Shit, yes. I'll be home soon. I got side-tracked."

"Everything okay?"

"Yes, everything's fine. I'll be home as soon as I can."

That was that. Evening would be approaching, darkness along with it, and my stomach was rumbling. I needed to get home and resume my efforts the next morning. Early. If this was a place of interest, Grady Allen would be here. There would be no way to miss him. He was an ugly son of a bitch, if the picture held true.

I'd try again tomorrow. I reached down to start the car just as a car pulled up to the curb in front of the coffee shop. Call it intuition, but I waited with my breath held until the driver's side door opened and Grady Allen stepped out. The picture had been accurate as far as what he looked like.

"Gotcha," I breathed.

I watched him stride into the coffee shop, but not before he took a quick glance around at his surroundings. With a gasp, I slid down in the seat. Shit! After a minute, I crept back up to see Grady had gone in and his car still there.

"That wasn't suspicious at all," I said. "Think you're being followed? You'd be one helluva smart guy. So let's see what your next move is."

When the door to the coffee shop opened fifteen minutes later, I surveyed Grady and another guy with shaggy dark blond hair with him. Both got into the car, and I immediately followed with elation thrumming through my veins. This is what I lived for. This is what I was trained for. Bring me to Queenie, I thought, in silence this time. I knew that would be too much to hope for. It could be too good to be true but following could bring me one step closer.

As quickly as I could, I called Hannah back to let her know I wouldn't be home for dinner after all. I'd have to settle for eating leftovers when I made it home. It wasn't a far drive from the coffee shop, into a normal neighborhood south of where I lived but not by much.

The neighborhood was characteristically middle-class with average homes, lush yards and decent size driveways. Trying to reserve judgement wasn't always fun, as I couldn't imagine a man like Grady Allen living in a suburb such as this, but maybe he lived with his mom and the guy he'd picked up at the coffee shop was his brother. I wasn't being paid for guessing things. I was paid to uncover things.

When they pulled into a vacant driveway in front of a separated two-car garage, I rolled my Jeep to a stop far enough away to be hidden from sight but close enough to still see them. When they disappeared into the house, I brought up the map on my phone to snap a picture so I could find it again. I waited to see if a Löwchen was let outside to potty, but the longer I waited the more my disappointment grew. No sign of the little lion dog.

After waiting an hour, I went home in disappointment. Queenie was here. I could feel it. Having rescued dogs before, I had a feeling. I wasn't an amateur. And if there was one thing I knew, it was that I'd be back. I was going to find her.

Chapter Five

I was in trouble. Big trouble. I may have been out of practice with picking pockets, but my stealth had improved and my ability to sneak around along with it.

Or so I thought.

My mistake was spotting the keys in the ignition of the beautiful machine parked on the patio between the house and the detached garage. It was a black Indian motorcycle, sleek and perched like the machine it was. Someone had left the keys, which very well could have a house key on it. Trespassing was against the rules, but I was a thief. What did I care? Winding my way around trees and bushes was easy. It took only a few minutes before I was squatting next to the bike. It wasn't until I reached up to pull the key out when I realized the key was stuck. The tug was just enough to jar the bike. The crack of the peg giving way echoed between the garage and the house. None of this would have happened had I known the key would get stuck, and the bike had a damaged peg.

In a crouch, I had no chance to get out of the way before the machine toppled toward me like lava oozing down a volcano, but then the weight hit me and knocked me off my feet. My feeble attempt to stop it almost made me laugh, but the sharp scrape of something against my shin just under my knee brought forth a gasp instead.

Now, laying on my back with the heavy machine on top of me, I could only stare up at the cloud-covered sky and wonder how

I would get out of this mess. The dangling of the keys, still in the ignition, mocked me. I didn't think anyone was home, having seen Grady Allen and the other guy from the coffee shop leave in a car only ten minutes ago.

My skill was usually on my side, but I couldn't think of a way out of this. I couldn't move my legs and at this angle, I wasn't sure how or if I could lift it off. It was impossibly heavy. This time was bad. They could have gone on a quick errand and would be back any moment. I knew the risks of my profession, but my years of thieving made me excel at sneaking around.

The creak of a door had my ears honed in, hoping it was the sound of something else. When a shadow fell over me and I looked away until I heard a smooth, deep voice above me.

"What the fuck are you doing? You knocked over my bike?"

Clearly, I was in bigger trouble than I thought.

Dumbfounded, I stared up at him. Of course, it had to be the same guy I had run into at the coffee shop when I had been staking it out. He crouched down next to me, his arm casually draped over his knee and a gun gripped in his hand. My heart thundered. Once again, I attempted to shimmy out from beneath the motorcycle, but it was a big bike. A heavy bike. All I was doing was hurting myself.

I'd be interested to know how he was connected to this. He was staring down at me, angry and expecting an answer. An answer that I wasn't about to give him.

His short hair, a summery blond color, stuck up like he had jabbed his fingers through it and not cared that it stood on end. He still stared at me.

"What . . . are you . . . doing?"

With ease, he stood and lifted the bike clear of me so I could scramble out. While he was busy inspecting it for damage, I rolled to my hands and knees and stayed there for a minute to catch my breath, waiting to see what he would do with the gun in his hand.

Out of the corner of my eye, I saw Mr. Blue Eyes coming toward me and quickly got to my feet. He could kill me. The tone of his voice was enough for me to figure he wasn't messing around. No one else was here. The houses in this neighborhood were close together, but not that close.

"I think you didn't hear me. What are you doing?"

"Looking for my cat," I said, the words rushing out of my mouth. "I thought I saw her come through here and I tripped." I sucked my lower lip between my teeth. Tripped and knocked over a motorcycle? He wouldn't buy such an outrageous lie unless he was stupid.

The doubt behind his eyes was clear, while he looked me up and down, almost lazily. Inwardly, I shivered at his perusal. There was something about him, something sexy in his sleeveless Slipknot t-shirt, his arms spotted with tattoos. I could tell there was a tattoo on his back because it extended out around his shoulders and peeked out from beneath his sleeves. Bad boys didn't attract me. Dog thieves definitely didn't attract me.

I watched him tuck the gun into the waistband of his jeans, breathing a sigh of relief he wouldn't use it. I turned to leave, but his strong fingers grabbed my upper arm before I could take one step. Uh-oh. The grip he had on me was firm, unrelenting. Of course, he wouldn't allow me to leave now.

With a tug, he pulled me around and released me as though telling me to stay where I was without so many words. I looked at the gun, still visible. It would be nothing for him to pull it out again.

Instead, he folded his arms in front of his chest, the muscles bunching in his biceps and drawing my attention to the smooth, golden skin of his upper arms. The sound of him clearing his voice snapped my eyes up to meet his, and the light in them was unmistakable. He caught me staring at him just as he had just been looking at me. *Shit, this wasn't good.*

"Maybe I can help you look for your . . . cat." His head angled to the side, the muscles in his neck stretching as he did so. "I didn't catch your name."

Years of living with a thief, then turning into a thief, reminded me of all the reasons I shouldn't give him my name. I couldn't reveal my original name to him. Too much danger linked me to it. I stepped back, but his hand slid around my arm again.

"I don't need to give you my name to look for my cat," I retorted.

"You knocked over my bike." He looked over at it, leaning against the garage wall. "And broke the peg."

"Riley," I whispered, slowly retracting my arm from his grasp. "If my cat was around here, he's long gone now. He doesn't like loud noises."

One golden eyebrow arched perfectly, giving him a look of a mythical God. "I thought you said your cat was a she."

What the hell is wrong with me? I could only blame his sinful attractiveness. I'd seen plenty of men that were good-looking. Of the few I had dated, none of them were as sexy as this man was. It had to be his eyes. Or the way he looked in that t-shirt. *Shit!*

"You're bleeding," he said, without releasing my eyes.

I looked down at my legs. There was a rip in my leggings on my shin just under my knee about three inches long, and he wasn't wrong. I was bleeding freely through the fabric. "Shit!" I said, out loud this time.

He was looking at me expectantly. "Come on."

He's inviting me inside?! After he just caught me tipping over his bike? It would be incredibly stupid to go inside with him. I had to assume he was alone since I had seen the other two leave. I didn't know when they would be back, or if there were more. It would be insane to go into the house with him. Alone. Then again, I'd be able to get a good look inside and possibly the layout of the house to come back.

"Lead the way. Then you can help me find my cat."

The house wasn't the sort of house I would imagine two, now three, thugs living in. It appeared to be a decent-sized rambler with white siding and colorful shrubbery.

He opened the creaky door, sweeping out his arm for me to go in ahead of him. "Your girl/boy cat?" he asked, his deep voice tense.

"My cat that doesn't like men."

The roll of my eyes went unnoticed when I stopped just inside the door. The kitchen was to the right, spacious enough with a center island and updated stainless steel appliances. There was a cute round table with a couple of chairs in a small nook next to the window I would have attempted to look in had the motorcycle not trapped me. If only I hadn't touched it, it wouldn't have fallen over. It wasn't as disgusting as I thought it would be with a house full of men. And criminals. Those I had known in my past were less than clean.

"Sit down."

I slid into one of the chairs at the small table, watching him disappear into the living room and around the corner. Quickly, I pulled out my phone and dropped a pin to Cassie so she'd know where I was. Just in case. Craning my neck, I tried to get a better look into the living room, but the dividing wall only let me see a couple of chairs and the front door. There was no sign of Queenie here, and I was wondering if they still had the dog. If they didn't, I was wasting my time and putting my life in danger for no reason.

He came back a minute later, carrying some bandages and a tube of ointment. My eyes widened, hoping he wouldn't try to get me out of my leggings. No way was that happening. Instead, he pulled out the adjacent chair. I gasped when he grabbed my leg and pulled it over his with ease. *Bold of him*, I thought. With deft fingers, he rolled the thin fabric up my leg. I hissed when he got to the scrape, marveling at how much gentler he worked the fabric over the area.

As he worked at dabbing away what blood he could, without removing my leggings or rolling them up any further, I was softening to his touch. His hands were . . .

"Ouch! What the fu . . ." I tried to pull my leg away at the burn of the ointment, but he clasped his hands firmly around my knee to keep me in place. He was bold, all right. Far bolder than he should be. "That hurts."

"When's the last time you had a tetanus shot?"

"What?"

He looked up, the seriousness in his eyes momentarily stunning me. "Tetanus shot? Have you had one in the last ten years?"

As soon as he bent his head to his task, I laughed. His head snapped back up, blue eyes sparkling. "You're lecturing me about a vaccination? Seriously . . . you haven't even told me your name."

He continued to work, making me wonder how someone learned to administer first aid this way. When I'd run into him at the coffee shop, he looked as though he worked in construction.

"Where'd you learn how to give first aid like this?"

"In my line of work, we take safety classes."

"Your line of work?"

He pressed the bandages to my leg, secured by medical tape and finished by rolling my legging back down my leg. Gently, he set my leg off his until my boot hit the floor with a thump. "You'll need a new pair of leggings," he said, and released my leg. "I'll see you out."

Just like that, and he won't tell me his name or answer my question. Wow! I stood up, walking to the door without waiting for him. Maybe it was my pride that he knew my name but wouldn't part with his, even though he just had his hands on my leg. Or maybe it was because I felt a powerful attraction to a man I had no business being attracted to. He was dangerous, and I was just sitting alone with him! I really was putting myself at risk too much.

As soon as I stepped out the door, I gave him one last look. One last chance to at least give me a name. Any name. He held the door open, almost leaning into it.

"Ty," he said, but his jaw flexed as though it pained him to tell me.

I turned to leave.

"And Riley? Don't come back here again."

I gave him a nod and limped across the lawn as quickly as my Doc Martens would allow, never once looking back. I didn't dare. But I knew one thing; I wouldn't take his advice. It would take more than being pinned beneath a motorcycle to keep me away. Until I knew one hundred percent, Queenie was not here; I would not go away quietly.

It wasn't until I was back in my Jeep that I realized my thigh was throbbing. I heaved an exasperated sigh, throwing my head back into the headrest. *That could have gone differently*, I thought. *It could have been terrible.*

"Is that your boyfriend's house?"

Shit! I jumped at David's voice from my backseat. "How did you get in here?" I asked, not daring to turn around while shivers danced along my arms.

"Come on baby," his voice crooned, sending fresh terror rippling down my spine. "Don't be like that."

"Be . . . be like what?" I whispered.

"Not exactly the reunion I was hoping for. Answer my question. Is this your boyfriend's house?"

"Yes," I whispered.

"How long have you been with him? Does he love you? Does he love you like *I* love you, Alexis?"

"I . . . don't know."

The sound of my heavy breathing filled the silence until I felt his breath against my neck, just below my ear. "I bet you he won't love you once he knows what you've done. Should I tell him?

Should I tell him how much blood is on your hands?" The sound of his laugh replaced the sound of my breathing. "Just remember that you belong to me. You owe me. It wouldn't be hard to leave the police a tip about where they can find a certain car."

I gasped.

When he abruptly opened the door and slid out, the fresh air slapped against me enough to spin me around to start the car and peel away from the area. I wanted nothing more than to be at home, safe. David knew how to rankle me. He always did. My hands didn't stop shaking until I was well away from the area.

Chapter Six

"I don't understand. You know the location, but you haven't seen the dog?"

I watched Maria pace her office from the small table where I always sat to the door. Unless she forced me to sit in front of the desk, I sat here. She was my supervisor, but I hated to sit at her desk. It made me feel small, and it was a feeling I hated.

"That's not what I said. I saw them bringing in a gigantic bag of dog food." I needed to slow down. My mind was working overtime. "That means they're planning for an extended stay for this dog or they have a large dog there, too. I haven't seen either."

She folded her arms in front of her, tapping her finger against her lips while continuing her track across the floor. "So they really are waiting for the publicity to die down. We need to know why they're holding this dog."

The reminder was unnecessary. She was right. After working for her for about six months now, Maria knew me pretty well. I wasn't a tough nut to crack. This job meant everything to me, and I'd do whatever possible to succeed. But I wasn't without personal issues. Panic attacks were rare, but that didn't mean I didn't have bouts of anxiety. Regardless of that fact, I did my job, and I did it well.

"Here's what I suspect. I think they're holding this dog until the publicity dies down and they'll make their demands then. What else have you found?"

"I've been digging around on Grady Allen. He did time for

carrying a concealed firearm without a license right out of high school, but his bigger issue is his Class C felony for possession parts of a short-barreled shotgun. He did two years in prison for that one."

"Hmmm," Maria said, sliding gracefully into her chair. "Sounds like we have a weapons dealer. But why keep a dog? Money? Trade?"

Cameron would know, I thought. I didn't want to bother him, but he might not mind if it was to find out information on dealing with arms dealers. He might lead me in a new direction.

"Miss Varro is offering a helluva reward. Who the hell wouldn't want money?" I offered. "If they're arms dealers, that would give them some serious buying power. I've been trying to sneak around the house, see if I can find anything."

Her gaze snapped to mine. "Riley, you know the rules. No trespassing, no taking pictures through windows. And for God's sake, be careful."

"I know, but I need to know if the dog is there, right?"

Her lips quirked up. "Yes. And I know it's your job, but it isn't worth your life."

Wrong. It was more than a job to me, but she couldn't know about my side jobs, so I said nothing. "I will let you know as soon as I hear or see anything else. I promise."

This time, she smiled. "As important as this is, being Ellie Varro's dog, I'm worried for you."

I gave a nod, rising. "I'm being safe."

My downfall in getting caught came to mind. No one knew about that. It hadn't happened again. I'd seen him coming and going from the house, but nothing outside of ordinary and nothing short of what the other two guys did. Except he'd spoken the truth that the motorcycle I knocked over had been his. Watching him come and go every day had been the best part of my stakeouts. He was yummy.

I left the office intending to resume my post at the house, but the aroma of the coffee shop down the street pulled at me. The weather was warm; the sun peeking out from the clouds occasionally, and there was no rain or even a hint of rain.

It wasn't busy for midmorning when I pulled open the glass door and stepped into the warmth, with the aroma of coffee beans assaulting my nostrils. I fought the urge to inhale deeply. The whir of the expresso machines was loud, but my attention was on the man sitting at a table near the front windows with a perky blonde. It was none other than Ty. As soon as his eyes lifted to meet mine, I shifted my gaze and moved toward the front register to place my order.

The man behind the counter, working the expresso machines I recognized as the one who'd been with Grady. Up closer to him, he looked like he should be in an alternative band rather than working as a barista. I didn't realize I was staring until he looked straight at me, then gave me a quick nod of his head and went back to work.

I gave my coffee order to the redheaded girl behind the counter, then moved along to wait for it while I considered Ty sitting with the blonde. I wasn't sure if I should acknowledge him or ignore him and warred with myself about it while I waited. I avoided looking in his direction as I added a bit of milk to my dark brew, hoping to slip out of the coffee shop without having a conversation with him.

My mistake was looking over at him when I tried to sneak past. He was alone now, his long legs were encased in a pair of well-worn light blue colored jeans and stretched out under the table. With his booted ankles crossed, he looked entirely too comfortable.

He waved me over. I was nuts to consider going to talk to him. The last time we had crossed paths, I was sure he was going to hurt me. How could I not assume that when he held a gun in his hand? And then he was sort of nice by taking care of my bleeding leg. Of course, I couldn't blame him for being angry at first. After all, I knocked over his bike while trying to sneak around. I wasn't sure I broke the peg, like he said I did. They didn't break as easy as that. Most guys that rode motorcycles were protective of their machines. We both knew my cat story was bullshit as soon as it came out of my mouth.

But our last encounter had me believing he would rather not fraternize with me. He was pretty adamant about me staying away.

"Come here," the rough edge of his voice reached me, pulling me.

I wasn't used to being commanded. It wasn't something I liked. But my feet moved of their own accord until I was standing next to his table. He waved toward the vacant seat across from him.

"Are you asking me to sit down?" I asked, pulling my tongue between my teeth and lightly biting down at my stupid-sounding question.

"Yes."

"Why?"

He laughed, the tremor deep in his throat. "You knocked over my bike. Maybe I want to find out why. What's the harm?"

There were several reasons I could think of, none of which I voiced. I slid into the chair, setting my coffee cup in front of me. The last time I sat down with a man over a cup of coffee, dinner, anything, had been over six months ago. And it hadn't lasted long.

"Did I break it?"

"Break what?"

"Your bike."

"No." I knew it! "The peg needed to be replaced, which is why it tipped over so easily. Of course, it wouldn't have tipped over had you not touched it." His eyes sparkled with mischief.

"What do you want?"

I caught his gaze, his eyes suddenly intense. I wasn't sure what to make of this man. He could have easily held me captive in that house until his friends returned. Or something worse. But he didn't.

"Did you find your cat?"

"My . . ." I almost laughed. "No."

"I thought it strange to find you, where I found you, after having just run into you, literally, here." My eyes narrowed, knowing exactly where he was going with this. "Don't you?"

"Coincidence," came my smooth reply.

"No, I don't think so, but it's obvious I won't get it out of you." He leaned forward in his chair, so close I could see the faint stubble of facial hair along his jaw and upper lip. "I meant what I said. Stay away from that house."

I cocked my head to the side, almost issuing him a challenge. "What's your name short for?"

His eyes intensified. "Tyler." He leaned closer to me. "Is Riley really your name?"

"What the fuck else would it be?"

He smiled, pulling back and crossing his arms over his chest in a way that made the material pull tight across his biceps. "Calm down. Just making small talk."

This was small talk? Okay. "Who was that woman you were talking to when I walked in? Girlfriend?"

"Ex. Like you, she just ran into me."

"I didn't run into you, *Tyler*. I was getting my coffee and was leaving when you waved me over." He continued to smile, a secret smile. He had the most beautiful smile I had ever seen. "I'm not having the best day today."

"Why not?"

I took a drink of my burning hot coffee to avoid answering for a moment, letting the sear of it warm its way down my body while staring at him. "I lost my cat."

The laugh that burst forth from him was full-bodied and easily believed. "I'm not sure I've ever met anyone like you."

I shrugged. "That's great. I'm glad. So . . . why's she your ex-girlfriend?"

His smile lost a little vigor. "We had differences we couldn't get past."

That shut me up. Nothing in this world gave me the right to ask anyone about their relationship, not having had one worth two shits. Not having had one that lasted longer than a few months and spaced out over the last seven-ish years.

"Ever had one like that?"

I shook my head.

"It sucks. How about you? Any ex-boyfriends lurking?"

"Nope."

"Not going to talk about it, huh?"

"Not with someone I don't know," I said sweetly. "No offense, but I don't know you."

"Yet you ask about my ex-girlfriend."

"You're right. It's none of my business. But it's not like I'll see you again. This is just a very weird coincidence that I've seen you a few times now." I glanced outside, feeling the need to get back to work. "I need to go."

He laughed again, this time quietly. "You should."

I stood up and would have turned away from him, but when I reached for my coffee, his fingers curled around my wrist. The shock of his hand on my skin sent a vibration up my arm akin to a thrill. My eyes snapped up to meet his. He turned my wrist up, his thumb tracing the black ink of my tattoo.

"I know what this means," he whispered, looking down at my tattoo. "If you want your story to continue, you'll stay as far away from that house as you can get."

When he released my wrist, I walked away from him and didn't look back to see if he was watching me. I was positive he was. I could feel his eyes on me, watching me through the windows while I marched back up the street toward my car with my coffee clutched in my hand.

Ty told me he had met no one quite like me. If I was being

truthful with myself, I had met no one quite like Ty. He was bold, but charming. Not overpowering, not bullying. And as much as he had tried to appear a hard ass when he busted me trying to sneak around, especially when I knocked over his motorcycle, he bandaged my cut leg *and* all but ordered me to get up to date on my vaccinations.

Chapter Seven

I ended up calling Cameron, but his information on arms dealers didn't lead me in any new direction. Money could be the reason, and the $200,000 reward Ellie Varro promised for the return of her dog would be motive enough–unless they wanted more. What better way than to wait it out until she was desperate? She'd be willing to pay a lot more than that for the return of her dog, or face the possibility of having to cancel her world tour and lose a lot more money.

It was good to talk to Cameron. He was still on his honeymoon with Regan, but they were in Lake Las Vegas visiting family. I knew they wanted to fly up to see me, but I still didn't want to bother them. That David found me unnerved me. Watching over my shoulder every minute of the day was exhausting.

It was my job to investigate cases and, in the cases of illegal activity, lead law enforcement to the bad guys. Under no circumstances was I to get in the middle of it. But to reunite dogs with their owners, who were always fraught with worry, was a side job that I loved. These dogs were a part of their family. It didn't matter that this dog belonged to a highly popular superstar. This was her baby. The thought made me sick as I drove my car back to my usual spot, far enough to stay hidden but close enough to see anyone coming and going. This made my job even more important.

It had been only a week since I'd run into Ty at the coffee

shop. The weather had taken a massive turn for the better, if you could call it that. Today, the drizzle had let up for once and the temperature had risen into the eighties with a sky full of bright sunshine. I craned my neck toward the windshield again, seeing nothing at Ty's house.

When my cell phone rang, I couldn't help but jump. At the risk of being approached by David, I had been on edge since that day. With a heavy breath, I answered the call. It had been a long time since I'd heard my mother's voice, and not nearly long enough.

"Simone."

"Baby, how are you?"

She sounded one of three things: fatigued, drunk, or high. It was hard to tell the difference now. This time of day, it could be all three. I never knew. She knew I had no money, but that didn't stop her from asking. Sometimes she didn't, and it was those times I think she called just because she was my mother.

"Fine. How are you?"

"I'm tired. I'm trying to find a job." If she was looking for me to say something, I didn't. "I know you don't believe me, but I am. Nobody's hiring."

"No one is hiring someone who can't hold down a job for more than a few weeks," I said, instantly regretting my biting words. It didn't matter if it was true or not. She knew her faults. There was no need for me to point them out.

"You still hate me."

I sighed, pinching the bridge of my nose. "I just wish it was different between us. But it isn't. I don't hate you."

"I told you I was sorry," she whispered. "I can't change it, Ale . . . Riley."

At least she called me by my real name now. It took a lot of reminding over the last several years, but she was finally understanding that I had started a new life the minute I walked out of her house. Naomi made sure of that.

"I know you can't change it. You can now, though. Get help."

She was quiet for a moment. "I shouldn't have let my mother take you and Ivy."

"It's Hannah now," I said, easing up on the snap in my tone.

"Why'd you have to change your names? Wasn't what I gave you good enough?"

A sigh slipped out before I could stop it. "We've been through this before, Simone. We needed to change our names because David kept coming after me. He's still coming after me."

"Why? What does he want with you?"

It was hard for me to put into words that she would understand, not knowing what state she was in. I didn't know how to describe it to myself. His sick perversion that we would be together when I had done nothing before to encourage it wasn't something that I even understood.

"I don't know how to explain it, but he wants me with him. And he'll use whatever means to make sure it happens, which is why we had to move." I tapped my fingers on the steering wheel. "Is there something you wanted? I'm on the job."

She gasped. "I'm sorry. I didn't know I would bother you."

"You need to stop apologizing. Please. I've moved on. It's time for you to move on, too. Get help, Simone. For yourself."

I heard a sniffle. There wasn't a time I talked to her over the phone that she didn't end up in tears. If this was her way of trying to make amends, I wasn't sure what else I could do to help her. There was not enough money in my bank account to help her with treatment, even if she stuck with it. Naomi had tried many times to get her to go. It never worked.

"I will. You'll see, baby. I'll change."

"Bye, Simone," I murmured, absently ending the call at the sound of a motorcycle approaching. I watched the man on the motorcycle, not taking my eyes off him, while tossing my phone to the passenger seat. "Well, well, well . . . nice to see you again, Ty."

Ty parked the sleek black motorcycle in its usual spot on the patio, off to the side from the two-stall garage. I waited, my breath held, while he sat there for a moment before swinging his long leg over and standing up. He unzipped his leather jacket to reveal another sleeveless t-shirt. It was too far away for me to see what band it was this time, but it wasn't so far that I couldn't see the finely sculpted muscles in his arms.

Shit! My mouth was drying up, and my bottle of water had only a swallow left. Yet I couldn't take my eyes off him. *Why does he have to look so good?* And what was wrong with me? I had to shake this out. He was just a man, even if he was sexy.

"You aren't the only sexy man in the world," I said out loud. "So you're sexy. I have a job to do and you will *not* get in my way, *Tyler*. I wonder if that's even your name."

Shaking my head, I reached for the binoculars, but thought better of it after a moment. I was close enough. I didn't want him to look over and see me spying on him. This was dangerous enough already. Although, he had rescued me when he could have easily pulled me further inside and never let me out.

No one knew where I was. Except David. I shuddered. He was the last person I wanted to rescue me. *No, thank you.* There was nothing David did unless it came at a price. I would *never* be under his control again.

I needed to stop talking to myself. Instead, I continued to watch Ty while he dug something out of his saddlebag and stuck it in the pocket of his blue jeans. With his black leather jacket slung over his shoulder, I watched him disappear through the side door. I nearly knocked the bottle of water out of my cup holder in my haste to grab it and suck down what remained after watching his ass walk away.

I threw the empty bottle into the backseat and tucked my phone into the narrow pocket of my leggings, about to slip out of the driver's seat when another car pulled into the driveway. This time, it was Grady and the other guy arriving home. They had to let the dog outside to do her business now. Maybe there was a spot in the far back yard.

Slipping out of my Jeep, I jogged across the street and down the block. Dodging between trees and bushes again, I used my stealth and the fading light of the day to get me closer to the back of the house. As soon as I slipped around the garage, another car pulled up and I flattened my back against the garage wall. A guy with dark, shoulder length hair got out of the car and disappeared into the house.

I waited a few more minutes before I crouched low along the back just in time to see Queenie get let out the back. If I wasn't trying to stay hidden, I would have let out a shriek after finally laying eyes on the tiny dog. Whoever let her out had gone back inside and left her alone. All I needed to do was grab her and make a run for it.

I needed to make a move, and soon. No one was around, but that didn't mean someone wasn't watching me. I was still on my guard.

The side of the house pressed against my back a few minutes later, just under the kitchen window, closer to the corner of the house. But I stopped. If she started barking at me, it wouldn't be good. They would certainly catch me. Instead, I waited until I heard the door at the back of the house open and close. On my tiptoes, I stretched up to peek through the window. This window wouldn't give me what I wanted, so I slipped around to the backside of the house.

Being inside had given me a one-up, thanks to the sexiest gang member ever, Ty. I knew which window would give me the best view of the living room, where they would most likely be. Sure enough, they were sitting around the living room enjoying beers, drugs, and video games. I gasped at the guns that were in open crates in the living room and some leaning up against furniture. The Löwchen, only a few pounds, laying on the floor next to one of those open crates chewing on a Mr. Bill toy.

Traitor, I thought. I could only see the one with dark hair through the window. No sign of Ty, and no sign of the other two.

If only I had tried to get a better layout while I was inside. My eyes widened when he suddenly stood, coming right toward the kitchen window where he would clearly notice me looking in. I sprang away, sliding back around to the patio and trying to keep as close to the house as I could. And coming face to face with the meanest looking guy I had ever seen. Grady Allen.

Someone must have fixed the creak of the door. I never heard it open, otherwise I would have stayed where I was. I had come across some tough thugs in my past, but I had never seen one as formidable as this one. Hard green eyes, accusing eyes, stared at me. True to his picture, he had a hank of dark blond hair that flopped over to one shaved side of his head. Other than his face and neck, tattoos covered most of what skin I could see.

Shit, shit, shit. He crossed thick, muscular arms in front of himself while sizing me up. If I could have guessed what he was thinking, it would be why a thin scrappy girl was sneaking around. It was my best try, but I stared back at him with hard eyes.

He cocked his head to the side, his jaw flexing when he moved toward me. There was nowhere to go. I had no plausible excuse to get out of this. I got caught spying. He knew it, and I knew it.

Reaching out, he grabbed my arm in his huge hand and I had to clamp my teeth together not to yelp at the strength. Damn, but he was strong. And less than gentle when he gave me a shake. He reached behind his back and pulled out a Glock. Dread washed over me when he pointed it at me, keeping his other hand wrapped firmly around my arm.

"Want to see inside so bad?" he asked, the chill of his voice menacing and hard. "Come on, then."

Chapter Eight

Digging in my heels would be pointless. He was huge and strong. There wasn't an argument to be made. I had no choice but to allow him to pull me through the door I had gone into with Ty. My only thought was that at least I knew what to expect when walking in.

Grady threw open the inner door with such force it banged against the wall causing the dark-haired guy's head snap up in surprise while Grady propelled me in. Grady was so much taller than I was. I was nearly dragging on my tiptoes while he pulled me from the kitchen into the living room.

There was barely enough time to see the guy on the couch before I was flung to the floor amidst the open containers of guns and ammunition. *Shit, that was a lot of firepower.* My cell phone popped out of the pocket of my leggings from the force.

"Looks like I found us a spy," he announced, kicking the phone away from me before I could snatch it back.

My knees hit the carpet painfully, my ponytail flinging forward and blocking my vision for a moment. Wasting no time, I pushed myself to my knees and threw my hair back over my shoulder. When I did, there was no sign of Ty. Only the tiny dog, who let out a small bark. My heartbeat thundered in my ears, a steady countdown to an unpleasant outcome. As many situations as I had gotten out of, I was sure I wouldn't get out of this one. My breathing tightened, but I took deep breaths and counted silently while I prayed for a panic attack to stay away. I needed to put on a brave, if not cocky, front with these men.

I was unsure of whether I should stay where I was or try to get up, but Grady decided for me when he took me by the arm and pulled me up. This time, I felt the gun pressing against my jaw. Dear God, this was worse than having David stalking me.

I looked at the coffee shop guy, who was playing video games and not paying attention to me. He was no help. "Please," I whispered. "I'm not any trouble, I swear."

The other one, bare-chested, sauntered back into the living room and sat down in a chair in front of me. Up close, I could see his hair reached his shoulders. He leaned back, appearing calm despite a woman in the living room being threatened with a gun.

"We're running out of . . ."

My head spun, eyes snapping to the hallway where Ty had stopped. He was wearing only a pair of his light blue jeans while towel drying his hair. No shirt, bare feet and looking sexier than he had all the times I had seen him before. He stared at me, his expression unreadable for the briefest second before it turned hard. Mean. It felt like long, stretched out minutes while I stared at him.

"What the fuck. Riley?" he growled, the towel dropping to the floor in his haste to get to me. "I thought I told you not to come here."

He hauled me away from Grady despite the gun, not gently, pulling me right up and into his arms.

The deep scent of manly soap assaulted my senses, creeping into all the emotions my head was battling. When he had pulled me up, my hands had instinctively pressed against the finely sculpted muscles of his damp chest.

What the hell was right? What the hell is he doing? Now, they'd all know my name, making me regret not giving him a fake name. Any other name but the two names I had held during my life. One linked to a thief and a murderer, and one linked to a private investigator in a den of illegal activity.

Ty tucked me behind him, facing off with Grady. Grady still

had the gun in his hand, but not aimed at me. It didn't matter. He still had it in his hand. The last thing I wanted was a blood battle with me in the middle, and I tried to get out from behind Ty, but he held me firm.

"Now might be a good time to tell me what the fuck is going on," Grady drawled.

"She's my girlfriend."

Wait. What? He claimed that awfully fast. But I couldn't say a damn thing. This was his weird way of getting me out of this mess, saving me for the second time, and I didn't know why. But I was going to find out.

"Sneaking around the house?"

"I wasn't sure this was the right house," I snapped, my eyes narrowing. I shouldn't goad him. "My bad for looking in the window."

"She's never been here before." Ty looked down at me, his eyes still hard. "And I told her not to come here."

"I followed him." It wasn't something I should have probably said, but if Ty was putting himself in a mess because of me, it was the least I could do. "He told me not to, but . . . I was curious."

Grady's jaw clenched. He gave me one more look, turned and left the living room while tucking his gun back into the waistband of his jeans and my phone into his pocket.

"You have my phone!" I yelled after him.

"And I'm keeping it, too, until you prove you aren't lying."

I didn't realize I was holding my breath until Ty loosened his hold on me. But he kept his hands on me. I hoped to hell Grady couldn't crack the code to get into my phone and find everything personal about me. The other two were looking at us, including the one who had abandoned his video game to enjoy the drama unfolding.

There were bags of white powder on the table in front of him. I could only assume was cocaine. This wasn't something I wanted to get involved in, and I tore my eyes away from it.

"Makes sense," came from Jack. "Don't pay any attention to Grady. He was born with a stick up his ass, and it's still there. I'm Jack."

His lips curled. This guy didn't give a damn that Ty had just claimed me as his girlfriend. This was going to be interesting. I had no intention of being a plaything for anyone in this house, no matter how sexy one of them was. Ty still had his hands on me, and I had done nothing to shrug him off.

Unsure what else to do, I nodded before I looked over at the scrawny one playing video games who reclined back but kept the controller in one hand while taking a pull from his bottle of beer.

"Merrick," was all he said.

"I get it," I whispered.

Ty said nothing, his fingers dancing down my arm until his fingers twined with mine and he pulled me into the hallway. There was nothing I could do. I couldn't argue with him about where he was taking me without raising an alarm to the farce we were playing at. The hallway split with two doors to the left and two on the right, one on each side. He drew me to the right.

My lips pressed into a thin line, boots stumbling a little while he drew me inside his room. I was in a house filled with men. Unless Cassie remembered I dropped a location pin here not so long ago, no one knew where I was.

Once we were in the bedroom, he shut the door and I pressed my back against it as though I was afraid to take one step closer to his massive bed. He turned, caging me in with his arms on each side of me. His eyes were a mesmerizing blue. He had slight stubble along his jawline, and his lips were full. He wasn't smiling.

"I thought I told you not to come back here."

The huskiness of his voice sent shivers down my spine. Not of fear, but of something completely different. *What the hell is wrong with me? I could be in real danger, and I'm acting like a lovesick teenager! And he's a criminal!* I couldn't find my voice to give him an answer. It wouldn't be the truth, anyway.

"I couldn't stay away," I finally said, a hint of tease in my voice.

I was playing with fire. That was the last thing I should have said when his lips curved into a roguish smile. *No! Shit, no!* He moved closer. I put my hands to his chest.

"Couldn't stay away, huh?"

I clenched my teeth. "That's not what I meant."

He needed to move back. I was suffocating with him so close, holding me hostage with his nicely sloped arms and wet, tousled hair that looked a mess, whether it was wet or dry. How could one man have such an imposing presence over me? He wasn't intimidating like some, but being this close to him was heightening every sense I had.

When his head slanted to the side, I could see a small dot on his earlobe where an earring once was, but instead of it raising more questions, it only raised my heartbeat. Our eyes met. My breath held. What was he going to do with me now that he had staked his claim? Announcing me as his girlfriend after catching me spying was bold. It wasn't as though I could just say goodbye and leave now that he had said that. It would raise questions I didn't need. Questions he didn't need.

"What now?" I whispered.

"I could think of a few things we could do . . ."

Despite the feel of his bare skin beneath my fingertips and palms, I pushed past him into the room. His bedroom was a decent size though the bed took up a good portion of it. There was a cheap tall dresser and a closet that was open with clothes spilling out. He wasn't a complete slob, but he wasn't neat either. I was far from organized, so I could lay no blame.

There was a chair in the corner with a small table and a lamp next to it. Wasting time, I wandered over to it and picked up the book. *The Count of Monte Cristo*, I murmured silently. I hid the quirk of my lips.

"Despite what you think, we're all educated." His voice seemed closer to me than I sensed. "Some of us more than others."

I whirled, finding him still across the room. "Why would I think otherwise?"

He stayed where he was, but I couldn't mistake the way his eyes traveled over me, as though seeing me for the first time. "A house full of men, in the company of guns and drugs, covered with tattoos. I think you would draw your own conclusions."

"Is that why you told me to stay away from here?"

Irritation lit his blue eyes. "I told you to stay away because it's dangerous for you to be around here. Yet, here you are again."

I didn't want anyone to overhear anything incriminating, but I had a strong desire to ask him why he had said I was his girlfriend. It was something I would have to wait to ask. I wondered how long I would need to stay in here with him before I could safely leave.

"What are we going to do now?" I asked, eyeing him cautiously.

"I told you, I can think of a few things to pass the time."

The look in his eyes didn't betray the hint in his voice of what he meant. I shivered, taking a step back until my ass hit the edge of the table. I was in a house full of men, and no one knew where I was unless someone got worried. It wasn't as though I hadn't staked out all night before. Investigative hours were long and could be anytime, day or night, weekday or weekend. We were in his bedroom and would be here for a while until I had a good excuse to leave.

"That's not why I'm here."

I didn't like how breathless my voice sounded, or the way my heartbeat increased at the thought of . . . that. With him. He didn't know what little experience I had with men. Not for lack of trying. It was my own shortfalls that were in the way.

"Why are you here?" he asked quickly, adding in a quiet tone: "And don't give me any bullshit this time."

I couldn't help but to laugh. "It's my cat. I know my cat is around here somewhere."

Ty moved quickly toward me, shushing me. Our breathing stopped when we heard footsteps in the hallway, strangely close to Ty's door. Were we being watched? That made me more suspicious. After being caught sneaking around, I can understand why Grady would suspect me. But Ty? Why would they suspect Ty? He was one of them. If he told them I was his girlfriend, didn't they believe him?

"I need my phone," I whispered as soon as the footsteps faded away.

The smell of him reached like fingers into my senses, wrapping around and squeezing parts of me. Intimate parts of me. He smelled so . . . masculine. I couldn't recall a time when anyone made me feel like this. Although none of my old boyfriends were criminals, I tried to remember that Ty was. He could have been the one that grabbed the dog. Or he could be innocent of it.

"Yeah, you aren't getting it back. Not anytime soon. Grady'll hang onto it until he's ready to give it back to you."

"Will he break into it?"

"Why? Afraid of what he'll find?"

By the look in his eyes, I knew I was treading on dangerous ground. I needed to back off a little, but out of all of them.

I had an intuition about Ty. Twice he had saved me when he hadn't needed to.

"Why did you tell them I was your girlfriend?" I kept my voice impossibly low, wary of anyone else listening to us. That, and the walls could be thin. For all I knew, they had the rooms wired.

When he leaned forward, his lips brushing against the skin below my ear, I held still. "Do you know what he'll do to you if you aren't?" came his whisper. "What else could I have done?"

I didn't have an answer. "And before?"

He pulled away. "Before?"

"You knew I wasn't looking for a cat, yet you invited me in. Patched up the cut on my leg." Talking in whispers was irritating me. "How long do we need to stay in here?"

His eyebrow rose. "I told you there were other things we could do."

When I tried to step away, his arms came around my waist. I pushed against his hands but couldn't dislodge them. "What the hell are you doing?"

"Why are you so skittish?"

"You're a criminal," I said through my teeth.

"Do you know that for a fact?"

"Considering what I saw in your living room? Yes, I'd say I know for a fact."

"Hmm."

By the company he kept, he was, but I couldn't give him that excuse.

"That and guys your size don't generally go for the Löwchen breed. You seem more like a Doberman kind of guy."

Recognition sparked in his eyes. "Is that why you've been snooping around? You're some sort of . . . *Ace Ventura*?"

I snorted. "Not even close."

His eyes narrowed. "Aren't you supposed to get the police involved?"

I smirked. "I work alone."

The laugh from his throat was deep and loud, causing him to step back from me. I admired his voice, and that he could find humor in this situation. I just about admitted to being a criminal myself.

"And you accuse me of being a criminal?"

My laugh wasn't as willing, but I couldn't stop it.

"How many times am I going to need to rescue you?"

My shoulders rolled. I needed to be more careful. Since I'd had been doing this job, no one had caught me. Not even once. Yet here I was, caught twice in the same assignment. In the few side jobs I had to recover a dog, I'd been successful except once. I'd been too late. The sadness of having to relay such information to a family waiting for their beloved to come home was terrible to have to do.

"What?" he whispered, suddenly somber. "Did I say something wrong?"

I blinked. He was worried about my feelings? "No. I was just thinking about a dog I couldn't recover. Having to tell the family is the worst thing."

"Has it happened a lot?"

Our voices returned to whispers, and suddenly I wanted to sit down. If we were going to be here for a while, I might be comfortable while doing it. I moved toward the bed, eying it cautiously. We had been in his bedroom for a while now, and he had made no moves. If he truly wanted to hurt me or force me, he could have tried by now.

The bed was neat, as though he had taken great care to make it presentable. Was he expecting someone before I showed up? Maybe he had a girlfriend, and I had just messed it up for him. The comforter was dark gray with two plump pillows neatly at the head. Simple, but neat. I sat down, cautious at first, then pulled my leg up almost like I was perching precariously on the edge. He was watching me.

Please don't make me regret this, I thought. Instead, he moved closer and sat down beside me, but gave me space as though he knew I was anxious about the situation.

"No. Only once I was too late."

"That has to make you feel good."

I offered him a half smile. "There isn't anything more gratifying in the world than bringing home a dog to a waiting family, especially when there are little kids involved." I met his gaze. "So why is this dog here?"

Long fingers raked through his hair, now dry, making the ends stand up. *Dear God . . . did he have to do that?* It flustered me. He was contemplating his answer or not answering me at all.

"I can't tell you that."

"Can't tell me, or won't?"

Stretching out, he reclined across the bottom portion of the bed with only his bare feet hanging over the edge. The way he looked, so casual and sinful, it tempted me to stretch out, too. *What the hell. Why not?* I leaned over, brushed my ponytail back and rested my head on my crooked arm until I was facing him. I didn't have to know him to be comfortable. It wasn't as though I was a virgin. Nearly, but not quite. I just didn't do one-night stands.

This was bizarre, lying in bed with a complete stranger. Although we weren't *complete* strangers anymore. We had three previous encounters, two of them including conversations. But I had never been in bed with a man I had not spent more than an hour's worth of time with. It seemed so normal. It was comfortable.

"I can't. I don't know."

"You . . . weren't involved in it?"

"No."

I had all but accused him of being a criminal when he was admitting to me he had nothing to do with it. Yet, he lived in a house full of crooks. With guns and drugs. There had to be a reason he was here with the others. It wasn't time to drop my caution.

I couldn't take the risk of telling him I meant to get that dog out of here. Not with so many dangerous possibilities of being overheard. He already rescued me twice. I would do better and save him from having to do it again.

"So . . . um . . . where's your actual girlfriend?" I whispered. "Won't she be mad?"

He stared at me, his eyes burning into me. "There isn't one. Guess you'd be my first one in a while. And in saying that . . . now that it's out, you're going to have to keep up the charade."

I played it off with a laugh, but I wondered how we would do that. The ruse would be a good way to stay in the house and watch Queenie. I doubted Grady, or the other two, would give away any information around me. But it wouldn't hurt to be here.

The smell of incense, earthy and spicy, wafted into the room. Patchouli. I hated that smell. It reminded me of . . . Simone's old boyfriend, her dealer boyfriend. He always lit incense when they were smoking something illegal in the townhouse.

Panic was rising, my pulse and breathing with it. I'd just turned fourteen when she came stumbling home, drunk and high, with Finnegan Caspian. It didn't take long before Simone was out cold, which meant I was vulnerable. He wasted no time in moving toward me, an available replacement for my mother.

I began my counting like Cassie taught me, but it wasn't working while I was struggling to breathe. I immediately sat up, gulping because I could, while my heartbeat erratically thundered. Ty bolted up, putting his arm around my heaving shoulders.

"Panic . . . attack," I gasped.

Sliding off the bed, he knelt down on the floor in front of me, taking my hands into his and sliding his thumbs over my wrists in a circular motion. *What . . . the . . . hell*?

I focused on his movements, my attention captured enough to count the circles until my breathing slowed along with the beat of my heart. Even when my breathing stabilized, he continued the motions while he looked into my eyes. I wondered what was happening. He didn't know me, and I didn't know him, but it was as though we were comfortable together. I looked down at his hands and slowly he stopped the movements.

"Riley," he whispered. "Does that happen a lot?"

I shrugged. He didn't need to know about my problems. Unlawful or not, he didn't need to know about my shady past. I didn't know him *that* well.

When I raised my eyes to his, he was still watching me and waiting for an answer. "No."

"I won't hurt you," he whispered, tucking wisps of my hair behind my ear.

His eyes promised honesty. After having saved me twice, how

could I not trust him? There were plenty of chances he could have hurt me, but he didn't.

A minute later, he pushed to his feet and was rummaging through his dresser drawers. "I'm taking you out," he announced. "To dinner."

Relief washed over me at the thought of escaping this room, this house, and that smell. But then I thought about my phone. I had to get it back from Grady. Somehow. Naomi or Cassie had to know where I was. Just in case.

He sat back down on the bed to pull on a pair of white socks and his boots before he went to the closet for a shirt, this time with short sleeves. When he turned around, I was still sitting on the bed. He was seriously taking me out to dinner? Every warning in my head screamed not to go out with him. I didn't date bad guys.

"It's just dinner, Riley," he said, capturing my hand. "Unless you want to spend the night here?"

I bolted up. He laughed.

"It's getting dark. They'll expect you to stay if you don't have an excuse that we're going out, so let's do this."

He had a way about him that made it so easy. Relenting, I smiled and nodded. "You win. I'll let you take me to dinner. Only because I don't have any money on me."

His grin was magnetic, making him even more gorgeous. "You don't have a jacket?" I shook my head. "You'll have to wear mine."

Swooping down to grab his jacket off a bench at the end of the bed, he opened the door a moment later. I realized I would need to walk back through the thugs in the living room with a grimace and the potent smell of patchouli. *Breathe*, I told myself. I got thrown into a living room full of thieves at gunpoint without a panic attack. I could get through this.

And I did. When we walked into the living room, they all looked at us. Including Grady, who sat on the end of the couch watching me with careful eyes. I was determined not to let Grady's distrustful look or the gang's reputation scare me, so I stared back with confidence. From what I'd heard, they didn't find people who were on the wrong side of these men, although no one could prove it. I was determined not to be one of those people.

Ty's palm pressed against my lower back, urging me across the living room toward the door. "We're going out," he said, his voice gruff and taking no arguments.

Grady stared at me. "I assume you'll be back."

"We'll be back," Ty said.

"You, too, Riley. Since you were so interested an' all . . ."

I swore under my breath and felt Ty stiffen behind me. This was not good. But I needed to keep up the scheme if I was going to be trusted here. And Ty had protected me enough. I had to make sure he didn't suffer because of my stupidity.

"Of course," I said, smiling at Grady. "I'll need my phone back."

"I'll consider it. *After* you get back."

Shit.

Ty had my hand firmly back in his, leading me toward the door before anyone else could say another word to us. I wasn't sure if he was in a hurry to go out with me or if he was in a hurry to get me out of the room with his roommates. Either way, I was glad to be away from Grady's glower.

Chapter Nine

Safely surrounded by Ty's leather jacket, I climbed onto the motorcycle behind him. The sleeves were too long, but I expected that. He was much larger than me. Once the engine roared to life, I sat there dumbly until he grabbed my hands and pulled them around his midsection. Heat crawled up my face, but the feelings shooting through me were something I might need to analyze. This wasn't at all normal.

There was something exhilarating about riding at high speeds on the back of a motorcycle. Once we hit the freeway, my arms and legs tightened around him and I pressed my cheek against his shoulder blade even when I felt his chest rumble with his laugh. When we veered off the freeway toward the pier, I relaxed my hold and looked up at my surroundings. Despite my ponytail, wisps of hair had escaped and flew around in my face.

I wasn't sure if I had my mother to thank for my hair or my father. It wasn't necessarily thick, but it was straight and fine. Simone and I shared the same eye color, a blueish-green, but my hair was darker than hers. Hers was a lighter brown, like Hannah's.

The evening was beautiful, almost balmy, with the sun beginning its descent in the western sky. We weren't too far south from where I lived, but I kept quiet. I knew all too well the beginnings of a relationship were usually idle chit chat about life. It made me realize Ty and I didn't have the normal beginning of whatever this was.

When he rolled the motorcycle into a parking spot, I hopped off and slipped out of his jacket. He folded it and put it in his saddlebag. It was warm enough not to need it, even with the night closing in. Confusion swept over me when he slipped his hand into mine, fingers intertwining and pulling me into a stroll. No one was around. He didn't need to pretend.

"Did you enjoy the ride?"

"I did," I admitted. "That was the first time I've been on a motorcycle. It was stimulating."

His laugh was so deep it rumbled through me. "Stimulating?"

"I went to college."

"Where?"

"In Sacramento." He was getting dangerously close to a history I didn't want to go down. "You don't ride in the winter, do you?"

"Nah, my car is . . . in the shop. I'm not sure when I'll get it back. I figured it was warm enough now for the bike to get me around, so it was time to get the car in for some much needed fixes."

Hmm, I had a pretty good idea when people weren't being honest with me. That smelled of a lie, maybe a white lie. But I said nothing, lapsing into thoughts of my own crappy car and its much needed fixes. Someday I would get to them. Or get a new car. Both seemed far off in the distant future.

We wound around until we were walking along the board-walk with the sound of the waves, seagulls, and an occasional blare of a boat horn in the distance. We agreed on wings for dinner, although I wasn't all that hungry. But I loved chicken wings, so I couldn't turn them down when he suggested it.

"Where do you live?" he asked once we settled in the metal chairs along the boardwalk.

I sighed, looking him in the eyes. "Can I trust you?"

"If you couldn't, you wouldn't be here. I wouldn't be here." At my passive look, he gave a chuckle. "Yes, you can trust me. I promise."

"I live near Magnolia Bluff." His eyebrows shot up. "No, no. It's not my house. I live with someone."

"A man?"

My cheeks warmed. "I live with my friend Cassie, my grandmother, and my sister. Cassie's a therapist. It's her dad's house. He's a drummer. Honestly, it's too big for even the three of us. I think it has five bedrooms."

He leaned back, considering the information given. Telling him that, even though I hadn't given Cassie's last name or address, was enough for anyone to look into and find me. He shouldn't have a reason to, but I had said it, anyway. Ty wasn't the person I was worried about finding out where I lived. It was David. He would use it against me. I knew he would.

"Where'd you meet her?"

My eyes met his again. "Her dad is a friend of my uncle's. When Cassie's mom died, she had no one to care for her since he was on tour. He asked Naomi to take her in. We became good friends. I was going through a rough time, and she was a good listener. Turns out, she's fantastic at it and she became a therapist."

"She sounds like a good friend."

"The best. Doing what I do is more about the glory and less about the money. Cassie takes pity on me. Naomi is a massage therapist."

"And your sister?"

"Hannah's still in high school. She's a junior, so one more year."

"Why does Cassie take pity on you?"

I pressed my lips together. "Enough about me. I've already said too much."

"You haven't said anything! Besides, we're about to spend the night together. Now's our time to get to know each other."

I shook my head. "We don't really have to, you know."

His eyes hardened. "Grady's not about to let it slide that he caught you spying. If you don't do this, you're putting me at risk, too."

My stomach clenched. I couldn't do that. Not after all he'd done for me. "I'll do it, but . . . promise me something."

When he leaned forward, I could see the glitter of mischief in his eyes. "You know that you're an attractive woman. You can't expect me to promise you something like I won't touch you."

I could try to be appalled, but the way he said it spread warmth through my midsection I didn't expect. "You don't even know me!"

"And you don't know me." He shrugged. "Does that matter? Are you seeing someone?"

My cheeks burned again. Ordinarily, I wasn't a timid person. Not after living through my youth of sneaking around and stealing from people. I blamed Ty. It was his fault I was blushing ferociously when he said things like that.

"Or maybe . . ."

"Stop that. It doesn't matter. This can't happen."

"Why not? I'm not seeing anyone, and neither are you." He grinned suddenly, as though he thought of something devilish. "This might have happened for a reason. And we've run into each other a few times now."

When our chicken wings showed up a minute later, I was grateful I could stop answering questions and think about what he was saying. What he was saying made sense, but that didn't mean I was going to fall for it. Being a twenty-four-year-old single woman who hadn't much of a dating life to speak of was embarrassing to me. Maybe it was time. I could spend the night with him and never see him again.

"Is Tyler really your name?" I asked, changing the subject between bites.

"No."

I let a chicken bone fall with a thump, surprised. "What else have you been dishonest to me about?"

"Is Riley really your name?" "Yes."

He used his napkin to wipe his fingers, looking away for a moment before looking back at me again. "We're getting into some real trust here. You can't call me anything but Ty. I'm serious."

I leaned forward. "I have no choice but to trust you. With everything."

"My name is Ty, but it's not short for Tyler. It's short for Tiberius."

My mouth fell open. "The Roman emperor? Shit, no wonder you told me it was short for Tyler!" It took effort not to laugh. "Which one of your parents named you that?"

"My mom's a history professor and obsessed with ancient Roman times."

"Siblings?"

"Two brothers, both younger."

I laughed. "What are their Roman names?"

"Marcus and August. Augustus. Obviously, we don't call them that. Marc and Auggie. Dad didn't stand a chance against mom."

"You grew up here?"

He nodded. "Born and raised."

From how he talking, it sounding like an idyllic family, but I was assuming. His voice was light, as though he was happy talking about his family, and his eyes danced. It made me wonder if he grew up in such a loving home, how in the world he got caught up in illegal activities. All it did was confuse me more.

"What about you, Riley?"

Laughter skittered away as the focus turned to me. I would much rather talk about him than me. What I had already told him summed up my life. It was simple and happy enough.

"Come on," he said, trying to coax me with his charm. "I showed you mine. Now you have to show me yours. You said you went to school in Sacramento, and you live with your friend, grandmother, and sister."

I swallowed the deepest breath I could. There were things I could tell him without revealing my true past. This wasn't the end of the world. "My upbringing doesn't seem as family friendly as yours." His eyebrows raised. "It sounds like your family is really fun."

His shoulders rolled. "They are. Maybe someday you'll get to meet them."

Wha . . . what? This was temporary, although it was entirely possible Ty and I could end up being friends. Looking deep into his eyes, the way it shot right to my loins, I knew it could never be. He was too damn sexy for a friend.

"So?"

"We lived in Fresno until Cassie's mom died, then we went to live in Los Angeles in her mom's empty house there. When Cassie graduated and went to school in Sacramento, it made no sense for us to stay in Los Angeles. Lex said we could move up here. That was during my junior year of high school."

I didn't add that the original reason we moved here was because David found me again. We had no choice but to move. He hadn't found me again after that. When I got the job with the agency, I conducted some digging and discovered that he'd been arrested for possession with intent to distribute and the court had sentenced him to two years in prison. Relief swept through me. Until now.

"Parents? Just one sibling?"

I shook my head. "I don't know my dad, don't want to know my mom. And I have no other siblings besides Hannah. At least that I know of. Naomi took us away from my mother when I was fourteen. Hannah was almost seven. Cassie convinced me to go to the same college in Sacramento as she did. She loved it there. It was an excellent school. Wonderful area."

"To become a pet detective?"

My eyes narrowed. "I'm a private investigator, if you have

to know."

He waved his hand, leaning back in his chair. "Investigating us, are you?"

Laughter escaped. I couldn't help it, damn him. "Originally, I wanted to be a veterinarian, but that's a lot of schooling and a lot of money. I volunteered in an animal shelter during college and did some odd jobs for people. When I graduated, I found the job at the agency. I applied and got it. The rest is history."

"How long've you been there?"

"A little over six months. I just graduated last year."

"Are you investigating us?"

I squirmed in my chair. "No." It was only a half lie.

Leaning back in his chair, legs stretched out in front of him and off to the side, he stared at me. Really stared at me. I couldn't look away.

"I haven't met someone like you."

"You've said that before." I tilted my head to the side, keeping my eyes locked with his. I could say the same about him. There wasn't anyone I could remember that was remotely like him. "Why do you say that?"

"I'm not sure I can answer that. You're bold. Like you're not afraid of anything."

"That's not true. Grady had me scared when he had that gun on me. And when I had the panic attack in your bedroom."

"You don't *seem* to be afraid of anything, but you're sensitive and *real*. Every woman I have ever known, including my ex, has not been as real as you are."

That was an awful lot to live up to. What he said sank in and made me think about it for a moment. If he knew the real me, knew about my past, I wondered if he would still say he hadn't met someone like me before.

"I like you, Riley," came his sudden announcement.

A smile curved my lips. "I like you, too, Tiberius."

We finished our wings, avoiding any more talk about our

pasts, then walked along the boardwalk amongst the twinkling lights. There was something about him, other than coming to my rescue, which made me feel safe. For someone who ran with criminals, I liked him more than I wanted to admit to myself. That wasn't true. He was like Cameron.

Cameron had stuck his neck out for me over ten years ago. Ty had done the same when I tried to sneak into his house. Cameron had come to my rescue on more than one occasion, and it appeared Ty was doing the same. And they were both in some type of illegal activity. I knew Cameron wasn't squeaky clean, just as I knew Regan wasn't. They had done illegal things. As I had.

I was condemning Ty for being a criminal when you couldn't get any worse than what I had done in my past. Stealing was one thing, but . . . David was right. I had blood on my hands. Finnegan Caspian's blood.

When I looked over at Ty, he was studying me. The way he watched me sent a burst of warmth up my body. Who was this man that he could make me feel like this? What was going on with me? No one had gotten this close before, slicing through my shield like it was a thin layer of ice beneath the blazing sun.

"Why are you looking at me like that?" I asked, whispering when we didn't need to whisper now.

"At the risk of sounding cliché, you're beautiful."

I glanced away, hiding my wide eyes. "I already told you I'd spend the night with you."

He stopped walking, and after a few more steps, I stopped. "You act like no one has ever said that before."

I closed my eyes for a moment before looking out at the darkness covering the water. If only I could tell him my deepest and darkest secrets. There were parts that Naomi knew and parts that Cassie knew. There were parts that Cameron knew. But none of them knew it all. Everything that I had gone through with my junkie of a mother and David. David, whom I had grown up thinking was my brother, then finding out he wasn't. He had damaged me more than anyone could damage someone else. He controlled me, and he still controlled me.

"Riley . . ."

Ty brushed his fingers against mine and curled them around until our hands intertwined. I felt it deep inside, so deep I had to suck in my breath quickly. He made no other moves. Just held my fingers within his, as though it was a silent way of saying he understood when I hadn't uttered a single word.

"No one ever has."

David, for insisting that he and I be together, had never once complimented me. Not on my looks, my personality, or anything that I had done right. Sure, he had his ways when I was a little girl of making me feel like I was safe with him, but that was just a way to manipulate me later in life. He had never once praised me. For anything.

"No one?"

"It doesn't matter. Let's keep walking."

I tried to pull my hand away from his, but he pulled my hand within his and refused to release his hold. "If no one has told you that before, then everyone is blind or stupid."

When he stepped toward me, it wasn't to make a move but to continue walking as I had requested. The night was growing cooler, and I knew we would need to get back soon or he would freeze on the motorcycle.

"We should get back," I said. "It's too cold for you without a jacket."

He chuckled. "Concerned? I'll let you warm me up later."

I shot him a look, but his eyes told me he wouldn't back down. "Ty, the woman you think I am, I'm not. I definitely don't do one-night stands, and I definitely don't sleep with men after a first date, if that's what this is."

"Fair enough."

Chapter Ten

It was past ten by the time we rolled up in the driveway after our boardwalk interlude. When he stopped the motorcycle and kicked the peg down with his boot, I slowly withdrew my arms from around him. The sudden absence of his muscles left me with an odd sensation in the pit of my stomach. I studied the faint color of the wings of the phoenix on the full expanse of his upper back through his thin t-shirt. It spread across his shoulders and curled around almost to his biceps, and I fought the urge to trace the swirls of red and black with my fingers.

When he turned to see what was taking me so long to climb off, I gave him an impish half-grin before accepting his hand and swinging my leg over. Being on a motorcycle twice now, it was an adrenaline rush I hadn't been expecting.

He was looking down at me with curiosity while my mind raced, trying to work my way around how I would spend the night with a guy I barely knew, was attracted to, and had done nothing close to this before.

"Okay?" he asked.

No, I'm not okay. But I'll have to be. I nodded. "I'm fine. Let's go in and see what your buddies are up to."

"We can go straight to my room."

"No." When I shook my head, my hair shook loose from the temporary bun holding it up. A light brightened his eyes. "I have to do this. I got us into this mess."

Taking up my hand, he looked at it for a moment, then tucked it firmly with his and pulled me along behind him into the house.

It was strangely dark and quiet, but I could hear the heavy beat of Slipknot playing in the background, along with hushed voices in the living room.

I was grateful he wasn't making me go in first. I didn't think he would, considering he'd saved my ass earlier. Why put me in danger now after going through all that trouble? We walked into the living room, finding Merrick playing his games with Jack. Queenie was curled between them.

Queenie looked like she was comfortable here. Jack's eyes met mine, and I smiled. They looked comfortable, and not nearly as dangerous as I thought. It was perplexing. The guns were gone, as was the white substance on the coffee table. It looked like a normal frat house setting, with guys sitting around drinking and playing video games.

"Want a beer?" Jack asked.

Suddenly, I was nervous. What if they grilled me with questions? "I'm actually pretty tired," I said, pulling my lip between my teeth.

Merrick, with his shaggy blonde hair, tore his eyes away from his game to look up at me. The sly grin that came across his face was unmistakable. He needed a shave, his jaw and upper lip sporting at least a few days' growth. If he wasn't careful, he'd start looking like Grady, that mean bastard.

"Leave her be," Ty growled, keeping my hand firmly in his and leading me across the living room toward his room.

As much as I would have liked to get the low-down on the other guys, it wasn't them I was interested in. I would have liked to see Grady, if only to get my phone back. When Ty closed the door behind us, I shuddered. Getting myself involved with Ty was one thing. I didn't want to get involved with anyone else. Not on this level.

I slipped out of his jacket and handed it to him. "Thank you."

"No problem. What do you want to do now?"

I hadn't been lying when I said I was tired, but suddenly I felt odd jumping into bed with him. There was no avoiding it. "I wouldn't mind chilling in here. You can hang out with your buddies. Don't worry about me."

He draped the jacket over the chair, turning back to me and crossing his arms in front of his chest. I felt stupid. If we were playing a part, he wouldn't leave me in here and go hang out with his roommates.

"No."

I had to laugh at his bluntness. "Like I told you, I'm not the woman you think I am."

"What's the harm in it?"

Everything! I wanted to scream. But I wasn't being honest with myself. This wasn't real. We weren't in a genuine relationship. There was nothing stopping me from walking away from him, and him walking away from me when Queenie returned to her rightful owner.

"You're right," I said, slowly. "You don't have a spare toothbrush, do you? Or a t-shirt I can sleep in?"

"I have a t-shirt. No spare toothbrush."

I shrugged. "I can use my finger. Not ideal, but I've dealt with worse."

"The bathroom is across the hall," he said. "Take your time."

When I got into the bathroom, I closed the door and leaned against it while my chest heaved. *Please, God, not now. I'm fine, and I'm safe. I think.* Ty made me feel safe, even being in the same house with Grady and two other guys I didn't know. I closed my eyes, counting to ten and back until my breathing evened out. Ty had done nothing short of saving my ass. He wouldn't hurt me, and I was almost positive he wouldn't do something I didn't want to do. It just didn't seem like he was the type.

After semi-brushing my teeth and splashing some water on my face, I returned to his room to find he had removed his shirt and jeans. A fiery flush crept up my neck to my cheeks at him, standing in his boxers. Even with his back to me, my mouth dried up. I studied the giant phoenix on his upper back. The tattoo was beautiful, making the urge to draw my fingers over the deep, colorful lines worse than before.

"Damn it," he murmured, turning. "I thought you would take longer."

I shook my head, unable to catch my voice while I crossed the room. He put a t-shirt on the side of the bed I assumed was the side I would sleep. Staring down at it, I wasn't sure what to do. Normally, I wasn't a shy person, but this was different. I looked up at him.

"Be right back," he said, quickly leaving me alone in the room.

Breathing a sigh of relief, I pulled my shirt over my head and pulled on his t-shirt that was just long enough to cover the important parts. I sat down and pulled off my boots, socks and leggings, thanking God I shaved my legs. While I thought about leaving my leggings on, these didn't slide smoothly with sheets and blankets. I didn't enjoy sleeping in anything but a t-shirt.

True to his word, Ty came back only a few minutes later. He stopped, taking in the sight of me in his t-shirt and legs bare to his gaze. I wanted to know what he was thinking, the way he was looking at me. Or did I?

Instead, he walked to the other side of the bed and threw the blankets back before sitting down. I was acutely aware of everything about him. The clean, masculine scent of him and the finely toned, muscular body. I sat down, turning to him.

"Is this weird?" I whispered.

"Absolutely. When can I see you again?"

I smiled. "You want to see me after this? Like, for real?"

He shrugged, leaning back against the wall. "Maybe."

"What do you do when you aren't riding around on your motorcycle or working?" *Or kidnapping dogs*? I asked silently, even knowing he wasn't directly to blame. "Do you drink beer and play video games?"

"I do a lot of lifting weights. Tinkering with my bike. Sometimes I read."

Damn it. Why does he have to be so likeable?

"What do you do when you aren't working, or trying to get into my house, pissing off my roommates?"

I laughed. "I read. A lot. Even cookbooks, even though I suck at cooking."

"Give me one secret."

"No! I'm not giving you shit!"

"Come on. I'll show you mine, if you show me yours."

Lord, he was charming. I was in his bed. And the room was getting chilly. Quickly, I joined him below the blankets, nicely surprised that he was like a ball of fire beneath. Even being about a foot away from me, I could feel his warmth.

I sighed. "I have tattoos."

He rolled his eyes. "Obviously."

I looked down at my wrist. "No, I have others."

After a minute, he said: "Are you going to show me?"

Uh . . . "Maybe someday."

"Riley," came his whisper. "Show me your tattoos. I won't look at anything private." He grinned. "Unless that's where you have them."

"You should have just stayed in the room while I was changing." I scooted out of the bed, raising a brow when he sat up with interest. "I swear if you laugh, I'm getting all my clothes back on and sneaking out your window."

Even his laugh was sexy. I turned and pulled the t-shirt up until it was partially off, fully aware that he could see my thong and full view of my ass. If I would have kept my leggings on, this wouldn't be so revealing, but it was what it was. I reached up to sweep my hair out of the way to reveal the colorful compass in the center of my upper back.

It wasn't nearly as large as his phoenix, but it was simple and it was a representation of where I was going in life. I was never going back, no matter how much David tried to pull me back in.

"Very nice," came his throaty purr. I wasn't sure if he was looking at my tattoo or my ass. "Are there others?"

"Yes."

This time he didn't have to ask me to show him, even though I hesitated. I turned halfway, covering my breast with my hand to show him the line of black stars, big and small, from my hip to just short of my armpit. Once I was certain he could see them, I slipped back into the t-shirt and climbed back in next to him.

"Now you know my secret. What's yours?"

"When I was a senior in high school, they voted me the one most likely to get a girl pregnant."

My mouth fell open. It wasn't surprising. He was charming and good-looking. I was more surprised that he told me that. "And?"

"Never happened."

"That's good. One thing about high school is that you never want what they think you're going to end up like to come true."

"What did they say about you in high school?"

"Nope. I gave you my secret. I'm not giving you more."

He folded his arms across his chest. "Can I ask you something, then?"

I slowly nodded.

"You didn't feel self-conscious about taking off your t-shirt in front of me?" I could only shake my head. "I can't promise to keep my hands to myself. You're a highly attractive woman."

"Thanks." I slid down, turning on my side and cradling my head in my hand.

"Were you telling the truth? About being tired?"

"Yes," I lied.

We continued talking well into the night. I didn't know what time I had drifted to sleep, but his bed was warm and comfortable. It was like a cocoon I could burrow into, and I realized I hadn't been sleeping much lately with the stake-out.

Chapter Eleven

"Don't forget to empty the rest of the coffee. Marianne will have a fit if she comes in tomorrow morning, and we forgot to do it," I told Paul as I picked up the two trash bags and gave the back door a hip bump.

Paul and I usually closed the diner on the weekends, being the most dependable teenagers that worked there. The owner, Marianne, opened in the mornings and needed someone trustworthy enough to lock up.

I had worked at the diner for over six months now, after school and on the weekends. At sixteen, I begged Naomi to allow me to work so I could have my own money. Ever since Hannah and I had gone to live with her, she insisted on giving us allowances for helping around the house with chores. Never once had I stolen from anyone or any place since leaving Simone's household, and Hannah was too young to know anything about what David and I had done. I didn't need to steal now. But working a job was different. It was a teenage rite of passage.

Naomi relented, even though she wasn't keen on me working in public. Los Angeles was a big city, and there wasn't much harm in allowing it. Especially since most of my shifts were with Paul.

The night was chilly, stars twinkling in the inky black sky. I could see my breath as I pulled the heavy bags over to the dumpster. The bang of the lid echoed across the empty parking lot and I threw them each in, glad that neither had leaked anything on my uniform.

I turned back into the warmth of the building when I felt a hand around my arm and I fell back. My back slammed against the cold metal of the dumpster, my head snapping back and catching the edge. I opened my mouth, but before I could let out a full scream, a hand cut it off.

"Don't do that, baby," David crooned in my ear. "Aren't you happy to see me? I'm happy to see you, although I'm a little disturbed by you working alone with some guy. Makes me all kinds of angry."

My cry came out muffled by his hand still over my mouth, but the tear that leaked out of the corner of my eyes spilled out unfazed. If he dragged me away from here, no one would know David had taken me.

He pulled me around the dumpster, keeping his hand firmly over my mouth. I was having a hard time breathing. I could feel the rising thump of my heart, the shallowness of my breathing as it slowed. If he didn't remove his hand soon, I was going to pass out.

"You're going to listen to me, Alexis. We're going to walk calmly to my car, and we're going to go for a drive. I don't want to hear another word about it, and if you scream, it's going to be the last thing you do."

I nodded, hoping by agreeing with him he would move his hand so I could get out a full scream and Paul would hear it. He was a football player and big. We weren't involved with each other more than working together and going to the same high school, but Paul would stand up for a girl.

The thought of Paul punching David eased some of my fears, but the back door still wasn't opening. Terror that this might be the time David could get me away sent my heartbeats into a new frenzy. Even when David eased his hand away from my mouth, I couldn't get a solid breath in and my heartbeat only sped up.

"I have a knife in my pocket. Don't think for a minute I won't

use it on you. I swear I will, if you try to get away from me."

The back door swung open, Paul taking up almost the width of the door. David faltered, his hold loosening and his hand falling away. I pushed away from him, falling to the pavement and scraping my knees.

"Riley? You okay?" Paul asked.

I turned, looking back at the dumpster to see no sign of David. He had fled into the darkness of the night like the coward he was. The tears came swiftly, but Paul helped me up and into the warmth of the kitchen.

I was gasping for breath, hoping I could catch it enough to speak with him.

"Are you okay? Should we call the police?"

I shook my head, unable to answer him. My knees throbbed where I had scraped them on the pavement, and I couldn't stop shaking. All I could wonder was when this would end.

"Riley?"

Clutching the blankets to my chest, I bolted up and searched in the darkness surrounding me. For a minute, I wasn't sure where I was until I felt a reassuring hand on my back. Ty. I breathed a sigh of relief. I wasn't sixteen anymore. And David wouldn't get the best of me again. Except even now, I still wasn't sure. He could ruin everything.

"I'm okay," I whispered. "Just need some water."

He moved to leave, but my hand on his arm stopped him. "No. I'll get it. I need . . . air. I'll be right back."

Ty said nothing as I slipped out of the cozy warmth of the bed and left the room. It was in the early hours of the morning; the house was completely dark. I knew my way easily enough and hurried into the kitchen, opening cupboards quietly to   find a glass.

It took me a few gulps of water to calm myself down, but at least it hadn't been a panic attack. Just a nightmare. Or a terrible memory. Had Paul not come out when he did, David would have had me. I shuddered, leaning my arms on the edge of the sink and dangling the glass loosely in my hands.

When I heard a noise behind me, I stood quickly and turned to see Jack leaning in against the wall. The look in his eyes was lazy, almost predatory. The t-shirt was barely decent, I knew that. Stupid of me to have been prancing around in a house full of guys like this, even though I thought they would have been asleep.

"I'm surprised Ty let you out of his bed," he drawled.

I scoffed, not sure what I could answer to something like that.

"Odd that none of us knew about you." He pushed away from the door, trudging toward me. I wasn't the type to back down, holding my ground even when he stopped just in front of me. "Why is that?"

It appears Grady wasn't the only one with suspicions. And here I thought Merrick and Jack were friendly enough. I should have joined them for at least a little while before going to bed, just to avoid this distrust.

I shrugged, snaking out my arm to slide the glass onto the counter. If I learned anything about predators, it was not to make any sudden movements. Calm and collected.

"Ty and I have been friends for a long time." He cocked his head to the side. "Seems to me he would have mentioned you."

This was dangerous ground. Was that a warning, or a double meaning? I wondered. "Maybe this is new, and he didn't want to mention it to you yet."

"I don't think so. Riley." He leaned closer when I thought he couldn't get any closer to me.

"Because you think Ty should tell you everything, even though you've been friends for a long time?" I asked, my voice laced with acid.

The smile that curved his mouth was devious. "We've been friends all our lives. But you . . . you've got balls for a chick. No one stands up to Grady. None that I've seen."

"Grady isn't the only one I'll stand up to."

His laugh was quiet. "I don't doubt that for a second."

"That's enough, Jack," came Ty's voice from the hallway.

I breathed a sigh of relief. Jack stepped back from me as Ty rounded the corner, wasting no time in striding over to me. His arm slid protectively around my waist, staking his claim on me again with a warning. My pride kicked up a notch. Jack seemed likeable enough when he wasn't acting like a douchebag friend. I wondered why he felt the need to tell me about their friendship.

"You okay?" Ty whispered down to me, his lips brushing my temple. I nodded. "Something you want to say, Jack?"

He threw up his hands as though he were innocent. "Nah, I was just welcoming her to the neighborhood."

When Ty's jaw tensed, I knew it rattled him. "Make sure that's all you do, buddy."

Jack inclined his head toward me, and we slipped past him with no further words. I didn't get the feeling that Jack was warning me about anything other than he was a suspicious. Or maybe he was.

Once we were back in the bedroom's darkness, I all but dove back under the blankets and waited for Ty. When the bed dipped and I felt his warm spreading, I could finally relax.

"Want to tell me about your dream?"

"No."

"Want to tell me what Jack said to you?"

I curled to my side, facing him, even though it was too dark to see him clearly. "It's like he said. He was just welcoming me to the neighborhood."

There was a moment of silence between us, almost as though he was distrustful of that. "I've known Jack for a long time. If there is one thing about him, he'll do anything to get a woman into bed."

"Even if it's his friends?"

"Even if she belongs to his friend."

I bristled. I didn't belong to anyone and I would never

belong to someone. "Has he ever taken a girl from you?"

"No."

"But?"

He sighed. "There's a first time for everything. Especially when the girl is standing in the kitchen in a shirt barely covering her very nice ass."

Thankfully, the dark hid the heat that crept up my face. "I'm sure he's seen a woman's ass before."

"I don't know that there've been any women in this house before, Riley. But, Jack is . . . well, it's been a while since he's had a girlfriend."

"He didn't touch me," I whispered.

"I might have killed him," he whispered back.

Confused, I frowned. "I don't belong to you."

"I'd defend you whether or not you were mine. And you would never belong to me. That's not what I meant."

That made me feel better, knowing that he wasn't that type of guy. I relaxed a little more, feeling protected, even when I didn't feel the need to be protected from Jack. Grady, maybe. Not Jack.

Chapter Twelve

"I'm not sure I've ever woken up in such a good mood before."

Ty's sinewy body molded against mine, with his arm casually slung over my waist as I peeled open my eyes. I was grateful to be facing away from him, so he couldn't see the redness rising in my cheeks. The length of him pressed firmly against the curve of my backside. I could feel nothing but the heat of his skin, the strength of his muscles, and how being in this position affected him.

We agreed when we returned to the house that we would sleep far apart in his bed, as the bed was large enough to do so. Somehow, that hadn't happened after we'd gone back to bed. I couldn't tell if it was my fault, his fault, or both.

"How could you be in such a good mood?" I murmured.

He laughed, and I could feel the warmth of his mouth at the nape of my neck. It would be rude to fling him off, as I was rather comfortable in the cocoon of his embrace. I hadn't been in bed with any man I'd known for less than twenty-four hours. This was new for me, but it was far from uncomfortable. It was . . . nice.

"How could I not?"

"I need to leave," I whispered. "Cass is going to call the police if I don't check in soon."

He stiffened behind me, the brawn of his arms pulling me even closer. "I wouldn't blame her. Quite a mess you got yourself into last night."

As much as I hated to move, I did, but only to turn myself

around so I was facing him. Odd that I wasn't panicking in this situation. "When is the last relationship you were in?"

Surprise flashed in his eyes. "What kind of question is that?"

"One that I want to know." I tried to flutter my eyes at him, like a girl. "I'm in your bed, Ty. In your *arms*. Tell me."

"When was yours?"

"I asked you first."

He closed his eyes, withdrawing his arm from me and flopping onto his back. "My last serious relationship was a few years ago. I've dated here and there, but nothing serious."

"I didn't mean . . ."

Damn it, why did I always need to push people away? I threw off the blankets, ready to escape, when his arm snaked out around my waist. He pulled me right back against him, except this time his mouth was on mine before I could think twice. At first, I stayed as still as possible until his lips moved against mine. My response was unstoppable. He groaned, deepening the kiss and sliding his hand down to my hip.

I thought if he was going to kiss me, he would have done it last night. I didn't expect him to kiss me this morning. Now that he was, my skin was instantly aflame, my heartbeat erratic, and all thoughts flew out of my head. I realized quickly after meeting him he was sexy, but I never knew he would kiss me like this. If I had, I might have encouraged him to last night. Instead, he had been polite, even understanding of the situation.

For a moment, his mouth left mine only to press against the sensitive skin on my neck while his fingers tangled with the hem of the t-shirt I had borrowed from him. My hands smoothed over the hills of his biceps, at last being able to trace the lines of his phoenix tattoo even though I couldn't see it. My fingers tangled with the hair at his nape. With one powerful arm, he lifted me up and pulled me effortlessly beneath him. We molded together perfectly, as if it was fate that we fit so well. The curves of my body were for him and him alone.

My legs hooked around his waist, his hands roaming up my hips to my waist and cupping my breasts beneath my shirt. The heat of his hands against my bare skin made me gasp. He groaned against my neck, returning his mouth to claim mine and sucking the gasps right out of me.

A banging on his door made us both stop, his mouth still on mine and his hands still on me. My heart threatened to pound out of my chest. Or was that his? His mouth left mine, and he lifted his head.

"Ty, get the fuck up. We have things to do today."

Grady. I really didn't like him.

We stayed without moving for another few minutes until we knew he was gone. Ty looked down into my eyes, his hands slowly sliding away from me. Suddenly, I didn't want him to stop. My body was craving more. It was him. I needed him like I needed nourishment. *Shit*, I thought, disengaging my legs.

His hands caught my hips, my skin felt like he branded it where he touched. "Damn it, but I don't want to stop." His voice was raspy, and I could only think how much I didn't want him to stop.

I offered him a smile, sitting up and giving him a chaste kiss. "Grady, as much as I hate the fucker, isn't probably someone you want to keep waiting."

When I slipped out of the bed, swooping down to retrieve my leggings, I heard his loud groan and turned to see him flop face-down on the bed where I had just been. I couldn't stop my giggle, even when he looked up with a teasing glare.

"Tell me when I can see you again."

I wiggled into my leggings, turning my back to him to swap his t-shirt for my shirt even though he had just had his hands on me. There was no use for modesty now. Making him wait for an answer was a little powerful, while I sat on the edge of the bed to pull on my boots.

"Riley," he growled.

"I suppose you can," I said, standing up and looking down at him. I knew I hadn't exactly answered his question. It was on purpose. I didn't know when he could. "Thank you for last night. I had a great time."

His laugh followed me out the door and stayed with me until I stepped into the kitchen. Grady sat at the small nook table, the glower in his eyes clear. I hoped Ty hurried up and didn't keep this miserable prick waiting.

I saw his jaw flex beneath his rough facial hair, his green eyes piercing. "Think you're smart, do you?"

"Excuse me?"

Grady stood, prowling toward me. *The men in this house could use some manners*, was all I could think. Trying to intimidate me.

"Girlfriends don't go sneaking around houses."

I sighed. "I told you, I didn't know if this was the right house."

"So text him," he snapped, making me flinch. He reached out, taking my hand into his forcefully. I balked at the contact, only to have him slap my phone into my palm. "I don't believe, for one fucking minute, you're his girlfriend."

Call me reckless, but I stepped closer to him. I would have pushed my face right into his if he wasn't a full head taller than me. "I don't give a fuck what you believe. Ty and I are together. So suck on it, Grady."

Before he could do something, like grab his gun, I pulled open the door and left the house quickly. Despite my shaking legs, I ran across the patio, down the driveway, part of the lawn, then down the street until I got to my car. While I extracted the key out of my pocket, I walked around the car to make sure David wasn't hiding before unlocking it and sliding in.

Right after locking the doors, I looked at my cell phone and groaned. It was dead. I'd be home before I had enough charge to call. Cass, Naomi and Hannah would be worried sick. It had been over twenty-four hours since I had checked in last. I was going to be in bigger trouble than I was just in. Except I didn't count spending time with Ty in big trouble. It had been so pleasant; it hadn't occurred to me to have him borrow me his phone. A simple phone call to one of them would have sufficed. I could only wonder again what was happening to me. It was so unlike me to let a guy in like this.

Ty got more out of me during the times we had spent together than anyone else had. Maybe this was what happened when you let someone get close to you. But he would never truly know me until he knew about my past. And that wasn't something I would willingly divulge. To anyone.

Chapter Thirteen

My anxiety was at an all-time high by the time I drove into the garage, slamming the shifter into park. No sooner was I through the door, than I could hear voices coming from the kitchen. Shrieks permeated the room when Gus and Gatsby noticed me, barking and running circles around me. I got down on their level, giving them love after having abandoned them. Gus sniffed me, then sat back on his haunches with accusing eyes. Gatsby didn't care if I smelled like another dog. He wanted all my attention to himself if Gus was going to be standoffish.

Cassie cleared her throat, leaning her hip against the counter with a steaming mug of tea in her hand. Naomi waited patiently for me to finish greeting the boys. Hannah bounced down the stairs and stopped next to Cassie. When I stood, I looked at Hannah first, then Cassie followed by Naomi.

"It wasn't my fault," I said.

Cassie raised her eyebrows. "Really? You're staking out a house and we don't hear from you all night, and it's not your fault? Where was your phone?"

I held it up. "Dead."

"Nuh-uh," Naomi said. "That's a rookie mistake, kiddo. You wouldn't let your phone die. Not during surveillance."

"Please, let me just explain what happened."

"Please do."

I whipped around at the deep voice behind me. The dark hair

and nearly translucent blue eyes of Cameron were unmistakable. I launched myself at him, keeping my arms around him even when Regan sauntered into the kitchen behind him. She paid no attention to me, sliding onto the stool next to Naomi.

"Why would you call him?" I turned my accusation to Cassie. "They're on their honeymoon, Cass! I had it under control."

Regan waved her hand. "It's all good. Nothing wrong with a little Seattle weather."

I snickered. "That's complete bullshit."

Cameron poured a cup of coffee, passing it to Regan. The look between them was that of two people in complete and irrevocable love. It was that which made me envious of their relationship. I could tell when I stayed with them in Regan's condo the night of their wedding. When she moved, he moved.

The look Regan pinned me with issued a challenge. "Are you sleep-deprived? Anywhere Cameron goes, I go. That's the deal we made. And if that's here, making sure you're not in trouble, that's where we'll be. Plus, we were visiting in Vegas, so we weren't far. All it took was a favor from a friend, and we had a private jet bring us here."

I sighed. "I don't know where to start."

"At the beginning," Hannah whispered.

"I got caught."

Cameron and Cassie became alarmed immediately. Everyone began talking at once, and my head couldn't take so many voices. I grabbed a mug from the cupboard and poured myself coffee. Not even bothering to cool it, I took a slug and relished the burn down my throat.

"Riley . . . you don't get caught," Cameron said.

"Tell us what happened," came the quiet command from Hannah.

My mind wandered to Ty. It was odd to wake up in the arms of a man I hardly knew and who had gone to great lengths to keep me safe. He made an impression on me, which said a lot, and I couldn't help but think about him all the way home. It made me wonder when I would see him again. If I would ever see him again. Had he not been there, nothing would have stopped Grady from hurting me. None of the others gave me a sense of what they would have done, but Grady scared me more than anyone had before. Ever.

"Riley?"

A hand slid into mine, my eyes opening when I hadn't realized they were closed. Regan was looking at me with concern. I managed a smile, but I was trembling. This wasn't a panic attack. It was something different I was experiencing. An aftershock to the danger I was just in?

"Do you want to talk, just you and me?" she asked softly. "I know you don't know me like you know Cassie and Naomi, and your sister. You don't have to . . . but I might understand."

I looked at Cameron. The smile that curved his lips was pride. I didn't know what I had done in this life to deserve the support system I had in this room, but it hit me that everyone here had my back. Without reservation and without question. They had come for me because I might have been in danger, calling in a favor from a friend. I was in danger. Except one unlikely person, not presently here, had been my shield.

"You can use my office," Cassie offered.

"No," I said, squaring my shoulders. Enough with the panic attacks and anxiety. "You were all worried. You all need to know what happened."

Without another word, I led them into the living room. I needed to be comfortable, and not panic right now. Gus and Gatsby were not to be left out again, following directly behind me. I had a feeling they would not leave me alone while I was home again. And I wouldn't let them. It was important that I get back to my job, but this was more important. My boys and my family were more important.

We got comfortable on the couches while the dogs laid down

on the floor to wait for us to conclude our business. As soon as I knew it was safe, I'd take them out to the park for a long run. They earned it as chaotic as it had been lately.

"Did something happen?" Hannah asked gently.

I laughed, keeping my coffee in my hands. "I'm so embarrassed."

Regan smiled, then laughed. "I've had plenty of embarrassing things happen. I'm sure we all have. Cam can tell you all about it. I put myself at risk, as angry as it made him, and I almost paid the price."

That summed it up. Putting myself at risk was sometimes a part of my job. It had never gotten out of hand before. "Like I said, I got caught." I took a deep breath. "Twice."

Everyone started talking at once again. I held up my hand, and Regan was bold enough to take charge again by shushing everyone. Her eyebrows remained perfectly arched. "Tell us how you got caught."

I sighed, beginning my tale from the moment they assigned me this monstrous case, leaving out any details about David. I still hadn't figured out how he'd found me there of all places. "I didn't know the key would stick and the motorcycle would fall on me. One of the gang members found me trapped under it."

A giggle erupted from Hannah, then Regan, and I smiled. Cassie and Naomi were remaining tight-lipped about it, but I wasn't worried about Naomi. She reserved her judgement until she heard all the facts. Cassie looked like she was brimming with questions she wanted to ask. Hannah and Regan weren't wrong for thinking it was funny. It wasn't when it happened, but it was now. Absurd, really.

"Obviously, you got out of it," Cassie said, her legs pulled up halfway beneath her.

"I did. I even cut my leg, and he brought me inside and patched me up."

Leaning back, Regan gasped at the new information. I had

told no one of what I had been up to. "You're kidding."

I shook my head. "He told me to never come back."

The smile that curved her lips spoke volumes. "You like him."

"There's more," I said, my voice small while I told my rapt audience about the events that unfolded yesterday.

As I described the part about Grady and the gun pressed against my head, I watched Cameron's body language become more intense. It angered him to know I was in that much danger. I couldn't blame him. One couldn't be friends for as many years as us and not feel affected by knowing that one of us faced down a gun. Unfortunately, it had been me.

"I thought I was dead. I should have been dead. And then he came in and . . ." They were all looking at me with wide eyes. "Told them I was his girlfriend."

After a moment of silence, Regan burst out into laughter, then Cassie, Naomi, and Hannah. Even Gus and Gatsby picked up their heads at the sudden outburst. Cameron was the one with the most unreadable look. I think my story baffled him. It stumped the hell out of me how any of this could have happened.

"Is he good-looking, at least?" Hannah asked, earning herself a shocking look from Naomi answered with a lazy shrug.

I nodded, and I couldn't help the curve of my lips.

Regan looked at Cameron, then her gaze shifted toward me. "From what Cameron has told me about you, I can imagine spending the night with him wasn't easy for you."

"No, but we managed."

"Did you . . ."

Shit! I can't believe she's asking that, and in front of Hannah! I blushed ferociously, not meeting any of their eyes. "He's off limits. I can't like him. He's a part of a job, and nothing more. This might be a good thing, though. I'm inside the house now. *Invited* in. I'm not trespassing."

I didn't mention that, besides trying to do this job for a well-connected popstar, I was also avoiding David. He'd found me at the airport garage. He'd found me at Ty's house, where I confirmed he was my boyfriend. I shivered. David was watching me.

Cameron finally couldn't keep his mouth closed and stood up to pace while Regan plopped back down where he had just been. "You put yourself in real danger, Riles."

"It's my job, *Cameron*," I countered.

I set my coffee calmly down on the coffee table and stood up. This was my life. He wasn't my father. Protecting me, coming to my aid, I got that, but he didn't need to say things like that with such conviction.

"You can't put yourself at risk like that," he said, putting one hand on my forearm. "This is too dangerous. I can't allow it."

I shook him off, anger rising. "I'm not your wife, and I'm pretty sure she won't allow you to dictate her life that way."

Regan was back on her feet, her eyes wide. "Okay, stop. Time out."

Cameron looked like he could throttle me for saying what I did, but I didn't give a shit. I stuck out my chin in defiance. There was a lot that I owed him, but he didn't get to command my life.

"Cam, let's take a walk."

As much as he looked like he didn't want to take a walk, he relented. I realized then how much hold Regan had on him. She was very smart. He knew that, and he respected her judgement. I collapsed on the couch as soon as they were out of the room and I heard the click of the back door.

"Well," Cassie said. "I've got some work to do, and as exciting as this has been, I'm going to get back to it. I'll be in my office. Glad you're safe, Riles."

I gave a nod while she removed herself from the living room, leaving Naomi, Hannah and me, along with the boys, alone. Naomi got up to go into the kitchen, leaving Hannah and me on the couch. My lips quirked into a wry smile at Hannah when she moved closer to me. I slid my hand into hers.

"I'm sorry I didn't call," I said.

"Sounded like you couldn't."

"Not sure what's wrong with me."

"You like this guy." She pushed her shoulder into mine. "I may be younger than you are, but I know you."

"I can't like him."

"But you do."

"What am I going to do, Han?" I whispered, leaning my head on her shoulder.

In return, she rested her head against mine. I was close to Cassie. Close to Cameron and Naomi. But no one could replace my sister. It didn't matter that we didn't have the same father. Hannah was my sister, and I would do everything to protect her.

"Day by day," she said. "Everything has its way of working out."

I lifted my head, looking into her green eyes. "How'd you get so smart?"

"Taught by the best sister in the world."

"I'd do anything for you, you know that."

"Good, because I have homework to do and I know you'd love to do it for me, but I have a grade point average to maintain for the best college options." I all but pushed her up from the couch. She laughed. "You'll be okay."

I wasn't sure if she was asking me or telling me, but I nodded. "Yeah. I'll figure it out. Like you said, it'll work itself out."

I watched Hannah leave, letting out a little sigh before I rose and went to the kitchen. Naomi was working her way around the kitchen, preparing breakfast for the house. She knew she didn't need to make breakfast for everyone, but she liked to cook as much as she liked to garden. Naomi stopped to refill my coffee, looking at me strangely.

"Riley, there are things you should know," she said slowly. "Things I'm not sure you're ready to hear. You've been through a lot of stress lately."

Is she serious?

"Naomi, if there is something you know . . ." I pinned her with my hard gaze, even though I knew she was only trying to be helpful, "then say it. Don't think you get to tell me what I'm ready for. Not after I just had a gun on me."

Her lips quirked, amusingly. "You two are a lot like each other."

"Who?"

"You and Cameron."

I smiled. "We kinda are."

Naomi lifted her hand to my arm, laying it there softly. "You okay, honey?"

I nodded, then smiled. "Never better. Don't worry about me. I'm fine."

I knew she'd still worry, but I had to try. "You can't blame us."

"If only I had placed my phone in a safer spot. I didn't expect it to pop out like that, or for the bastard to take it." My hand covered hers. "I got caught but was saved. And here I am."

She pressed her lips together but stayed silent for a minute. "I called Cameron. Not Cassie. And I think it's about time you know why. I know who your father is."

"I know you do. You tried to tell me when I was eighteen," I said. "I told you then I didn't want to know. Why do you think I'd want to know now?"

That part of my life was over. As far as I was concerned, both of my parents were gone. Simone was more like a distant family member anyway, although I would help her if she decided she wanted to get clean.

"I don't think you were ready when you were eighteen. I think you're ready now."

My eyebrows drew together. "What does this have to do with you calling Cameron? You're really beginning to freak me out."

"You met Cameron's family at the wedding?"

I raised my eyes to meet hers. Of course, I met his family. His family was wealthy and impressive, and yet I liked them immensely. And Regan's family. They were very engaging, especially Reno, although Cameron's mother was less than welcoming. I talked to everyone else but her that night.

"So what? Cameron's family knows my father?" I laughed. "Let me guess, I'm actually Regan's sister! That's it, isn't it? Shit."

"Regan . . . your father . . ." She stopped talking, looking into my eyes. "Reno Moretti is your father."

The air sucked out of my lungs. What the hell? What was she talking about? My head was spinning, trying to remember the wedding reception and meeting Cameron's family. Reno had looked at me oddly at first, but he was understanding, especially when I panicked after thinking I saw David. But they were very nice. Part of me didn't believe it.

"Why are you telling me this now, Naomi?"

She withdrew her hand. "I knew Simone had an affair with him, and I knew she was trying to keep him for the money. Reno has a reputation."

"Yeah, he's a gangster, just like Regan's father. So?"

"I thought it was a blessing he wasn't in your life."

I gasped. How could she think that? The only blessing in my life was Hannah, and until Naomi took us away from Simone, there was nothing else for me in that life. If he had been in my life, would it have been different? And Cameron? I gasped again, my hands coming to my mouth.

"Does Cameron know?"

I didn't wait for her to answer. This time, I pulled back and paced around the kitchen, causing the boys to wonder what was happening. "If Cameron knew he was my brother, why didn't he ever say anything to me? Why?"

"I can't tell you that. You would have to ask him."

Aggravated beyond words, I abandoned my coffee and went into the living room. Cassie's office door was closed. With deep breathing, I willed the anxiety away. I would not panic now. No.

Instead, I would just do what Cameron and Regan did. I would go for a walk to cool down, to clear my head.

"Where are you going?" Naomi asked, following me.

"For a walk," I said, just as the back door opened with Regan and Cameron calmly strolling in, hand in hand.

"What's going on?" Regan asked.

My glare was only for Cameron. "How could you not have told me?"

He looked surprised at my outburst. "What didn't I tell you?"

"Shit, Cameron, just tell me why! How long have you known?"

"Known what?" Regan asked.

"Doesn't she know?"

"Calm down!" he said. "If you would just calm down for a minute, I'll answer your questions, but I need to know what the hell you're talking about."

"That your father had an affair with my mother?" He stared at me. "How long have you known?"

Regan looked shocked at the revelation, leading me to believe he hadn't told her either. I wanted to know why there was secrecy. I slammed my hand down on the counter.

"How long, Cam?"

"I've suspected, but I've never been able to get him to say anything about an affair. I can only assume the picture tucked in his desk drawer is of your mother. But . . ."

"But?"

Regan and I held our breath together. "You and Zoey look very similar. Most people wouldn't be able to tell because she dyes her hair, but when my father saw you, I was waiting for a reaction. And he gave it to me."

I let out a shaky breath, dangerously close to having a meltdown. Cameron didn't deserve my wrath. Regan didn't either. Hell, Naomi didn't, and she's the one who spilled the truth about my parentage when I hadn't wanted it. I couldn't be mad at anyone.

"You are my sister. In all ways, Riles. Even if we don't know it."

Chapter Fourteen

No one moved. No one spoke. I stared at Cameron. Everyone stared at me. The urge to laugh came to me, but the look on Cameron's face was pure seriousness, and if he was telling the truth that would be rude. I wanted to be angry. Everyone who knew me knew I had no desire to know who my father was. I didn't want to know anything about what my mother had done before I was born. I knew enough about what came after.

"Riley?" Cass asked gently. "Are you okay?"

So engrossed in this new shitstorm, I hadn't heard her come out of her office. I ignored her and instead raised my eyebrows, still looking at Cameron. "Are you serious?"

"Dead serious," he said. "He all but confirmed it with his reaction."

"So?"

"If it's true, and you are his daughter, he won't let anything happen to you. And neither will I."

I crossed my arms over my chest, leaning my hip against the counter. This was too much to take in. There were plenty of reasons I wanted to leave my past where it was, but it seemed like everywhere I turned, it was popping up. David. Now this.

Cameron reached out, but I moved and his hand fell away. He looked crushed. I couldn't deal with this right now. Brushing past him and Regan, I ran out of the room with tears burning my eyelids.

"I need some time," I murmured, hurrying into the garage,

getting back into my car and hightailing it out of there with tears in my eyes.

I was suffocating in the house. I needed to get out, at least until I cooled. My head spun, trying to figure out why Naomi felt the need to tell me now. Why didn't Reno come for me if he wanted nothing to happen to me? Questions bounced around in my head that I wouldn't get answers to unless I sat down with Reno and asked him, but right now, I was reeling from it. How long had Cameron suspected it? Did he know when he caught me stealing from him?

Cameron had always been there for me, just like a brother would be. Like David should have been, even though David was the farthest thing from a brother. His own father had abandoned him. My mother had been involved with Vic Martin, who had taken off and left three-year-old David behind. Simone had no choice but to take him in.

I drove even though tears threatened to blind me. It was this or stay and have a major meltdown. I drove into the city, ending up at a coffee shop where Merrick worked and where I had seen Ty the first time.

My mind wandered to when I might see him again. When we parted ways this morning, we hadn't exchanged numbers. We hadn't made plans to see each other, though his roommates expected to see me around the hideout again or prove Grady right. I stayed in my car for a few minutes to compose myself before I went in for coffee and to collect my thoughts. It was nearly noon on a Sunday, so it wasn't busy like it would be on a weekday, although coffee was a big deal in this town.

Merrick wasn't working today, I noticed.

I sat at a table alone, deep in my thoughts and nursing a cup of dark French roast. When Naomi had rescued Hannah and me, I was fourteen. Cameron caught me stealing the month before I turned fourteen, before the incident with Finnigan. Before Naomi took us away. I wondered if he had suspected I was his sister then. Is that why he had been where he was that night? Things changed after that, since I was no longer in the neglectful care of my mother and under the control of David. Of course, David had a chilling warning that he would find me. And he had. Twice now.

The devil must have invaded my thoughts because after sitting there for a short time, David slid into the chair across from me. I glanced up, closing my eyes and heaving a deep sigh. His eyes sparkled with mischief when I opened my eyes. He must have noted my exasperation.

"Happy to see me, are you?" he said, the familiar drawl of his voice slithering across my skin like a snake.

"Not exactly," came my tight reply. "I'm not in the mood for this."

Leaning back in his chair, he stuck out his lower lip. "Oh, poor baby. Sorry to throw some lead balloons into your party, but we have a problem."

God, what now? I felt like crawling under a rock. Anything to hide from everything that was not going right in my world right now. But with David, I couldn't. He had something on me I could never run far enough away from or hide under the tallest rock. Something he could ruin my entire life with, my entire future.

I didn't take the bait and waited for him to continue with explaining why *we* had a problem. As far as I could tell, he had a problem. But I wouldn't say that.

"Seems you're still seeing that guy."

"What is it you want me to do, David?"

"Stop seeing him."

I tilted my head. "I'm not sure I want to." I should goad him, but I was tired of this. I knew the consequences. I couldn't just stop seeing Ty. I had a job to do.

"It's not as easy as you think."

"I don't give a fu—" He abruptly leaned forward, stretching

his hands across the table as though he were reaching for me. But he stopped short, but his eyes softened. "Baby . . . Alexis . . ."

"Don't call me that," I snapped.

When he shook his head, I knew I was running out of time. David wouldn't let me off the hook this easily. He'd found me, and he could tip off the police and I'd go to prison for manslaughter. Letting me free now wouldn't happen.

"Riley?"

My gaze snapped up, widening when Jack strolled into the coffee shop. I couldn't miss the washboard abs, quickly disappearing beneath the t-shirt he was shrugging into. *Yep, my day just can't get better, can it?* Who else would walk through the doors? Grady? Ty? I waited, watching the door instead of Jack walking toward us, praying Ty wasn't coming in behind him. I wasn't ready to explain David. Not to anyone.

"What are you doing here?" he asked.

It was delightful that he was ignoring David. The darkness in his eyes was only on me, a gleam there that shouldn't be since he knew I was the supposed girlfriend of one of his friends. A friend he'd known his entire life, he'd said. It seemed more than a moment of staring at me before he realized I was not alone.

He turned to pin David with his stare. "And you are?"

David leaned back again, his arm casually draping over the back of the empty chair next to him. I wanted to puke at his wanton display of male dominance. I fervently hoped that Jack wasn't buying this bullshit.

"Riley's boyfriend."

"The hell you are," I snapped. "You are someone from my past, and nothing more."

The corner of Jack's mouth quirked up, creating a charming dimple. If I wasn't mistaken, he seemed to like this banter. I felt the powerful need to get him alone and tell him not to mention this to Ty, but that would seem guilty when I wasn't doing anything of the sort. David was like a rash I just had to get rid of.

It wasn't anything I couldn't handle, and it didn't matter whether Ty knew.

The glare from David suggested otherwise. My rebuttal hadn't helped, but I didn't care. He was determined to get me into the role of being completely his. There wasn't a time he wasn't. For whatever reason, he thought he and I would be together forever.

"Will you be around later?"

That caught me off-guard. It was foolish of us to part ways without talking about our next moves unless he was planning on telling his roommates we had broken up. That would be suspicious, I would imagine.

"I'm not sure," I said. "Probably."

"We're counting on it."

The flash of his straight, white teeth and the lilt of his voice made me wonder how dangerous he was if he was a part of this gang. Jack and Merrick seemed the least dangerous if I had to go on appearances only. Grady was by far the most intimidating. But Ty . . . he was a different story. At our first meeting, I would have pegged him as dangerous, but I knew differently now.

"I'll see you soon, I guess."

He gave a nod, then continued on. I watched him go in curiosity. The encounter was so casual. David was watching me stare after Jack, his brow raised in suspicion.

"Who the hell was that?"

I shrugged. The less he knew, the better. If David didn't know who was in the house I visited, he didn't need to.

"Seemed a little chummy with you. I don't like it."

"I'll break it off with him soon." Irritation was thick in my voice. "Is there anything else?"

His eyes slid over me. "If I hear that you're screwing him, you'll pay for it."

My eyes narrowed.

When he stood up, he leaned over me until his lips brushed my cheek. I jerked away from him, but he grabbed my arm to pull me back toward him.

"You'd best do it soon, Alexis." The emphasis on my name sent terror anew shooting down my spine. "Ivy's gotten really pretty since I last saw her."

The front legs of my chair came off the floor, precariously close to tipping me over, as he released me abruptly. He walked out without looking back, just as Merrick came in, leaving me with a feeling of complete dread. There was no doubt in my mind he meant what he said. David always followed through on his threats. I looked out the window, watching him pull up the collar of his jacket while striding across the street. *Bastard.*

Apprehension washed through me. I wasn't the only one he was watching and I would be damned if I'd allow him to ruin Hannah's life. And I was not having that. Not when she was so close to having a bright and beautiful future.

I had just slumped in my chair when Jack returned with a cup of coffee and Merrick following. Merrick didn't look pleased. I could only guess he had been waiting for Jack, and had been waiting too long, bringing him into the coffee shop at the untimely moment David was all but assaulting me.

Jack sat in David's vacant chair, and I groaned when Merrick picked up a chair nearby with one hand and swung it around. He sat in the chair backward and stared at me, along with Jack.

"Problem?" Merrick asked.

My eyes darted to Jack, then back to Merrick. He was asking me?

"Um, is there a problem?" I whispered.

Jack chuckled. "I couldn't help but to notice the . . . rudeness of your friend. Are you all right?"

Absently, I rubbed my arm where David had grabbed it. I didn't know where to begin explaining him, or if I should. It had taken a considerable number of years to escape my past. Mixing it in with my life now wasn't an option. David would not be staying in it long.

"I also saw it," Merrick said. "Not good company to keep, Riley."

I scoffed. "No shit, really? He's a blast from my past, who won't stay away."

"Need us to take care of it for you, or will Ty do it?"

Ty roughing up David was an intriguing picture. I knew it wouldn't help matters, but it was a pretty thought. Maybe I would consider having someone rough David up when this job is done, but hopefully, by that time, David would have left. I doubted it. David wanted something more than just me breaking it off with my pretend boyfriend. He was withholding something from me.

"It's fine. I appreciate the offer, but it's fine. Really."

"So, you and Ty, huh?" The smile curving Merrick's lips was endearing. With his shaggy hair and light eyes, he looked less than formidable. But when he smiled, it made all the difference in the world.

"Yeah, me and Ty."

"Where'd you meet?"

To cover up my alarm, I smiled. This could be a setup. Ty could have already told them something, and they were asking me to see if I had the same story. It wasn't a trap I would easily fall prey to.

"I'm not talking about my relationship with Ty to two dudes I don't know."

Merrick's smile knocked down a peg, but he continued to stare at me, as did Jack. Was this an interrogation? Didn't I just go through with one? An overwhelming need to go home came over me. Running away was bad. I shouldn't have done it, especially to Cameron. They were probably worried. Again.

"Come on!" I said. "I'm seriously not talking about it. Ask me anything else, but not about Ty. It's fairly new to us. Just give us some space."

"Obviously," Jack said. "We've never met you, and he's not had anyone spend the night before. Next time, keep it down a little so you aren't keeping us all up."

My eyebrows shot up. *What the hell was he talking about?*

Nothing even happened between us last night. How could we have been loud? Instead, I shook my head and rolled my eyes.

"Don't you guys have something better to do today than hassle me?"

Merrick's laugh was deep, but he pushed away from the table and set the chair back where he found it. Jack followed him up, but they both hovered over me. Intimidation? I leaned back to look at them.

"Tell Ty I'll see him soon," I said, hoping it would cool them off from the trail.

I watched them walk away without looking back at me, chuckling when Jack pulled off his shirt before even walking out the door. Apparently, he didn't like shirts. It didn't make any difference that the weather was awful. I couldn't say I blamed him. I let out a deep breath, as though I'd been holding it all along, when they were both gone. This was turning out to be a hell of a day. One I would gladly like to be over.

Chapter Fifteen

When I walked into the house an hour later, Cameron was the first to greet me after Gus and Gatsby. He said nothing, just pulled me into his arms and held me for a few moments. I knew I had hurt him by leaving, but I was hurt by learning what I never wanted to know. That wasn't his fault, I knew. That he was my brother comforted me, though.

I hung my head. "I'm sorry."

"No. Don't be." His tone was firm. "I should have told you a long time ago what I suspected. But you should talk to Pop."

"Absolutely not." The words rushed from my mouth so fast and so loud that Regan came swiftly around the corner. "I need time to digest this, Cam. It's not something I can just accept. You as my brother, without question. But a father after never having one? No, not yet."

Regan appeared to be biting back words. I couldn't be certain whether they were harsh. After all, I had hurt Cameron regardless of whether I meant to. Her steps slowed when I pulled away from him, unsure of what I was going to get.

Instead, she stopped at the edge of the kitchen and pressed her lips into a line. "I can't understand what you are going through. I grew up without a mother, but it's not the same. But I know Reno. He's a defender. He would protect you like no other."

"I appreciate it, but I'm not ready to meet with him yet."

I wasn't sure I wanted to meet with him at all, but I knew eventually Cameron—or Regan—would wear me down. When he wanted something, he always got his way. I sighed.

He gave me a nod. "I respect that."

Interesting. "Can I ask how you found out? It's a little odd that I've known you for so long and this is only just coming up now."

Without warning, I unexpectedly had several questions I would ask Reno. I wasn't sure where I would begin. First, I would ask why he didn't say something at the wedding, but then I remembered he asked where I was from. My answer had only been the partial truth. I'm from Seattle now, but Naomi didn't raise us here.

"I told you before. I found a picture. Of him and presumably your mother."

"When?" I rushed to ask. "When did you find the picture?"

He shook his head. "Meeting you was pure coincidence, I promise. But as our friendship developed, and you grew up, I noticed the uncanny resemblance between you and Zoey."

I scoffed. "I saw her at the wedding. Talked to her. She is breathtakingly beautiful, even at her age. And that doesn't answer my question, Cam."

Blowing out a breath, he looked up in thought. "After I graduated from college. Before I went to Spain for my master's degree. Let's see, you would have been seventeen then. And you're as breathtakingly beautiful. Don't sell yourself short."

That calmed me to know he was telling the truth. "Fine, I believe you."

"He wasn't about to discuss it with me. I knew that."

I couldn't validate what Simone was up to back to then. She had multiple partners while I was growing up, and I believed most of them were in exchange for drug money. The thought that I was the kid of some random guy paying her for sex made me want to puke. I'd much rather be Reno's biological daughter, as much as it pained me to know that he might have known about me and done nothing about it. How my life could have been different.

"There are only two people who can confirm it," I said.

"Yes. Talking to him about the situation would be better, since I don't have any information to go on."

Huh. Simone was a gold-digger. Reno Moretti was a wealthy man. My mind raced with what might have happened between them. I thought about meeting Cameron's mother when I met Reno, and while he had a surprise in his eyes, she was surprised but recovered quickly and excused herself. I could only imagine what Simone had done to lure Reno into her life. Disgust filled me.

When I pulled away from Cameron, there was alarm in Regan's eyes and she stepped in front of me as though she would block me from running away again.

I laughed. "I'm not running this time, but I should take the boys to the dog park for a run. They need exercise, otherwise they get hyper." I laughed again. "Like kids."

"We took them for a run this morning," she said through a sideways smile at Cameron. "They were good boys."

"Thank you."

I leaned down to scratch each of them behind their ears, earning myself some nudges and attempted kisses. If it weren't for Gus and Gatsby, I wouldn't be as far along in my therapy. They were my saving grace, and they had been a big help. Other than the occasional panic attack and some bouts of anxiety, I managed well. I didn't consider myself totally cured of my mental health issues. I glanced down at the small black semi-colon tattoo inside my wrist and flooded with memories of Ty touching it and showing him my other tattoos. Heat rushed to my face, and while Regan noticed, she only smiled.

My wrist tattoo was one of the first gifts I gave myself after I graduated from high school. That Ty knew the meaning behind this symbol impressed me, too. The other tattoos came later, and I wasn't certain they would be the only ones I would ever have.

When I stood up, Regan had sidled closer to me. *What is she up to now?* I thought. Having only known her for a short time, I liked her a lot. Cameron's admiration for her made it impossible for me not to. She wasn't perfect, but neither was I. She made him happy, and that made me happy.

I sighed. "I'll let you know when I'm ready to meet him. Okay?"

"You're going to like him." She was so matter of fact about it, as though she were issuing me a challenge.

"I met him at your wedding."

"That doesn't count, and you know it."

I grinned. "It does! I talked to him for a while. Not only that, but he also seated me at his table when he knew I didn't know anyone else there. At no point did he mention he thinks I could be his."

"He is too proud to come outright and ask who your mother is," Cameron said. "Even if he suspects it."

"You mean, he still might not know I'm his daughter?"

He shrugged. "I don't know what happened between them, Riles. I only know that he had an affair, and I think it was with your mother. Sounds like your grandmother confirmed that."

It was time to move on to something else. Nothing was going to come of this conversation unless we had one or both parties in it, and I had no intentions of contacting Simone with questions. If, and when, I spoke to Reno, I would need to accept his side of the story as the truth.

"How long are you staying?"

Cameron's lips curved into a knowing smile. "Eager to get rid of us so soon? I thought you enjoyed having us around."

"That's not what I mean. We have plenty of room here. You and Regan are welcome to stay as long as you'd like to."

Gus and Gatsby followed me into the living room. When I settled onto the couch, the boys jumped up to flank me on both sides. Cameron and Regan had no choice but to find another spot on the couch or in the matching oversized chairs. They settled closely on the other end of the couch.

"I have to admit, it's been a while since I've been here. I'm up for reacquainting with the fine coffee of Seattle while we're here," Regan murmured. She tucked her legs under her while leaning against Cameron.

"Decaf?" Cameron asked.

"Give her a break, Cam," I said. "Coffee will not hurt the baby. You can't believe everything you read. Geez."

"*Thank you*, Riley."

"Can't I be an overprotective father?"

"No," Regan and I said, rather emphatically.

We dissolved into laughter while he rolled his eyes, drawing his arms closer around her. It was good to lighten the mood after such a heavy discussion. I was happy to be in their company, not having had enough time while I was in California. With the baby due in September, I wasn't sure how long I'd have with them.

"Seriously, though. Where are you going after this?"

"Cameron thinks we're going back to Cape Haven, but I'm thinking it would be nice to go to back to Las Vegas for a bit." I knew what was coming next. "You could join us . . ."

"I'll *think* about it," I said. "It's going to depend on this job and how quickly I can wrap it up."

It seemed to appease her. For now.

Chapter Sixteen

When I walked into the living room a few days later, Ty sat comfortably on the couch beside Merrick, with Jack in his usual spot and Queenie curled in his lap. There was no sign of Grady today, eliciting a sigh of relief when I stepped in.

Queenie let out a tiny bark when she saw me, so I walked over to Jack, scratching her tiny head. I couldn't help but muse how I was used to rescuing bigger dogs. Queenie would be the tiniest dog I had ever rescued. I didn't remember seeing a dog so small as she was. Maria told me specifically not to grab her, but to find out what the plan was.

Jack looked up at me. "How're you?"

I shrugged. "Getting by."

"You're okay after the other day?" I nodded. "You'll tell us if you have problems?"

I shot a glance over at Ty, who raised his eyebrow in question, then over at Jack. He listened intently to the interchange, keeping his eyes on me even when he took a drink from his bottle of beer.

"Of course."

I gave Queenie one more pat on the head and crossed the living room, causing a groan from Merrick. My distraction must have caused an issue in his video game. I rolled my eyes. I'd seen Merrick enough times now. I imagined video games were his sole activity outside of normal daily things to do.

"Do you like your job at the coffee shop, Merrick?" I asked, stopping next to Ty.

He didn't take his eyes off the television. "Yeah. Why do you ask? Where do you work, and do you like it?"

Shit. I didn't want the questions to land back on me. Instead, I held up my hands. "Sorry! Didn't mean to strike a nerve."

Never once did he take his eyes from his game, even when I gasped at Ty's arm around my waist a second before he pulled me down into his lap. Cradled across his thighs, my face turned red.

"Someone giving you a hard time?" he murmured.

"Yeah, you." He squeezed. "I ran into Merrick and Jack the other day while I was getting coffee."

"Popular place to run into you."

"So, where do you work?" Jack asked.

Sitting on Ty's lap while having a conversation with the others in the room made me self-conscious, but the way his arm slung around my waist was comforting. It was as though he put up a shield of protection with the simple gesture. It was casual to Ty, but it wasn't so much to me. A part to be played, I knew, but this was a familiarity I didn't know.

Eyes wide, I watched Ty's fingers dance up my thigh, followed by a deep-throated chuckle I felt against my side. My gaze snapped to his, finding his blue eyes full of mischief. His arm tightened when he leaned up, his mouth almost touching my ear.

"Relax," he whispered.

"Jesus, Ty," Jack growled. "You gonna make out with her right here in front of us?"

My face burned with embarrassment. He didn't kiss me. All he did was pull me into his lap and put his hand on my thigh. Afraid of my lack of knowledge in this was showing, I pushed up from his lap and sat down between him and Merrick. Merrick paid no attention, but Queenie did when she jumped from Jack's lap, right over into mine.

I laughed when she looked at me with her puppy-dog eyes, giving in to her silent demand and petting her while Jack pinched his lips together as though he lost a prize.

All I could do was murmur an apology, but Merrick laughed. "I think the dog prefers a woman's touch, Jack. Not that yours isn't feminine enough."

Jack shot him a nasty look.

"Hey, calling it like I see it. Don't blame me for the dog's preference."

"She's my dog."

Merrick continued his laughter while Jack stood up, leaving the room. "For now. Don't get too used to it," Merrick called after him.

I looked over at Ty, his eyes still lazily watching me. The last time we spent time together felt different from how it was between us now, like he was possessive of me, and I couldn't understand if it was an act, or if the real Ty sat beside me. Jack returned, passing a beer to Merrick, then to Ty.

"Can I get you one, Riley?"

"No. Thanks."

"Don't like beer?" he asked, returning to his chair.

Ty chugged from his bottle like it would disappear if he hadn't downed it, half gone before he pulled it away, hanging his arm loosely over the side of the couch with it dangling in his hand. I could only ask myself what I had gotten into. Seemed like I was getting in deeper and deeper.

"It's not my favorite," I said, biting my bottom lip.

"What is?"

I shrugged. "Tequila, I guess. But I'm not really in the mood for drinking." At his frown, I added: "Don't worry, I'm fine."

Ty, despite the tiny growl from Queenie, slid his arm around my shoulders and pulled me toward him. I expected him to smell of beer, something I had smelled often in my youth when Simone brought home someone new, but he didn't. I didn't know how many he had before I arrived. He didn't smell like anything but his masculinity, as he had the time I was here before. Queenie discovered she didn't like him and hopped down, rejoining Jack.

When I met his eyes, he smiled. "See? She prefers me. I think she wanted to sniff out the competition."

"No doubt," I said.

"You didn't answer my question, Riley. You work around the coffee shop?" Jack asked.

Here we go, I thought. Here came the barrage of questions I tried to prepare myself for in advance. If Ty and I were going to pull off a relationship while I tried to get closer to getting Queenie out of there, I needed to face his roommates, and I knew they would question my life.

"Yes, I'm a receptionist at a dental office over there." After a minute, I added: "Part time. It's all they had, so I had to take it until something opens up."

"Did you graduate?" he continued.

"High school?" He nodded. "Barely. I'm not as smart as you think I am."

"You from around here?"

I couldn't tell if Jack would continue to pepper me with questions. Ty tried to relax me by running his fingertips along my arm. "Not originally, no. I'm from California."

"LA?"

"Jesus, Jack," Merrick snapped. "Are you interrogating her?"

Jack shot him another nasty glare. "It's called getting to know her. Since she's sleeping with a friend of ours, don't you think we should know something about her?"

I laughed, hoping it didn't sound nervous. "Yes, Fresno and LA for a time. What about you? Did you grow up here?"

"We all did. I went to school with Ty, and Merrick knew Grady. They went to another school, but they were buddies."

"I can talk for myself," Merrick said, his thumbs clicking on the control and his eyes remaining on the screen. "Thanks though."

Jack rolled his eyes.

"What about you, Merrick? Did you go to college?"

"Finished school. That was enough," he answered. "Working at the coffee shop, that's all I need. Don't need a college degree."

Ty's patience for the conversation leaving him out was admiral. The trail of his fingers along my arm and the steady beat of his heartbeat against my shoulder blade made me aware of his presence. Otherwise, he remained quiet.

"You go to college, Jack?"

He laughed. "No. No job either, although I am lookin' for one."

"How do you pay for shit?" I laughed.

"Living frugally. I have some money saved up I live on. It's gotten me far enough. Not in too much hurry to get a job. That and I'd have to wear a shirt."

I noticed. "Maybe you should move to California and get a job as a lifeguard. They don't have to wear shirts."

He rolled back, laughing, nearly tipping over his beer. I glanced up at Ty, whispering: "Not that funny."

The back door slammed, my muscles instantly tensing. Ty's fingers continued their trek along my arm, the other tightening around me when Grady rounded the corner. His gaze immediately found me, eyes hardening.

I stared back, seemingly unfazed. Only Ty knew how his presence affected me. Grady set a brown grocery bag on the coffee table, blocking Merrick's way and causing him to throw the control down with a colorful curse.

"Divide that up," he said, then looked at me. "Make yourself useful since you're here and make us some dinner."

My mouth popped open. "I don't cook. I can order some pizzas." And dip into what money I had in my checking account.

Grady crossed his arms in front of his chest, staring down at me. I thought he'd push the issue, forcing me to cook them something. Reading cookbooks was a silly thing. I didn't actually pay attention to the recipes. Other than basic things, I wouldn't have the first clue what to cook.

"I've got it." Ty moved me to the side.

"Sit the fuck down. If she's going to be here, not paying rent, she can earn her keep."

I sucked in a breath, waiting to see what Ty would do. He stared at Grady, and I could feel how tense he was. He didn't like this.

"I've been here twice," I ground out. Three times, actually, but none of them knew about the time I knocked over Ty's motorcycle. "I'm not living here, but I don't mind shelling out for pizza in return for a beer now and then." *A beer I'd never drink.*

If looks could kill, I'd be dead. He pointed at me. "Order the damn pizzas."

Shaking, I shrugged off Ty to go into his bedroom and call for some pizza while Grady left the room without saying another word to me. I cursed him every which way I could on my way to Ty's bedroom, almost in tears by the time I closed the door. I vowed not to let him get the best of me, but he was right. If I came here more, played my part more, I would have to do something to make them like me. Dividing up drugs for sale wouldn't be part of it. I'd need to learn how to cook. Fast.

The door opened behind me, Ty slipping in. I didn't need to turn around to know it was him, and when his arms came around me, all I could do was lay my head back against his chest.

"I hate him," I whispered. "How do you live with him?"

"He isn't that bad when you get to know him."

I whirled, Ty's arms dropping away. Anger didn't come quick to me, but I felt like I was going to explode. "The way he talked to you was crap! I understand why he talks to me like that, but not you."

He shook his head, lifting his hand to brush my hair back. I shivered when his hand slipped around my neck and his mouth lowered to mine. At first, I didn't know if it would be a repeat of a few days ago when we had woken up. Thrills electrified my body, waves of flames rising when he pulled me closer.

"Let it go," he murmured.

I set my hands on his ribs, sliding them to his lower back when the pressure of his mouth on mine increased. Sparks were flying around me, creating a cascade of fireworks in my head. I didn't need to question how one man could wreak this havoc on me. It was as though he was the master of my body, promising me more to come.

When I felt the bed hit the back of my legs, I gasped in surprise that he had walked me back without knowing it and he took full advantage of it. A groan slipped from my throat when a second later, there was a knock on Ty's door.

"Ty?" Jack said through the door. "I hate to bust up your party, but I suggest ordering them pizzas up quick. Grady's in a temper."

Our foreheads met, and Ty released a heavy sigh. In this house, there would always be an interruption. There would be no way to get away from it. But Jack was right. I needed to get the pizzas ordered or suffer the wrath of Grady.

"I'll be out in a minute," I whispered.

"We like everything," Ty said. "And I'll pay you back. You shouldn't have to pay for them." He turned toward the door, adding with a snicker: "Not on a part-time receptionist's salary."

The corners of my mouth tipped up. Light amidst the darkness. I waited until the door was closed behind him before pulling my phone out to order pizzas from the closest place the internet could tell me would be. Once the order was in, I walked to the door. Ty's empty beer bottle was on the dresser. I frowned, expecting he would have tasted like it. But he didn't.

Chapter Seventeen

The text from Ty was simple. *It's Ty. I need to see you. Right now. Tell no one.* I stared at my phone, which I held carefully in my trembling hand so I didn't drop it. A new phone wasn't exactly in my budget. When my phone vibrated on the counter, I didn't think it was a big deal. But now that I was seeing the sender, it made me question everything. I was careful, very careful, who had my phone number. That wasn't the worry. My fear was something was wrong. Grady had no issue voicing his doubts about me. Icicles of fear skittered up my spine.

The address he gave me wasn't the same location as the house that I had spent the night with him again only a few days ago. Adrenaline rushed through my veins like the rush of a river. I loved it. But this was a unique situation. Although I had spent time with him, having a different glimpse of him than what I originally thought, he was still a part of a group that had kidnapped a dog, had more guns than they should have, and were clearly selling drugs. I didn't want to know what else they were involved in. I definitely didn't want to know what else Ty did, even if this relationship was short term.

I punched the address into Google maps. Warning signs echoed in my head. This house was in the middle of the woods, heading toward Mount Rainier. *Was he insane? Was I insane to consider doing this?*

I looked at Cameron, sitting at the kitchen counter with his laptop. He was the only one home. Cassie went to her office in the city to work, Naomi was at work, and Regan took Hannah and was out enjoying the city. If I told Cameron, I knew what he was going to tell me. He looked up.

"What is it?"

"Work thing," I said, quickly. Too quickly.

"Riles." The tone of his voice was enough to tell me he knew my lies. "It's Memorial weekend."

"I know," I whispered.

"I'll go with you."

"You aren't coming with me. No way. I've got this."

"Now is not the time to be stubborn."

Despite my own reservations, I could drop a location pin just in case I came up missing again. I needed someone to know what I was up to, despite the possibility it was just Ty wanting to meet with me outside of the scrutiny of Grady.

"I understand this is your job, but this is more than a job. This is your life, Riley. And I'm not about to let you put yourself at risk. No. It's out of the question."

"It's not up to you. And it's more than a job to me." I pinched the bridge of my nose, swallowing deep breaths. "You don't know what I went through when I was a kid, Cam. No idea. This is my therapy."

"Risking your life?"

"Yes!"

I didn't hide the truth. It was the truth. It didn't matter that this dog belonged to a famous pop star with issues. My gut instinct told me this was a dog that was taken for selfish reasons, and I was going to get it back.

"I'll call you when I'm on my way back," I added.

"I wish I had a tracker on you," came his grumble.

Despite myself, I smiled. There was no doubt in my mind that he'd have a tracker on me, and probably his wife, if we'd allow it. But I'd drop a location pin, all the same.

Another text from Ty came in, this time more insistent.

"I have to go. Call you later."

I didn't wait for Cameron to protest further before I raced from the kitchen. *Please*, was all it said. I wanted to text back and ask why the secret location, why the urgency, but something in the last text made me pause. Maybe he knew something and wanted to share it with me, away from the other house. Maybe there really was trouble. There was no way for me to know unless I went.

Even after I started driving with the remote address plugged into my phone GPS, I was questioning whether it was a good idea to go without backup. If Ty knew something and wanted me to know, he could have done so anywhere but a distant, and likely isolated, place.

By the time I had wound my way through the city and was on a two-lane road heading into national park territory, I convinced myself he had information for me. There were too many times he could have hurt me and didn't. That had to count for something. It took a while to get through the city, but now as the dense forests closed in around me, I felt a calm I shouldn't feel.

The view of Mount Rainier was beautiful, the lush surrounding forests breathtakingly serene. There was a tranquility in the air out here that held me like a hug, making me feel at peace. I wondered if living in urban cities, something I had done my whole life, wasn't what I should be doing. Maybe I should live outside of a peaceful little town, like the ones I was passing through.

I pulled off the main road over an hour later and headed down a paved road canopied by thick, leafy trees that blocked out what little sun there was. Every once in a while, the trees would give way and it would lighten. I rolled down my windows a bit, smelling the deep, earthy smells of nature. Having the top off the Jeep would have been better, but there was a drizzle that wouldn't allow it that day.

My pulse picked up speed when I turned down a dirt road.

I didn't drive more than a half mile when I pulled up to a picturesque house, sitting on a small rise under thick trees not unlike those I had been driving under for the better part of the last half hour. Amazed at its perfection, I threw the shift into park and hopped out without taking my eyes away.

Lights illuminated the inside and twinkled warmly at me, appearing to have more windows than not. It didn't look overly large, but it looked comfortable. I tore my eyes away from the house to look around. Ty's motorcycle sat in front of a separate two-car garage off to the left, but to the right was a wide open lawn framed on both sides by trees that led down to a lake. A dock led straight out, and I saw a canoe upside down off to one side. Wide open space and water. Gus and Gatsby would love it.

The creak of a door snapped my attention back to the house. Ty, wearing only a pair of jeans, stood in the doorway much like he did the day Grady caught me sneaking around. The saliva in my mouth dried instantly when my mouth popped open.

His head cocked to the side, blue eyes piercing me. "You gonna come inside?"

Adrenaline resumed its fiery spurts through my veins again. I slammed my door and bounced up the wide stone steps to get to him, thinking he would move or lead me into the house. It didn't seem like there was trouble, and he was obviously comfortable here with nothing on but a pair of jeans. Before I could say anything, his hand slid around my neck and his mouth was on mine.

The sensation of his lips playing on mine brought forth memories from only days ago when I woke up in his bed, in his arms again. I was playing with fire, and for the first time in my life, I wasn't blocking it. Not this time. It was almost like we were actually dating. My reaction to him surprised me, my hands coming to rest on the bare skin of his ribs. Skin that seemed to radiate heat. Boldly, I smoothed them around to his back and he groaned, his kiss deepening until my knees grew weak.

"Riley," he murmured. "What in God's name are you doing to me?"

I pulled away. His eyes sparkled. His lips were parted slightly. It seemed like he was going to pull me back into another kiss, but he stepped to the side.

"Whose house is this?" I asked, stepping cautiously into the small foyer and kicking off my boots.

The house was beautiful and brightly lit. The inside was just as inviting as the outside, with a big open room that had a kitchen, dining room, and living room all in one. Windows surrounded the room, except for the back where the bedrooms presumably were, and the stone fireplace across from the couch. I was in love. Everything about this place, inside and out, was perfect. The city was doing me all wrong. I belonged in a place like this.

"It's mine."

I felt light-headed, looking around. He was a bigger criminal than I thought to own something like this, assuming he owned the land that stretched down to the lake. It looked like it was straight out of a home décor magazine or the HGTV network.   It was a place I would imagine an artist or a writer would live a quiet life in, not someone who did illegal things for a living.

"I have things I want to tell you about me."

There *was* trouble, I thought, unsure of whether I should hang around the door in case I had to bolt or step inside and look around more. I wanted to do both.

"I have to trust you not to say anything. Grady really isn't a person either of us wants to fuck with." He stepped around me, waving me in. "Can I get you something? Coffee, water, hot chocolate . . ."

"Coffee, if you have it."

Ty walked into the kitchen with a stainless steel refrigerator and range on the back wall. He grabbed a mug out of the cupboard next to the refrigerator. I was afraid to step onto the gleaming hardwood; it looked like I would slide right across if I had socks on. Cassie was right. I really needed to take better care of my appearance. Having left in such a hurry, I hadn't even put on socks.

I smiled. At least I was doing regular maintenance, like shaving and putting on toenail polish. And although I always threw clothes on rather than meticulously picking them out like Cass and Hannah did, my clothes were clean. My room was messy, but I did my laundry on a regular schedule and when I couldn't, Naomi helped me out.

"Come in," he said, pouring two cups of steaming coffee.

I met him in front of the fireplace. He set the mugs down on the coffee table, and I folded myself onto the cozy couch. It was a beautiful, deep brown couch with a soft fabric. One could easily take a nap on it, surrounded by the serenity of nature.

"Look," I said. "I have a lot of things in my past. I would rather not share with anyone. You don't have to give me the gory details about how you came to own such a beautiful place."

He grinned. "You like it?"

"I love it! How could you not love a place like this?" I would have liked to look around more, but I didn't want to be rude and ask where his bedroom was. "I've lived in cities my whole life. Guess I didn't know what I'm missing out here."

I picked up my mug, bringing it to my lips and inhaling the strong fragrance. If I lived out here, I'd miss the coffee shop by the agency, but I was almost positive there was a coffee shop somewhere out here. It might be miles away, but I was sure there was one or two to be had.

"Look, I'll be honest with you. I know everything about you. I ran your license plate."

My hands remained firmly around the mug as though it were a barrier, while I remained frozen in place. My heart picked up a familiar speed when panic eased in. What did he mean by *everything*? Did he know about the murder? My pickpocketing days?

"Between your record with Maria at the agency and what I learned about you, I feel like it's safe for me to be completely honest with you."

I frowned. Okay, maybe he didn't know everything about me. *What the hell was he getting to*?

"I'm not the criminal you think I am. Yes, I live in a house with someone who kidnapped the dog you're trying to rescue and illegal activity. But..." I took a sip of the coffee, feeling the searing burn down my throat. "I'm a cop. An undercover detective."

The knee-jerk reaction jolted my body, and coffee sloshed out of the mug, down the front of my shirt and lap instead of in the cup or in my mouth. Of all the things I expected him to admit to, being a cop was the last thing I would have thought. Why did he have to be a cop?

"Jesus!" he said, jumping up to grab the mug out of my hand. He set the mug on the coffee table and ran into the kitchen, returning a minute later with towels.

The coffee was hot but not boiling. I opened my mouth, but nothing came out while he pressed the towels against my shirt, which only stuck to my chest. Apparently, he didn't care where he was touching me.

"That wasn't the reaction I thought I would get," he said, looking at me. "Riley? Are you okay?"

I shook my head. "It burns."

Throwing the towels to the side, he drew my shirt up and tossed it away. Redness marked my pale skin between my breasts where the coffee had scalded me. He shook his head.

"I'm sorry," I whispered.

It was hard not to be hyper-aware of his own bare chest when he stood, pulling me up from the couch and leading me by the hand toward the back of the house and into a bathroom. I was barely aware of how small the bathroom was with a simple one sink vanity, toilet, and shower. He grabbed a washcloth from a rack over the toilet and ran it under cold water before pressing it to my chest.

"Why is it I am always patching you up?" he murmured, looking into my eyes as though trying to distract me from his hand.

It was no use. Even with a towel between us, his hand only heightened my yearning. I wasn't sure what it was about this man that held my attraction to him so firm. No one else had secured it enough for it to last.

"Riley?"

"Ty?" I whispered.

"Does it hurt?"

I shook my head, but I wanted to nod. My entire body was burning, and it wasn't from the coffee. He lowered the towel, and with widened eyes, I watched his head dip to replace the towel. The breath caught in my throat at the feel of his lips on my skin, the heat from the coffee swiftly replaced by the heat of his breath. My head fell back, my hands gripping the edges of the vanity behind me.

Confident hands slid up my waist, to my back, and I gasped when my bra fell away a second later. The press of his lips trailed a path up to my neck, his thick arms came around me, and my heart burst into an erratic rhythm. It seemed like his hands were studying the curves of my body while his mouth was learning the taste.

When his teeth grazed my earlobe, I inhaled sharply and my hands slid up to his back where the phoenix was spreading its wings. The course of his mouth changed to mine, his lips catching my gasps. Expertly, he lowered his hands and lifted me until I was sitting on the edge of the vanity with him cradled firmly between my legs.

Every place he touched me tingled, bursts of flames spreading throughout my body while he continued his quest with his mouth. The feel of his palms molding around my breasts nearly undid me, and my head fell back again.

"Do you want me to stop?" he murmured before his mouth pressed to the swell of flesh just above his hand.

My body trembled, and I couldn't find my voice. When he looked up at me, his blue eyes penetrating, all I could do was shake my head. His arms came around me, picking me up and walking me out of the bathroom and into a large bedroom.

I was barely aware of the giant windows facing the yard and lake beyond before he lowered me to an enormous bed, continuing his teasing assault with his mouth. He pulled away from me, grasping my leggings at the waist and peeling them away. Heat rushed to my cheeks, realizing I was completely bare to his gaze. I shouldn't be self-conscious, knowing he had already seen much of my body when I showed him my tattoos, but the glaze that came over his eyes was of pure desire. He quickly stepped away to shed his jeans.

"Ty . . ." I whispered, halfway between a moan and a gasp.

"If you don't want to do this, tell me now, Riley." His voice was raw. "Tell me . . ."

I couldn't. It was the first time in my life I was one hundred percent sure I didn't want someone to stop. I stared up at him while he stared down at me. I said nothing. All I could do was shake my head. That was enough for him to lean down, his tongue traveling from my navel to neck while his hand slid up my inner thigh in perfect tandem.

My fingers curled into his hair at the feel of his hand between my legs, his fingers doing the most delicious things to me. I wanted to clamp my legs together, but I also wanted to open them wider. I felt the rumble of his chuckle against my neck when my fingers clenched.

My breathing was erratic, coming out in inconsistent gasps while my head pushed back against the pillows at the feel of his hand. Dear God, I was going to die . . .

"How can one person be so . . ." His words evaporated when a strangled sound I didn't recognize escaped from my mouth, my legs shaking at the feelings he invoked. "Should I stop?"

"No," came my rushed reply. "God, no. Don't stop."

Boldly, I loosened my fingers from his hair and slid my palms down his back. A shudder shot through him. A groan ripped from deep in his throat before he reached over to his nightstand to pull out a condom.

I didn't want to think about how many other women he might have had in this bed, so I closed my eyes and concentrated on the sound of the tearing of the wrapper. A second later and his hands were on my knees, gliding up my thighs.

I inhaled sharply at the pain of him pushing into me. It had been a really long time since I had done this. *Really* long. He stopped instantly. My eyes were open wide.

"Ty," I whispered.

Guilt for not telling him about my past snuck in, but I slipped my hands around his neck while my legs locked around his waist. I wasn't a virgin, but I might as well be.

"God, you're so tight. I don't want to hurt you," came his throaty murmur. "Give yourself a minute."

"I'm fine," I whispered, squeezing my legs until he moved, slowly at first.

I groaned softly as he moved his hips, but then his mouth covered mine, and a wave of pleasure I'd never experienced swept through me. My fists grabbed at the bedding, twisting it while I let the feelings of pure ecstasy sweep through me. I saw stars bursting behind my eyes from the orgasm that hit me. He continued the gentle roll of his hips, his mouth continuing the quest to taste me everywhere he could reach while his hands molded to my hips. If I could have burst from the orgasm that hit me, I would have, but he continued the gentle rock of his hips. His mouth continued to taste me everywhere he could reach, his hands anchoring me to the bed.

Floating away could be entirely plausible, given the sparks of flames I experienced. Abandoning the fists full of bedding, I plunged my fingers into his hair and met the pace of his hips with mine.

"Ty," I cried. "I can't . . ."

"You can," he murmured.

The trembling I felt with the first orgasm couldn't compare to the tsunami of the second. My abs clenched, my heels drug a hard line down his calf, and Ty wasn't far behind me. He pulled me tighter into his arms, continuing his pace until he couldn't hold back, gathering me close to him it when his muscles trembled.

Time stood still for several moments. He pulled away enough to look at me. Neither of us moved after that, though we stared at each other. I was in shock at what had just happened, but Ty was looking at me with a softness in his eyes. When I opened my mouth to speak, he shushed me and pulled away.

"Stay there."

Turning my head, I watched him walk into the private bathroom and couldn't help but admire his naked backside. A flush came over me, from my head to toes. I heard water running, and a moment later he was scooping me up from the bed.

I squealed, but he only chuckled and carried me into the bathroom where he had a deep bathtub at the far wall that looked big enough to fit at least three people. The double vanity in this bathroom was topped with bright bulbs over the enormous mirror. Across from it was a shower that rivaled Cassie's, which was mostly open with a small, frosted glass door only partially enclosing it.

He set me down next to the tub, leaning down to test the water temperature before he stepped in and held out his hand for me to take. At his grin, I must have been blushing again, but I took his hand and allowed him to pull me into the warmth of the water.

Once we settled in the water, he pulled me closer to him until I straddled him. This soon after, I wasn't sure I could do it again. I shook my head, but he nipped my mouth with his lips.

"Why didn't you tell me?" he whispered

"It's not something that comes up in conversation. You might think I was a virgin, but I'm not. It's just been a long time. A very long time."

"I might have taken my time had I known."

My eyes flashed. "Would you still have had sex with me, knowing I'm not experienced?"

His arms slid around me, slippery from the water, and his fingers wrapped in my hair until my head tilted up. The feel of his mouth on my neck summoned feelings in my lower extremities all over again, and I exhaled. On second thought, maybe I could go again. Flames ignited, settling low in my body.

"Yes," he murmured against my neck. "Is there a reason?"

"There's not been anyone worth it. And the one, the only one, was just a very crappy decision in high school. I'm lucky I didn't get pregnant from it."

His lips tipped up at the corners. "I'm flattered." He tucked my hair behind my ear.

There were very few men I had spent a considerable amount of time with. I'd had boyfriends, but none lasted long. I wasn't interested in getting tangled up with someone who wanted to control me or leave me stranded with a broken heart. I had my wall guarded well. Until Ty.

Chapter Eighteen

Darkness had fallen by the time I realized I had left everything in my car when I got here. I hadn't dropped the pin location like I intended to do. Ty insisted on cooking dinner, which didn't cause any complaints from me, and I excused myself to get my things from my car.

As soon as I reached for my phone, I cursed colorfully. Several text messages and calls from Cameron and Cassie. *I haven't been gone that long.* Quickly, I sent them each a message to let them know I was fine and I would call them when I could. It wasn't good enough for Cameron, apparently. My phone was ringing before I reached the door.

"I said I was fine," I said.

"That isn't good enough for me," he said. "Anyone can send a text from someone's phone. Where are you?"

I looked around, a smile tickling my mouth. "In the middle of the woods. With someone. No need for you to worry."

Cameron was quiet for a moment. "What's going on with you?"

Happiness, I thought. Glancing through the window, I could see Ty working his way around the kitchen, and my body warmed. Wearing only his blue jeans, I couldn't help but admire his courage to cook without a shirt on.

"Riley?"

"Your impatience is showing, Cam. I'm fine."

"When are you coming back? Who are you with? It would help

to know where you are just so we know. Especially since it's a holiday weekend."

"I'm not sure when I'll be back."

"You are absolutely infuriating!"

I laughed. "I know. Call you tomorrow."

The pungent smell of garlic permeated the air when I opened the door, hearing the sizzle of whatever Ty was cooking at the stove. I wondered what he was cooking, but then again, I didn't care.

"Who was that?" he asked, without looking up from whatever he was chopping.

I slid around into the kitchen, leaning against the kitchen counter to watch him deftly chopping onions.

"My brother." It didn't come as a surprise how easily I could refer to Cameron as my brother, as though I knew he had been all along. "He's very overprotective. I was going to text him when I got here, but I forgot and he's worried. I drove out into the middle of nowhere to meet with a guy I barely know."

Ty looked up, his eyes sparkling. "You know me well enough by now. But I am sorry about the secrecy. It was too risky to tell you anywhere but here."

"So? Now what?"

"I can't convince you to give up your case, can I?" I shook my head. "I'm undercover, Riley. You being there is putting us both at risk."

"I have a job to do, just as you do."

Putting my life at risk was one thing, but the more I thought about it, the less I wanted to put him at risk along with me. I understood he was in the same position. The issue was that while we were both doing our jobs, he had to protect me in the meantime which meant more risk for him than me.

I glanced at Ty, who smiled out of the corner of his mouth while returning to his chopping. It was more important now than ever that my past stayed where it was. David could never know about this. He wouldn't think twice about outing me.

"What do we do now?"

"We figure it out later. Are you up for spending the night? Maybe the weekend?"

Taking care of Gus and Gatsby was a group effort. They weren't just my dogs, they were all of ours. Cassie, Naomi, and Hannah never took issue taking care of the boys. And Cameron and Regan were there, too. We all adored Gus and Gatsby. I glanced out the windows at the yard they would love to run in. *No need to get ahead of myself.* He wasn't asking me to move in with him.

There was a thrill of waking up in his arms again, but under better circumstances, shooting through my limbs. "I can do that. It's not like we haven't spent the night together before."

He chuckled. "Dinner will be ready soon. I'd offer you some wine, but I don't drink."

My gaze snapped up, meeting his. I didn't think he was a liar on top of being a criminal. It hadn't been but days ago I'd seen him drink a beer.

"I . . . you don't drink?"

"No. I have a problem with drinking. Or I did. I can't drink anymore."

"But I saw you have a beer."

"You saw me have water in a beer bottle. Jack knows I have a history of drinking. When he gets me a beer, he dumps the beer and rinses out the bottle, filling it up with water. That way the others don't suspect."

Of all the things we didn't have in common, how could this be the one thing? Simone was the reason I didn't drink.

"I don't drink, either. My birth mother, Simone, is an alcoholic and a junkie. Growing up like I did, I never wanted to be like that. She was always high or drunk."

"I'm sorry," he said. "I didn't grow up with it, but I became it after college. Went to rehab after my girlfriend almost died in an accident and haven't touched it since."

I couldn't relate or understand, but I hoped with my vow not to touch it, it would help him. Those were two things I had no desire to touch, knowing both could lead me to the life my mother lived. I would never live like that again, regardless of how low paying my job was.

"Don't be sorry."

That was all I was going to say about it, hoping he didn't interrogate me with questions. He admitted to being a cop. Questioning people was what they did. Instead, he continued cooking, every so often putting something in the pan that would sizzle. I watched him pour pasta out of a pot and steam rise from the sink.

"So, you had a rotten childhood, but now have a decent life?"

That summed it up. I nodded.

"I had a terrific childhood and went through a horrible start to an adult life. It's better now, though. Are you ready to eat?"

"What did you make?"

"Nothing special, I'm afraid. Fettuccini alfredo. I hope you like pasta."

Ty grabbed two large bowls and scooped me some, sticking a fork into it before handing it to me. "I am the least picky person you will ever meet with food. It smells great. Really."

It was the best fettuccini I had tasted in my life. I hadn't realized how hungry I was until we were sitting at the table in front of double French doors looking out toward the lake. The moon was peeking out from clouds, casting a shimmer on the water.

Once we finished, he asked, "Do you want to walk down to the water?"

"Yes! My dogs would absolutely love this yard. I can imagine they would run as fast as they could right into the water. Then they would stink and need to be bathed."

"You have dogs?" he asked.

Ty didn't bother with the dishes, just put them in the sink and returned to me. He opened the French doors, and we walked out toward the water.

"Two black labs. Gus and Gatsby. They're brothers I rescued, almost two years old and full of energy. We all take care of them, but I was the one that rescued them. They sleep with Hannah when I'm on the job."

"You didn't steal them?" he teased.

That made me laugh a little. "No. Someone adopted them for their kids for Christmas, then found out they were too much to handle. Bugs me when people do that. They were puppies. They needed to be trained."

"Why Gus and Gatsby?"

"Gus was my grandfather, Naomi's husband. He died before I knew him, but Naomi told me about him. From what she told me, he was a saint. Gatsby because well, you know . . . The Great Gatsby? It's my favorite book."

"I'd like to meet them."

Surprise lit my eyes. "You would?"

When his fingers brushed mine, I tried not to let the jolt go to my head. When his hand closed around mine, walking hand in hand down to the lake, I tried not to let any of it go to my heart. Sleeping with him and pretending to be his girlfriend were one thing. Starting a genuine relationship was a completely different matter. And dangerous. I liked Ty. I liked him more than I should have. But there were things in my past he could never know, especially since he was a cop, otherwise he would never look at me the way he did now.

How can a cop who cleaned up his life be with someone like me? Someone with a biological father who's a big-time gangster? I flushed. I was in deep. Ty could never know about my past. Not if we wanted to keep a relationship. No need to dwell on it. I shook it off.

"Is that okay?"

"Sure. They love people." I laughed. "I took the time to train them."

It was easy to talk to Ty. It was easy to like him. From what he told me, he grew up in a normal family with two younger brothers and two great parents. He always wanted to be a cop, a detective to be exact, and despite his troubles with alcohol, succeeded.

"Do you want to tell me about your ex-girlfriend? You said she almost died?"

He sighed. "Yeah, I should probably tell you. It had a big impact on my life, and probably why I haven't been able to have another serious relationship since. Like you, I went to school in California for criminal law, and I stayed there to do my police training. Seemed like a good idea to join the police force there."

"Seems normal."

"Not quite. During college, I partied pretty hard although I eased up while I was going through police training, but after that started back up again. Layla and I met at a party, and we hit it off. The longer we were together, the more we argued about my drinking. One night, she was going to run out on me. I tried to stop her, but she left anyway."

"I can understand how that would happen, having lived with it."

He nodded. "I woke up the next morning to missed calls from my mom, her mom, my chief. Jack."

"Jack?"

"He's my partner. If you blow my cover, you blow his, too."

"Ty, I would never."

He offered me a smile. "I only told you because I don't think you will. You know the danger that we face now. And Jack." I gave him a nod. I would take it to my grave if needed. "Anyway, Layla had been in an accident. Hit by a drunk driver. Could have just as well been me, as far off drinking as I was. Jack begged me to get help, get treatment. And I did. Layla broke it off with me, and after rehab, I moved back here."

"Was that her in the coffee shop that day?"

He nodded. "She's from here, too, which is part of the reason we hit it off so well. She moved back here to be closer to her parents after the accident. They had to help her get back on her feet."

"You're on better terms now?"

He laughed. "You could say that."

"Why do you say it like that?"

"She's wanted to get back together with me for a while now. Now that I'm sober. We aren't the same people we were. I'm not the same person."

I understood that. And because I did, I told him about my life with Naomi, leaving out several things—namely David. I also mentioned nothing about my recent discovery of having a father suddenly surface.

"Where do we go from here?" I asked once we stopped by the lake. "If you're working undercover and living there. What do you tell them you do for a job?"

"Lucky for me, I'm a man of many talents. I work for a construction company, along with Grady. The force installed there me on purpose to meet Grady. Grady is lethal. If I hadn't been there that night, said you were my girlfriend, you might have died that night."

I wasn't daunted. "I need to get information on that dog. On what the plans are."

He ignored me. "That's not gonna happen. Grady doesn't trust me yet, and he definitely doesn't trust you."

"The longer we keep this thing between us, the more risk we're in," I said. "They already ask questions. They're going to ask me deeper questions. Lies that I'll need to keep straight. I hate lying."

"I'm hoping you aren't around long enough for them to ask you those questions." My expression must have conveyed that his words hurt. "I don't want you around Grady. I don't want you around that house."

"If I get this dog, what happens to your case?"

He shrugged. "Extends it, probably. I need to get to the core of this operation, and then I need solid evidence to bust it."

"I can give you a week."

Ugh, why did this have to be so complicated? Was everything working against me? I pinched the bridge of my nose. Getting the plans to get Queenie safely back to Ellie would be detrimental to Ty. There was no easy way out of this mess.

Chapter Nineteen

Waking up in Ty's arms the next morning differed from the first time I had woken in his arms. There was no one in the world who could pound on the door to interrupt us. This time when he drew me beneath him, it was as though we were two people meant to be together. It couldn't have been more perfect.

Curved in the warmth of his arms, I stared out at the sunlight glimmering on the lake. This was truly a perfect place, and I had to remind myself that this was temporary. It wouldn't go beyond me getting this dog. He was a cop. It was a bad enough situation.

"What are you thinking about?" he whispered, his finger drawing a line over the curve of my bare shoulder before I felt his lips in the same spot. Shivers swirled deliciously down my spine.

"How different your bedroom is here than your bedroom is there." I bit my bottom lip, flipping over to my back and looking into his eyes. He didn't know me well enough to know I was lying.

"Have a reputation to keep up."

His mouth was trying to sidetrack me. Dear God, he was insatiable. It made me wonder if this was how it was in an actual relationship. Is this what Regan dealt with all the time? If that was the case, she would have a hard time not being pregnant constantly. And I couldn't blame her. I could lie in bed with Ty all day, his mouth coaxing me into a blissful state.

"My bedroom would disappoint you."

His mouth moved to my neck. "Doubt it," came his muffled

reply.

My fingers threaded through his hair. "I'm not nearly as neat as you."

It was all I could manage before his hand slipped between my legs, his mouth catching my breathy gasp. We would never make it out of bed if this continued. I didn't have it in me to argue, his hand and mouth doing their best to make sure I couldn't utter a word. My only thought before pulsating raptures engulfed my entire body, shooting in all directions, was that I was in big trouble.

Once my breathing slowed down, he took my hand and pull me out of bed, toward the bathroom.

"But . . . aren't we . . . ?"

"That was for you," was all he said.

After we showered and partially dressed, I told Ty I would make breakfast since he made dinner. While I whipped up some scrambled eggs and toast, he watched me while sitting perched on the counter in his blue jeans with no shirt. Heaven help me, but I was in trouble.

"I thought you said you couldn't cook," he said when I handed him a plate of fluffy eggs.

"I'm learning. But I can do pretty basic stuff. Eggs are easy. I'm finding that I can read a recipe but as far as creativity, forget it. That's Naomi's area."

He took a bite, giving me a nod of approval. "I'm confused."

I leaned against the opposite counter. "About?"

"Why the hell you're single?"

Shit. "Like you, my work takes a lot of my time."

I shoveled in another bite before I could bite my lip. He seemed to accept my answer, and I didn't need to ask him about his reason. I knew what detective work was, my job being similar with surveillance taking me away from home much of the time. His was much more complicated, taking him away from home for months at a time. Maybe longer.

"Is it hard?" I asked, suddenly.

"Is what hard?"

"Being around the guys while they're drinking beer." I set my plate down. "You said you went to rehab. Grady's house is a nicer-looking frat house, even if it's just you four living there. And Jack dumping beer so you can drink water out of a beer bottle. That's got to be hard."

He took a deep breath, setting his own plate down. "I battle it every day," he whispered. "There will always be a voice inside that tells me that one won't hurt. Except, I know it will. I may be a different person now than I was then, but I know in my heart that I'll go down the same road the minute I take a drink."

I moved toward him, wrapping my arms around his mid-section and laying my head against his chest. My heart hurt for him to have that weighing him down day after day. It made me think about Simone. So many times she could have gotten help, but she never did. I couldn't help but to be convinced she never would. The drugs and the drinking would kill her.

Ty's hand curved around my neck, his fingers sifting through my hair, and I felt his lips on my temple. "Thank you," he whispered.

I wasn't sure why he was thanking me, but I oddly felt his pain. The future had me scared shitless that I was falling for a man I couldn't ever be with, especially when we had conversations like this and I saw deeper into the man. He wasn't the criminal. I was. Not on purpose. And if he ever knew, he would hate me.

"Did you decide to stay the weekend?"

I pulled away with a smile. "I don't see why not. It's not like I can run in with guns blazing and grab little Queenie now. I don't even have a gun."

He laughed. "You'd never get her away from Jack. He adores her." I moved so he could hop down from the counter. "I want to bring you some places today. Around town. Is that okay?"

I shrugged. "It is a holiday weekend. I don't have to check in at the office until Tuesday. I guess I'm all yours."

Ditching our breakfast, we went to put on more clothing before we headed out. The drizzle had let up, giving me the elation of another ride on his bike. The first place he brought me was the closest town with all its charm, the locals waving at him from the sidewalks as we rode the motorcycle slowly down Main Street. We stopped for coffee at the local diner, where everyone knew him by name and he knew everyone.

The town made me fall all the more in love with this part of the state—the part I had never known existed with its tasty coffee, clean air, and breathtaking views.

After our coffee, with a pastry added in, we hopped back on the motorcycle and Ty hesitated for a minute while he texted someone. I looked at the two old men sitting on the bench in front of the drugstore, one of them holding two fingers up to his baseball hat in a gesture of greeting to me. I smiled back.

"Where are we going now?" I asked, curious to know who he was texting but minding my own business by not looking over his shoulder.

"I have someone I'd like you to meet. Is that okay?"

"It's not another criminal, is it?" I teased.

"No, not quite. But I'll give you fair warning. If you fell in love with my place . . . this place is going to make you think my place is a dump."

Not likely. I wasn't sure it was possible after all I'd seen so far. I clung to him as we sped down the narrow corridor of trees, much like those on the way to his house from the city. Every now and again, it would open and I'd get a clear view of the mountain.

When we pulled off the main road, I saw the name Cavanaugh on the mailbox, just before we headed down a private, paved road that was framed on both sides with low, white fences. We rode for another half mile before the trees cleared away and I saw a huge brown house with mountains and a lake in the background.

My mouth refused to shut when we came to a stop in front

of a three-car garage. I got off the bike and waited for Ty, wanting desperately to know whose gorgeous house this was. We hadn't even gotten inside yet, but I knew it would be equally impressive. As though sensing my hesitation to walk in alone, Ty took my hand and led me around to the front porch and door.

It swung open before we got to the first step, revealing a woman with light blonde hair stylishly swept up. My steps faltered, but Ty tugged my hand. She wore a pair of capri-pants and a sleeveless blouse.

"Tiberius Cavanaugh," she said, stepping out as we reached the top step and kissing his cheek. "You didn't tell me you were bringing someone home."

Ty grinned. "Mom, this is Riley."

Mom? Shit! He gave me no warning. I could have stopped and bought some different clothes, instead of wearing the same ones from yesterday. Even laundered after spilling the coffee, I felt like a slob. I looked down at my boots, swearing under my breath. Not even any socks.

As if sensing my distress, Ty squeezed my hand. I looked up at him for a reassuring smile. He was so damn smooth, he charmed me into meeting his mom without telling me about it. I couldn't even be mad at him.

"Riley, it's nice to meet you. I'm Suzie. Come in, come in. Your dad and brothers are watching baseball."

I inwardly groaned. Not just his mom and dad, his brothers were here too. We stepped into a spacious foyer with gleaming hardwood floors and a brown stone interior matching the exterior of the house. There was a closed in staircase to my left and a formal dining room set with six chairs on the right. We passed into an open area with kitchen, nook, and living room. A giant stone fireplace, visible from both rooms, separated the living room and dining room.

A man sat on the brown leather couch, immediately coming to his feet when we were walking in. He was the spitting image of

Ty except older, the same twinkling blue eyes but with a shade of darker blond hair. The two other men, sitting in the adjacent chairs, stood as well. Dear God, but there was no mistaking that they were brothers, both with blond hair, and all of them had blue eyes.

"Ty!" he said, smiling at me. "And?"

"Riley," I said, extending my hand.

Ignoring it, he pulled me in for a hug instead and I heard Ty chuckle. "William, put her down," I heard his mom say from behind us.

The shortest brother stepped over to me, folding me into his arms. "Auggie," he whispered dangerously close to my ear.

"August, you'll not be stealing your brother's date," Suzie called from the kitchen.

When Auggie released me, the other brother pulled me into a hug. Good God, but they were all huggers. I wasn't used to being manhandled. He was at least taller, so his voice wasn't directly in my ear.

"I'm Marc," he said.

When he released me, I turned to see Suzie in the kitchen. She gave me a knowing smile, and I wondered how she dealt with four men in the same house. One would have to be a strong woman. The kitchen was partially closed by a stone half wall, set with a few bar stools in front of it.

I wandered over to her, keeping one ear on the conversation Ty was having with his dad and brothers. "Do you need any help?" I asked.

"No, no. I appreciate it, but lunch will be ready soon. You just go relax."

"When did you get into town?" William asked Ty, settling back down on the couch while Auggie and Marc sat back down.

"Yesterday."

"Aren't you on assignment?"

"I had some things to do at my place, so I made an excuse to get away for the weekend. Jack's got it under control," he said. "I wanted to show Riley around town."

"Well, it's very nice to meet you, dear," his mom said. "It's a beautiful day. We can have lunch in the back."

"We just ate, Mom. I just wanted to bring Riley by to meet you."

"We didn't even know you were dating anyone," his dad said, not taking his eyes from the game. "Is this part of the assignment?"

I pressed my lips together, waiting for Ty's explanation. Part of me was hoping what was happening between us was more to him than just an assignment. From our conversations, he led me to believe it was more.

"No," he said. "I can't tell you more than that, as we're both on assignment and it's dangerous." He looked over at me, taking my hand. "For both of us."

"Are you a detective, too, Riley?" Suzie asked from behind me.

"Private investigator. I get to do the surveillance, interviews, reports, but I'm limited to what I can do. Not like Ty."

"Say no more," William said.

"He's right," his mom cut in. "Don't tell us any more, honey."

"I want to hear about it!" Auggie shouted.

Suzie came out of the kitchen, placing a vase of brightly colored flowers on the center of the table in the nook next to the kitchen. "We certainly hope we get to see you again, Riley. Ty has brought no one home for quite a while."

I smiled. "It's nice to meet someone who doesn't drink."

That perked her up, and she stopped arranging the flowers to look directly at me. Her mouth curved into a smile. It was impossible to tell what she was thinking, but I swore there was admiration in her eyes.

"You also don't drink?"

"No, I don't. My mother had issues with it when I was growing up. My grandmother took me and my sister from her when I was fourteen. As far as I know, my mother still has issues."

Ty's arm slipped around my waist. Though we had different situations, the outcome in our lives was the same. We were trying to become better people because of it. One slip up and we could both end up back at square one.

"That must have been very difficult for you."

You have no idea. "We've tried many times to get her to get help."

"Ty needs as many people on his side as he can get," William called from the living room.

Ty sighed. "Let's go out to the back."

He led me out a glass door between the nook and the living room that led to a wide open deck and barbeque area. It was astoundingly stunning with the lake and the mountains behind it. Extracting my hand from his, I wandered to the edge and gasped when I saw the shimmering pool below.

I didn't know what to say. It wasn't a mansion like the De Luca estate, but this estate was in the middle of tranquility. It was better. Peaceful and private.

"Say something."

I turned, leaning my butt against the half-wall to face Ty and crossing my arms. "I feel like I'm missing quite a few things, but then again, you don't know everything about me. Don't your parents work?"

"Yes. Dad's a lawyer, and I told you about my mom. They have an apartment in the city for during the week. This is their weekend home, and their retirement home."

"I'm not sure I've seen a house so beautiful. But yours is cozy."

His laugh was quiet. "I like it. I like you in it."

"Ty! We just met."

"That isn't true. We met a while ago."

"You running into me at a coffee shop doesn't count as meeting."

"I feel like I've known you for a long time," he said, his words drawn out slowly. "Still can't explain it."

"If you tell me I complete you, I'll punch you."

"Let's just enjoy it for now and worry about the semantics later."

I could do that. No. It wasn't a matter of whether I could do it. I had to. And then he had to introduce me to his family, and now there was no turning back. When he slipped his hand into mine, tugging me into his arms, I smiled.

"What do you think of our little bit of paradise, Riley?" Suzie said, coming out the side door with a tray laden with a pitcher of lemonade and glasses.

I watched her set it on the table in the barbeque area, William and Ty's brothers following her out with hands full of trays and bowls. If I had to guess, we'd be eating again.

"It's lovely," I said, walking with Ty up the steps to the table.

Auggie set down a tray with meats and cheeses while Marc put down a bowl with a bright green salad. I felt like we were eating like royalty, especially when William set down the tray with assorted rolls and breads.

Ty released my hand briefly to kiss his mother's cheek before pulling out a chair for me. "How do you feed all of them?" I asked her.

"Oh, it was never just these boys. They almost always had friends over to feed when they were growing up."

"Mom's got a way of planning things out perfectly," Auggie said, his mouth full of shaved turkey.

"Augustus Richard! Don't talk with food in your mouth."

I laughed when he snapped his mouth closed, but not until after he mumbled sorry to her. With food in his mouth. Ty's family charmed me, just like he did. I couldn't help but love the lively banter they fell into with ease.

Suzie handed me a porcelain white plate, waving her hand to the array of food. "Help yourself, Riley. Before they eat it all. And trust me, they will."

"I trust you." I helped myself to a bun and some meat, catching the twinkle in Ty's eye watching me while he made up his own plate.

"You live in the city, Riley?" Marc asked.

"Yes."

"She stays with me sometimes," Ty said, then instantly grimaced. "You didn't hear me say that."

"Whereabouts?" William asked.

"Over by Magnolia Bluffs. I live with my friend Cassie. It's her dad's house. He's a drummer. He's never there."

"A drummer?" Auggie leaned back in his chair. "Rock band? Heavy metal? Anyone we might know?"

"Lex Edwards. I believe it's metal."

"Hooooly shit," Marc said. "You live in the drummer of Skeletons of Disciples' house? And his daughter is your friend?"

"Is she single?" I looked at Auggie, wondering if I should have lied instead. I didn't want to lie to Ty's family unless I absolutely had to.

"Yes, I live in his house. He's best friends with my uncle. Cassie's kind of dating someone, but I haven't been able to sit down with her and have a long talk for a while. I'm not sure how serious it is."

"Can you introduce me to her?" Auggie said.

I laughed softly. "Guys, give her a break," Ty said.

Suzie poured me a glass of lemonade and I gratefully took a drink to get a break in answering their onslaught of questions. At least they weren't all about my life. I'd gladly talk about Cassie and her dad. They were a unique pair.

The conversation veered away from me, thankfully, and they conversed lightly about what was going on in their lives. I noted they were careful about discussing what went on with Ty, as he was undercover, but they included me in with questions when they could. By the time lunch concluded, I liked his family a great deal. They'd been as easy to get to know, and get along with, as Ty.

Everyone helped bring the dishes back into the house, and I helped Suzie with the dishes while Ty joined his dad and brothers in the living room.

Every once in a while I'd catch Ty looking at me, a warm feeling settling low in my stomach. It took effort to pay attention to what Suzie said to me, getting sidetracked by Ty and his mischievous eyes.

"I have never seen him like this," Suzie whispered to me.

I turned. "What? Seen who like what?"

"Ty." Her voice was intentionally low, and she glanced over at the guys before looking back at me. I assumed it was to make sure they were watching the game instead of us. "I've never seen Ty like this. He can't take his eyes from you."

"But he's had other girlfriends."

"Not like you, dear. Not like you."

It momentarily stunned me. When I looked back into the living room, Ty was looking at me again. This time, the look on my face must have worried him and he stood up, coming to the breakfast bar.

"Okay?"

I nodded.

He stabbed his fingers through his hair. "Mom, what did you say to her?"

"She didn't say anything," I said. "I'm fine."

"You look like you saw a ghost or something."

When I laughed, it came out shaky. "No, it's fine. Why do you keep looking over here? Are you making sure I'm not spilling your secrets?"

He grinned. "Pretty sure she knows my secrets."

"Of course, I know all your secrets. Thank you for your help, Riley. We're all done here."

Ty took my hand as soon as I stepped out of the kitchen, guiding me back to the living room. "I hate to bust up the party, but I think we'll be heading back to my place. Thanks for lunch,

Mom."

Suzie put on a pout but smiled anyway. "Thank you for coming, Riley. And thank you, Ty, for bringing this lovely woman to meet us."

"Figured you'd want to know what I've been up to."

My eyes widened and my face burned. He squeezed my hand in return. "Dad, Auggie, Marc, I'll see you next weekend on Sunday. I'm skipping Sunday dinner tomorrow."

"What?" Auggie said, put out by it.

"I've got something planned with Riley tomorrow."

"Why don't you bring her to Sunday dinner?" William asked. "It's not like you to miss a Sunday dinner."

"It's fine, Will. If they have plans, let them go."

Ty looked at me. "Can you handle my family for another meal?"

"Can they handle me?"

Everyone started talking at the same time, but Suzie had the last word and I assumed she always had the last word. The respect each man had for her was admirable.

"You are welcome anytime, Riley. If it fits into your plans tomorrow, we'd love to have you for family dinner."

I nodded. "I'd be happy to come back. It's been fun."

It took another few minutes, but we finally said our goodbyes and walked down to the motorcycle. No one followed us out, and Ty stopped before we got on. He put his finger beneath my chin, leaning down to place a soft kiss on my lips.

"Thank you for that."

"For what?"

"Putting up with my family and agreeing to put up with them tomorrow."

I shrugged. "I like them." He climbed onto the bike. "Do you have family dinner every Sunday?"

"When I can. Being undercover has its drawbacks."

I slid on behind him, drawing my arms around his waist. "I

love it. Everything about your family, and about how you are with each other. That's how I imagine a family is supposed to be."

"Careful, or you'll be falling in love with them."

I laughed, and the roar of the motorcycle drowned it out. Minutes later and we were riding back down the driveway toward the road. If I wasn't careful, he would end up being right. In more ways than one. The danger of losing my heart to him was already there. His family was only the icing on the cake.

Chapter Twenty

If I could have stayed in bed with him all day, I would have. I nearly did.

But Ty needed to get back to the house before it raised suspicion of his whereabouts. And I needed to get back home before Cameron sent out a search party. The smile plastered to my face stayed with me until I walked in the door to nothing.

Silence greeted me. There were no telltale clicks of dog nails across the hardwood floors, no voices wafting from the living room or Cassie's office. There was no one home. It was a holiday. Cassie and Naomi wouldn't be working, and Hannah wouldn't be at school. It was eerily quiet in the house.

I didn't like the way the silence sounded. It raised the hairs on the back of my neck and I dropped my bag heedlessly on the bench just inside the door, stepping in cautiously. There was nothing that would cure me of ever thinking David was in my house. He would always find me.

I was lying on the bed Hannah and I shared in the room, some-times, with our mother, when I heard the front door open and close. The sound of the front door had dread coursing through me. Ever since Finnegan Caspian had made his advances toward me, I'd been uneasy. Either Simone found another to replace him, or the police had found the car David said he hid.

Straining my ears, I didn't hear any loud bellows from a male entering. I relaxed a little. Sometimes I wished I was old enough to have a job. An actual job. I had no desire to deal with her tonight, either disgustingly drunk or in a haze-like high. Even David had a job. At least he wasn't home.

I went back to reading the book I had checked out from the school library. Stores were difficult to steal from with their detectors and cameras, and I was grateful David didn't make me do it. Instead, we stole from unsuspecting tourists in the area. Typically downtown and along the strip, where I could slip in and out undetected.

The loathing I felt after taking someone's money took several days for me to get over. But stealing wasn't the worst of my crimes. David had a way of making me do his dirty work, but stealing was the least of it. I killed someone. Intentionally. And I would never forget it.

Voices raised in an argument from the living room piqued my interest. It was a woman's voice I could hear Simone arguing with. I dog-eared the book and set it aside, rolling off the mattress and jumping to my feet. The door was open a crack and as I crept closer; the volume increased.

"You cannot think this is a fit place to raise them, Simone. Please! Think about someone other than yourself for once!" the woman's voice said, high-pitched but whimsical.

"They are my daughters. Not yours."

"You're right! I raised you better than this!"

My back pressed against the battered wall, sliding along slowly as I slipped into the hallway. I wore my shoes still, the carpeting in our house too disgusting to go without. The few pairs of socks I owned would be dirty quicker than I could launder them, so I wore my shoes most of the time. I looked down at the hole beginning to form at the top of one, a testament to the fast rate at which I was growing.

I gasped when I felt something touch my hand, before realizing it was Ivy. She was so tiny, even at almost seven years old. I pulled her up into my arms, cradling her close against my side and pressing my fingers to my lips. She nodded silently, clutching the stuffed dog Bobo to her chest. I didn't mind sharing him with her, as battered as he was.

The woman's voice was vaguely familiar, as though I'd heard it before. I stepped closer to the living room. When we reached the end of the hallway, I stopped and closed my eyes, trying to remember where I'd heard the voice before. I blinked.

"Naomi?"

My grandmother stopped coming to see me when I was eight. Ivy was only one at that time and didn't remember. If it wasn't for her, I would not have had decent clothes and things to play with when I was younger. I looked down at my ripped jeans and threadbare t-shirt. It seemed like so long ago.

I turned the corner, coming to face the two arguing women.

"Alexis, take Ivy and go back to the bedroom." Simone pointed to the hallway behind me.

I wasn't a little kid anymore. Instead, I stood my ground and looked at Naomi. She looked older, her hair still blonde, but I could see the gray strands even though they were well-hidden. Her eyes lit with softness when she saw me.

"Alexis! Ivy! Oh my, how much you've both grown!"

"What're you doing here?"

Naomi looked at Simone, who was eying her like she was the devil. "Simone may have forbidden me from coming to see you years ago, but I've been watching you and I can't leave you and Ivy in this house any longer. I want you both to come live with me."

There was nothing in this world I wanted more than to leave this nightmare of a life behind me. To take Ivy out of this life. A life of living in poverty wondering when we would have money for a decent meal, and the life of wandering the streets stealing from people. The life of a criminal. Every day there was a knock at the door, I thought it was the police coming to take me away. We were nobodies here, but that didn't mean someone didn't see what happened. They would put me in jail and Ivy would be at the mercy of David. It was only a matter of time before David started getting her to steal. I would do anything to make sure that didn't happen. I would do everything to make sure it didn't happen.

"Well?" Simone said. "Is that what you want?"

I used my free hand to pinch the bridge of my nose, immediately dropping my hand when I thought the front door opened. This was our chance to leave before David got home. He'd have no way of finding us if we went with Naomi.

If David were here, he would never allow me to go. He'd do everything in his power to make sure I stayed. I was his tool. I couldn't do that to Ivy. But this was my only chance to get out of here, otherwise I knew what would happen if I stayed. I saw how he'd been looking at me lately. We both knew he wasn't my brother. There was nothing stopping him from abusing me more than just emotionally and verbally. And I think Simone knew it. I could tell from her eyes.

"Alexis, go," she whispered, her eyes shadowed with sorrow. "You and Ivy go with your grandmother, and you have a better life."

I ran for Naomi, despite Ivy in my arms. Naomi's thin arms came around us, and I could feel her strength as she walked us cautiously to the door. I didn't care about bringing anything with us. We had Bobo. He was enough. I just wanted to be out of the house and away from David for good.

I couldn't believe it was ten years since Naomi had pulled us out of that house, bringing us to live with her outside of Las Vegas. She put her house up for sale almost immediately, and we moved to Fresno. We weren't there long before she got the call from Lex about Cassie. We headed to the big city after that.

I poked my head around the corner to look into the living room from the kitchen, breathing a sigh of relief to find it empty.

Still not convinced that David hadn't found out where we lived, I stepped carefully into the living room and looked around.

When I heard the door open, followed by the scrambling of dogs on the hardwood floors and voices, my chest lurched in relief.

"Riles?"

Cameron came into the living room first, after the dogs danced circles around me in greeting. I had to give them their attention first before standing up to look at him. His eyes were hard. He knew something spooked me.

"What's wrong?"

"Everything's fine. It was weird that no one was home."

"We went for a run," Regan said, coming in behind Cameron. She didn't look like she had been running. "Naomi and Hannah went to the grocery store."

Regan looked like she had just been out for a stroll with her hair in a messy bun and not a single drop of sweat on her. Cameron did. I could be envious of her, but I didn't run. I exercised the dogs, and that was my exercise. No yoga, no health club membership, nothing that would make me sweat that much.

"I'm going to take a shower," he announced, then pinned me with his brooding eyes. "Then we're going to talk."

When his back turned, I rolled my eyes. Regan caught it and gave me a knowing smile, following him out of the room. *Oh, how I like her.* I smiled. Regan was not the type of woman to be maneuvered. I liked that immensely. Cameron loved her more than life, but that didn't mean she had to bend to his every command. And she didn't.

I sat down on the spacious living room floor with the boys. "You would not believe where I was," I told them. "The yard was so big even you two would get tired from running."

They soon got bored with me and started rolling around with each other while I stretched out, leaning against the couch. I looked at my phone, hoping for a text from Ty. *I'm being silly. I just left him. He won't text me so soon.* My thumb itched to send him a text, but I didn't. We agreed to be cautious, although I agreed to go to Grady's house in a couple of nights. Jobs aside, we had to continue the appearance. And I couldn't wait to see him, my stomach fluttering anxiously.

A half hour later, Cameron and Regan came back downstairs and settled on the couch across from me. He stared at me, and I pretended to be looking at my phone to rattle him. Petty, I knew. I was trying to be like Regan and not let him bulldoze me.

"Talk to me," Cameron said, his voice softening.

I looked up. "About?"

"This guy you spent the weekend with."

Calmly, I set my phone aside. Regan was on her phone, but I could tell she was tuned in on our conversion more so than her phone. I would disappoint her. There wasn't much I could tell either of them about Ty. It would put both of us in even more danger, even though I could trust them. I wouldn't even say his name.

"What do you want me to say? I met someone." Shrugging, I shifted my eyes around to avoid eye contact before uttering my next words. "I like him."

"Where did you meet him? What does he do for a living? *Where* does he live? When can I meet him?"

"Stop it. I might be your sister, but I'm an adult."

Cameron sighed. "Give me more than this. I'm worried. This job you're doing is dangerous. Then you take off to meet this guy at this house, spend the entire weekend with him."

A smile threatened to crack on Regan's face. I laughed. "You're telling me, after you met Regan and got to know her a little, you wouldn't have jumped at the chance to spend an uninterrupted weekend with her?"

He stabbed his finger in the air at me. "Don't turn this around on me. It's not the same situation."

"This wasn't the first night I've spent with him, you know that."

"But it's the first time you've willingly spent the night with him," Regan said.

My face warmed. "Yes. He's different."

"Just be careful," Cameron said, lightly. "You know I would do anything to protect you. Whether you were my sister or not—"

I snorted. "We don't know that for sure yet."

"You've always been family," he added. "You know that. Morettis protect each other."

"I'm not a Moretti," I reminded him. "I'm Riley Parker."

"That wasn't your name when I met you."

"I told you after we went to live with Naomi that Ivy and I were going by different names. I made it official after I turned eighteen."

"Why?"

I sighed, not wanting to have this conversation with him. I didn't want Cameron to know about David. Now or ever. There was no reason he had to know about David.

"Cameron, do you have to interrogate her?"

He could interrogate me all he wanted. It didn't mean I was going to give him the answer to every one of his questions. There were some things he didn't know, and there were some things that he would never know.

"I need to know what I'm up against."

My eyes flashed. "You aren't up against anything. I am. And I will handle it. I always do."

He leaned back against the couch, folding his arms in front of his massive chest. "And David?"

Goddamn Cassie. I shot forward. "How do you know about David?"

"Cassie told me. She was worried that he might have found you again." He stared at me, daring me to argue about it. "Did he?"

I should have known it was Cassie. I had sworn Naomi into secrecy about speaking about David to anyone, including Cassie. Hannah was too young to remember much of David.

Cameron was one person I couldn't lie to. It was bad enough

that I met him while trying to lift his wallet. The least I could do was be honest with him from that moment on. And I never lied to him. Not once.

Shit. "Yes."

"Cameron." Regan's voice, although quiet, was thick with warning. "Calm down."

"Tell me," he said, surprisingly calm.

"There isn't anything you can do. Please, don't get involved in this. Trust that I can handle it."

His eyes narrowed. "From what Cassie told me, he abused you when you were younger. He would have sexually abused you had Naomi not pulled you out of that house. And you don't want me to get involved with it?"

"Cam . . ." Regan said.

"No." His tone was firm. "I'm not staying out of this. Where is he?"

I laughed, my laugh coming out shaky. I wasn't sure there was a time I had seen Cameron this angry. "David finds me. I don't find David."

"When is the last time he found you?"

"The coffee shop on First Street a few weeks ago." I leaned forward. "Unless you're planning on killing him, don't bother. You're going to put me in more danger by getting involved."

The consideration was behind his eyes, and I didn't think for a moment that he wouldn't do it. Or get someone to do it. I knew who Reno Moretti was. And I knew that none of his sons would hesitate to take someone out of the picture for the sake of family. Cameron would, without a doubt, protect those he loved. That I knew.

"What does he want?"

"Me."

Regan's eyes widened. "What do you mean? Is he stalking you, Riley?"

"Yes. I don't know what he's up to, but he is certain that I should be with him and only him. I've dodged him for ten years and he's been in prison until recently. He found me again. He won't stop until I'm with him."

"Oooohhh, he'll stop," Cameron said, his tone chilling. "He won't have you, Riley. I'll make certain of that."

And Cameron would. I just hoped that David wouldn't spill his guts to the world about my past. Telling Cameron about what I did was no big deal. Telling Regan wasn't either. But if anyone else should find out, it would ruin me.

Chapter Twenty One

I found Maria in her office when I strolled in the next day, looking perfectly put-together as she always did. Perched behind her desk, she typed prettily on her laptop without the need to look up to know I had breezed in. I went to the window and looked out, waiting for her to finish.

"What's your update?" she asked.

"I'll have Queenie by the time Ellie needs to leave for her world tour."

She took a deep breath, the tip-tap of her keyboard stopping abruptly. "Publicity has died down. I'm almost positive they're hunting for a higher reward. What are your plans?"

Completely out the window, I said silently. There was no way on earth I was going to admit to Maria I had gotten caught, now stuck in a situation I wasn't soon going to get out of. After the weekend, I wasn't sure I wanted to yet. In the haven of Ty's home in the woods, I felt the safest I had ever felt. I wasn't sure if it was Ty, his house, or both.

"Riley?"

I turned away from the window, meeting Maria's eyes.

"Your plans?"

"I'll get the dog, Maria. It'll be much easier than I thought it would."

"Do we need law enforcement involved in this?"

I shook my head. "Nope. I have a plan, and it doesn't involve trespassing. Trust me in this, though. Ellie will have Queenie back."

Primly, she folded her hands in front of her, considering the information. I couldn't imagine what she might be thinking. It was a high-profile case, but it was risky. And I was asking her to put all of her trust in me. Blindly. Maria had one job, and it wasn't much different from mine. She just had more experience than I had. And she didn't look convinced.

"I've always put my life on the line for this job, Maria. Never once have I ever backed down from a case, and I'm not about to now. I will get that dog, and if I can't, I promise to notify   you immediately so we can get the police involved."

I watched her digest my words, hating to put such a dramatic force behind them. This was my biggest case. I had to make an impact.

"Riley," she said, and something about the way she said my name made me catch my breath in my throat. "I know what you've been doing."

"What I've been doing?" I swallowed the lump in my throat.

"You've used this agency to recover other stolen dogs."

I blew out a breath. "I'm not sure what you mean."

"I know you have. There isn't any point in denying it. Why do you think I gave you this case?"

"Mandy backed out."

She shook her head. "I've been a private investigator for over twenty years. Do you honestly think I don't know what you've been doing on your extended vacations? That you've been using the records system to find things out?"

"But Mandy. She didn't back out?"

"I never assigned this case to her. I had to buy myself time until you got back into town, Riley. This case was meant to be yours, and I fully expect you to handle it."

I nodded. My steps were silent as I walked over to her desk, staring down at her for a moment before I placed my hands on her desk and leaned down. Damn, she was good.

"I will not let you down," I said. "Give me a half hour to type up my weekly report and I'll be out of here."

I pushed away from her desk and left her office without another word. If I got caught in the crossfire from this, I was going to feel even worse for putting her in this position. Maria might be a hard-ass boss as much as I was a stubborn-ass junior investigator, but she had a heart and I knew deep down she didn't want me to be in this much danger. If only she knew how much I was in.

True to my word, I had my report typed up and emailed within a half hour and I was on my way out of the office. Nothing would happen with Queenie today. I would go to the house tomorrow after promising Naomi that I would be at home for dinner tonight. I owed Cameron and Regan some of my time while they were here, at least. They hadn't said when they would leave, but from what I could tell, Regan had dug in her heels and wasn't in the mood to rush anywhere.

As a strategic consultant, she could work from anywhere. Same as Cameron. He was the executive officer of several businesses and had dozens of people working for him. Money wasn't an object for them. The only possible dilemma was that Regan was almost six months pregnant. I hadn't asked where they planned to have the baby, but I was betting Seattle wasn't the place. Regan's father, Gavriel De Luca, lived in California, north of Los Angeles. Regan's mother lived in Cape Haven off the coast of South Carolina, and Cameron's family lived in Lake Las Vegas. Seattle would be the farthest place they would want to give birth.

My thoughts were so deep, I didn't notice David fall into step beside me. I gasped when he grabbed my arm roughly, propelling me around the corner of the brick building into the narrow alleyway. When my back slammed against the building, it knocked the breath out of me and brought tears instantly to my eyes.

David was against me a second later, his body wedged firmly

against mine and his mouth just under my ear. "I think you misheard me the last time," he ground out. "You . . . are running out of time."

I tried to shove against him, but he wasn't moving. Instead, his hand slid around my neck and tears stung my eyes when his fingers dug painfully into my neck. Words failed me at the pain shooting down my neck.

"What is it going to take to make you understand the issue here?"

"I'm trying," I choked, tasting the saltiness of my tears.

He slammed me against the building again. "You've been with him after I *warned* you. You have one week, Alexis. One week, then the police. And once that's done, I'm going to reacquaint myself with our little sister." His voice was ominous in my ear. "I know where you live. It won't be hard to get to her."

His fingers dug further into my neck, hot tears burning my eyes. Any more force and I was sure he could snap my neck. Using all my strength, I managed to loosen my hand and shove it up as hard as I could. My palm connected, blood immediately gushing from his nose. When he released me, I gasped and doubled over. My hand went to my neck. He had grabbed me so hard. It was tender but not bloody.

"Don't think I won't do it," he said, then stumbled away with his hand holding his nose.

Gulping in deep breaths of air, I fell to my knees and threw up the contents of my stomach. My hands shook, my neck throbbed, my throat burned, and I couldn't collect myself enough to get back to my car.

Shaking, I pulled my phone out of my back pocket and when I heard Cameron's voice a second later, I sobbed and couldn't get the words to come out of my throat.

"Riley?" His voice was fraught with worry. "Where are you?"

"Office," I croaked. "Alley."

When the line went dead, I slumped against the wall and

curled into a ball to wait for Cameron to rescue me yet again. David's words echoed in my ears again and again. The realization that it would never stop hit me. He would always find me, and he would always use me.

I was barely aware of anything when Cameron and Regan arrived. Mortified at having to be carried out of an alleyway and placed in a car to be driven home, I could only cry in the back seat of the car into Regan's lap while she stroked my hair.

"I'll kill him," Cameron muttered.

I jumped when his palm hit the steering wheel. Regan pressed her hand against my shoulder when I only sobbed harder. When her fingers brushed against my neck where he had grasped me, her breath caught in her throat and she moved my hair to inspect the angry red marks.

"I'll kill him," she murmured.

"What does he fucking have on you, Riley?"

"Cam, she can't talk right now," Regan reminded him. "She needs time to get over whatever she just went through. But I can tell you he hurt her. Bad."

"I'll fucking kill him," he muttered again. "And I don't give a shit what he has on her. I'm going to find him, and this is going to stop."

"Call Reno," Regan said.

"No," I said, struggling to sit up. Regan pressed me back down. "Don't call him. He doesn't know me. He doesn't know this situation."

"I can handle this," Cameron said. "We don't need him here. I've got this."

Everything would be better if Cameron handled this. All of my issues with David would go away. Wouldn't they? All I could do was hope that Cameron could find him and do this for me. My past would remain buried. But I would need to confess to them what I had done. And if I had any kind of future with Ty, I would need to tell him, too. But I couldn't.

Regan tucked me into bed when we arrived home, Gus and Gatsby eager to snuggle with me regardless of what time of day it was. Naomi was beside herself with worry, but Cameron assured her he would handle it. Cassie was at the office and in the dark about any of it yet, but I was sure she would notice what was going on. Hannah would definitely not know any of it.

Cameron sat down on the end of my bed, reaching out to grab Regan's hand. I couldn't miss the exchange between them, my heart lurching at the thought of Ty. If it had been Regan in this situation, Cameron would protect her without fail. I wanted to think Ty would protect me without fail, even if he knew what I had done.

"What happened?" he asked, his voice low.

"David grabbed me coming out of the office."

Cameron gave me a look. "And?"

"He slammed me against the building, grabbed me around the neck." I swallowed the lump in my throat. "He told me I have a week to . . . to break it off with Ty, or he goes to the police."

"With?" Regan whispered. "What could you have done?"

Shame burned inside me. "I killed someone."

"So have I," she said. "So has Cameron."

I shook my head. "If he goes to the police, and this gets out, it will ruin me. It will ruin my career and my life that I've worked so hard to build. I killed someone in good conscience. It wasn't an accident."

Cameron pressed his lips into a thin line. "I'll take care of him before that happens. You don't need to worry about it."

"David is sneaky, Cameron. You won't find him."

"Is there anything else I should know about what happened when you were younger? I need it all. No judgement."

"He's always wanted me to be . . . his. In every way." I whispered, my face burning in shame. "I don't know how long I'll be able to keep him away. He'll take Hannah if I don't."

Cameron's jaw tightened. "I will make damn sure that never

happens. What about this guy you've been spending time with?"

"He can never know about this. Never."

"It isn't good to hold secrets," Regan pointed out, looking at Cameron. "It might not work out if you really like him . . . or love him."

My face flamed. "I don't love him. I hardly know him."

She shrugged. "Seems like you're headed in that direction, to me. And I like it."

I smiled. "I wish it could be, but when this is over, I'm sure he'll go his way and I'll go mine."

"Don't discount it," Cameron said. "We'll let you rest."

Gatsby crawled closer to me when I remained the only one left in bed, and I idly stroked his black fur. Gus, not to be ignored, crawled closer, too. Sighing deeply, I closed my eyes and burrowed deeper into the blankets with thoughts of Ty on my mind.

Chapter Twenty Two

When I stopped the car in the driveway behind Ty's motorcycle and the other cars, it still felt weird to be in plain sight when ordinarily I wouldn't be. The garage door was open, the blast of heavy metal crashing against me when I walked over.

Ty, Jack, and Grady were in the garage listening to Slipknot pounding out of the Bluetooth speaker while they lifted weights. I stopped for a minute to watch Ty, admiring the ease with which he lifted the barbell. When I looked at Grady, he had a sinister gaze deep in his eyes when he saw me approach but continued to deadlift. The man had massive muscles covered with tattoos, rivaling Cameron's. He was possibly the most dangerous man I had ever met. I would have thought he'd get over his suspicions since I'd been here multiple times over the course of the last few weeks.

"Riley!" Jack said, dropping his dumbbells and coming over to me before Ty had a chance to.

Grady continued to stare at me. If he was thinking he was intimidating me, it was working. It wouldn't stop me from at least trying to grab this dog, but I would have to watch my back after it was done. He was bad news.

"Glad you came by."

"Stop it," Ty said from behind him, giving him a gentle push out of the way before he pulled me roughly into his arms.

His sweat-covered chest didn't bother me, especially when his mouth was on mine in an instant. Despite his workout, I couldn't help but to get weak in the knees from his assault on my senses.

"Wish we were alone," he murmured in my ear before pulling away.

"Hmmmm . . . I agree."

"Have a seat. We're almost done here."

He led me to a lawn chair in the garage's corner and I sat down to wait patiently for him to finish his set of reps. Jack seemed perturbed. He didn't talk with me after being interrupted, but Grady . . . Grady was not saying a damn word but staring at me nonstop. *Fucker*, I smirked. *I can't wait for the day you get brought to your knees.*

The way he looked at me told me to not bother with conversation. He didn't trust me, and he never would. And if he didn't trust me, I was certain he didn't trust Ty. That didn't sit well in my stomach. The only way out of this mess would be to let this case go so Ty could solve his case and put the person responsible behind bars. But I couldn't, in good conscious, let Ellie cancel her tour when I could get Queenie back for her.

The result would end the same between us. I would lose him no matter what I did. He was a cop. I was a criminal. Whatever we had together wouldn't last, anyway. I'd enjoy it while it lasted, even though knowing it would end left a pit of despair in my stomach.

Ty mopped the sweat from his face with a towel, walking toward me. He slung the towel over his shoulder and held out his hand. When I slid my hand into his, allowing him to pull me up, his eyes never left mine. The intensity of his gaze left me breathless. The promise there held something deep. I tried to look away, but he wouldn't let me.

Without a word, he pulled me out of the garage, away from Grady. I resisted a shudder when we were around the corner of the garage, walking across the patio to the door. It didn't seem so long ago I was being led through this door with a cut on my leg after being clumsily busted sneaking around. Being grateful that it was Ty who had been the one home, who had investigated and not Grady, was easy. I couldn't be more grateful for that.

We were in Ty's bedroom only briefly before he led me into the bathroom. My eyebrows shot up when he locked the door. The wicked gleam in his eyes took my breath away. I had known him for more than a month now. I recognized that look. He backed me up against the bathroom door, his mouth molding against mine and leaving me weak in the knees.

"They won't bother us," he whispered, gathering my t-shirt in his fists and lifting it away.

The feel of his palms sliding up my ribs created a weakening that I felt all the way to my toes. He left me for only a second to turn the water in the shower on, turning back to me and wiggling his eyebrows.

Oh, what the hell . . . I thought. I kicked off my boots, peeling out of my leggings a minute later. The rest was barely off before he was pulling me under the spray of water, continuing his assault on my mouth. Water washed down around us while my head spun with the feeling his lips were invoking. His lips were one thing, his hands were another. I grasped his shoulders, my back arching.

I wasn't sure I would ever get enough of this man. The way he made me feel would be my undoing. I knew it would. His tongue gave chase to mine, a game of cat and mouse, while his hands memorized the curves of my body. At the feel of his hand between my legs, I let out a squeak swallowed by his mouth.

Moments later, I was panting as his mouth trailed kisses along my neck, sending fresh waves of fire throughout my body. Or maybe it was his hand, doing the most indecent things until I was crying out in agonizing torture.

"Ty," I said, my head falling back against the wall of the shower.

"God, say it again," he growled.

"Ty."

He grabbed my legs and wrapped me around him before reaching down to shut the water off. With ease, he stepped out of the tub and walked across the small bathroom. The cold air of the hallway hit me briefly before he opened the door to his bedroom and slammed the door behind us.

I laughed, my voice shaking when he dumped me on the bed without losing contact for a single moment. We had walked naked across the hallway, regardless of who might have seen, although I wasn't sure it would surprise them at what we were doing. My fingers tangled in his hair, my back arching off the bed while his tongue swirled and his teeth scraped against sensitive flesh.

◆

Wrapped in his arms, I didn't know if I had ever felt so thoroughly content in my entire life. It was as though I could stay here forever. But I knew it wasn't possible. We led two entirely different lives, and yet Cameron and Regan's words of wisdom rang in my ears. They were newlyweds, of course. They were in blissful happiness after being married only a few months and expecting their first child together. But there was something when they looked at each other. Something that went far deeper than just being newly married.

I stroked the back of Ty's hand while it trailed along my thigh. It didn't matter where we were; I was happy to be in his embrace. How I had gotten to this stage of my life so quickly was a mystery. No one had broken down the barrier I had built around me. How did he do it?

I would have turned to look at him, but he brushed away my hair to place a kiss on my neck. I felt him stiffen behind me. Every muscle in his body strained. I didn't need to turn to know he was seeing the bruises on my neck.

"Who did this to you?" His voice was deadly.

I turned, looking into his eyes. The look in his gaze was intense. "It's fine, Ty. Nothing to worry about, and nothing I can't handle."

"Who did it?"

It would be useless to avoid answering, so I spilled what I could without giving away too much. Involving him in more of my life would be a waste of time. I wasn't sure how to describe David, so I gave him the only thing I could think of. "My brother. We had a disagreement."

The line of his jaw clenched. I slid my hand along it, raising my mouth to his. I hoped to clear his mind away from it, and that he would forget about it. There was no other way to describe David, but instantly I regretted referring to him as my brother.

"I'm fine," I whispered, pushing him to his back and continuing my assault on his mouth. "Let it go."

"I'm not sure I can let it go. Someone put their hands on you. In anger." He raised his hand to my jaw, his hand simply cradling my face. "I can't allow that."

"You're going to have to. He's long gone."

The feel of his body relaxing beneath mine was enough, his arms coming around me and pulling me against him. All thoughts of my ordeal the previous day fled when he sat up, filling me at the same time. I gasped, my head falling back at the feeling of content.

"Riley," he murmured, his lips burning a trail against my collarbone. "I love you."

I stilled, pulling away from him with wide eyes. There was nothing in his gaze that said anything short of truth. What was worse was Regan had been right. I was falling in love with him. Except I couldn't.

I shook my head, a smile playing on my lips. "I think I love you, too," I whispered.

"Think?"

"I do. I shouldn't. Not sure how we're going to make this work, but I do."

He growled, flipping me over at the same time. "We'll figure it out later."

A shiver of unexpected excitement, different from what was flowing through my veins, washed over me. The feel of him gathering me against his body, his hands confident while they molded over my skin. Lips cruised along my jaw until they connected with mine, pulling possessively until I opened to him.

My body arched like a cat as his hands grabbed my hips, pulling me roughly against him. If my head wasn't already lying against his pillow, it would have fallen back as tidal waves of desire washed over me. A yearning deep in my belly was build-ing while his hands traveled down my thighs, pulling them further apart. A moment later, I gasped as he pushed me deeper into the bed while I felt his muscles ripple with the effort.

His mouth swallowed my first cry of pleasure, the pounding of his hips creating a cacophony of emotions deep in my body. My hands slithered up his neck, tangling in what little hair he had at his nape.

Not to be dominated, I pushed him over until I straddled him and took him deep until his eyes half closed. The murmur of an epithet escaped from his lips only a second before his hands gripped my hips and I moved above him as though I had done this dozens of times before.

"Dear God," he whispered. "What are you doing to me?"

My head kicked back, my hair cascading halfway down my back. Our hands found each other, fingers intertwining while our bodies beat a steady rhythm together until a guttural cry wrenched from my throat. There wasn't a care in the world for who might have heard. His hands grasped my hips once more, not to be outdone by my release, his face marked concentration until he shuddered his own blast of pure pleasure.

I stretched out on top of him, relishing the feel of our sweat-slicked bodies pressed together. The strength of his arms banded around me, his lips taking a nip at my shoulder.

"I meant what I said," I whispered against his collarbone. "I love you."

"Didn't think you were lying," came his reply.

"I've never said it to someone before."

He pulled away, his eyes searching mine. "They're powerful. You should mean them when you say them. I didn't intend to fall in love with you, but I'm glad. No matter what happens. I will protect you at all costs."

The corner of my lips lifted. "You won't need to. But I appreciate it."

When his fingers brushed aside my hair, revealing the marks David had left, the guilt stabbed at my heart. Now would be a good time to be honest with him about my past, and everything in it, but my mouth couldn't form the words. Something was making me stall and I couldn't. It would just drive him away faster. I couldn't do it after just admitting to him I loved him. And he loved me.

"Will you stay?" he asked.

"Of course."

That was the easiest decision I could make. I finally relented and moved off him, flopping beside him onto my back and staring at the ceiling. It wasn't possible to get enough of him. I turned to my side, resting my head in my hand.

There were too many ears around. My smile was inevitable. After what they probably heard coming from this room, there shouldn't be any doubt that we weren't acting. Grady could shove it up his ass if he thought he couldn't trust us.

I still needed a plan. It wasn't like I could just swoop in and grab the dog. I would be taking the chance of blowing Ty's case apart and the possibility of his cover getting discovered. Jack was at stake, too. There was too much risk to do it, yet risk not to do it.

The consequences still lingered. And I was running out of time. Fast.

Chapter Twenty Three

Cameron sat on a stool at the breakfast bar with his laptop open, so engrossed in whatever he was doing, he didn't look up when I walked into the kitchen. I got home from Ty's earlier but escaped to my room with Gus and Gatsby to get some much needed sleep, then shower. It was nearly dinnertime, and luckily not my scheduled night to cook.

Regan was nowhere to be seen. After I gave the dogs a treat from the cookie jar, reserved for their treats instead of actual human cookies, I leaned against the counter and waited for Cameron to acknowledge me. My irritation grew the longer I waited.

"Cameron," I snapped, instantly regretting the bite in my voice when he glanced up at me.

"Your issue is proving to be harder than I thought to find." He tapped a few more keys, then pushed the laptop to the side. "Every time I think I've located him, he's gone again."

"Not surprised. I told you before. You don't find him, he finds you."

His gaze leveled with mine, the look in his eyes chilling. I had never seen such a look behind his blue eyes, and I was sure I would never want to be on the wrong side of him. Cameron was determined. He didn't need to say anything to know that he would not stop until he found David.

"Who?"

I turned to see Hannah breezing into the kitchen, looking

refreshed in a tank top and skinny jeans with her brown hair swept up in perfection. She and Cassie were so much more alike than she and I were. I smiled.

"It doesn't matter," I said. "Are you going somewhere?"

"I wish you'd stop treating me like a child." She folded her arms in front of her, eyes glimmering with hurt. "I hear you whispering around here. I know something is going on."

There was no point in avoiding it. She needed to know the truth so she could stay cautious. Even though I was still in the middle of this assignment, I didn't trust David not to approach her. If he was being truthful, and he knew where she was going to school, I couldn't take any chances.

"Do you remember David? From when you were little?" She stared at me, but her eyes gave no sign of whether she remembered.

"Vaguely."

"He's back, and he's creating some issues for me. I need you to be very careful, Hannah. Do not talk to anyone you don't know. It's extremely important that you are always with someone."

Her arms loosened. "Is he after me?"

"He's after Riley," Cameron said. "Until I can get to him, we're afraid he might grab you to get to her."

She nodded. "Okay, I'll be careful. I'm going out with some friends. Is that okay?"

I nodded, pulling her into a hug before she could escape, and murmured in her ear to be careful. When she skipped out of the kitchen, leaving out the back door, I turned back to Cameron.

"Where's Regan?" I asked, in a hurry to get away from the subject of David.

"Out shopping with Cassie. They didn't think you'd want to go with." I wrinkled my nose and his lips curled up. "Not your thing, huh?"

A snort slipped out. "Me? Shopping? More like shoplifting."

"Come on, Riles. I thought you were past that."

I sighed. "Maybe I am. After all, I'm sleeping with a cop."

As soon as the words slipped out of my mouth, the surprise that lit his eyes couldn't be unseen. *Shit.* The last thing I needed was Cameron getting freaked out with a cop being in my life, albeit temporarily. The thing was, I wasn't sure how temporary it was going to be. I hadn't been lying when I told Ty I loved him. But I couldn't move on without confessing to him what I had done in my past.

"You are *what*?" Cameron asked, his tone clipped. "Did you say you're sleeping with a cop?"

"It's not . . ." Not what? Not what it seemed? I didn't know what to tell him. "Yes, Cam. The man I've been sleeping with is an undercover detective, and I swear to God if you tell a soul, I will kill you myself. If you do anything, say anything, you are jeopardizing both of us."

He looked like he was going to say something, but changed his mind and snapped his mouth closed. He appeared to be torn between guilt and anger, and I know he wasn't happy about the situation, but neither was I. We were both guilty of doing things on the wrong side of the law.

"Does he know?" he finally asked.

"That I'm a thief? No. He does know I'm a private investigator. After all, he did bust me trying to sneak into the house."

He leaned back. "Oh my God."

"What?"

"You're in love with him."

"Shut up."

He had the decency to not outright laugh at me. It was shocking enough that I was sleeping with a cop, but now my heart had to be involved. Something I had never felt for someone before. I felt my cheeks warm.

"Admit it."

"It doesn't matter. We can't stay together. I'm a criminal."

Cameron pushed up from the chair, coming around to stand in front of me. His hands came up to my arms, but he didn't pull me into a hug. "Little sister," came his whisper. "You're doing your job. Maybe you were a criminal a long time ago, but you've changed."

I shook my head. "Cam, when I told you and Regan I killed someone . . . I was telling the truth. He knows something that can put me away for a long time."

When Cameron stepped away, staring at me, I knew I'd have to tell him the entire story. Of all the people in my life who knew me, Cameron would understand the most. He had blood on his hands as much as I did.

"It was after you busted me. Two months after. Simone came home with her boyfriend, drunk and high, as usual. Except she was more out of it than usual . . ."

"Alexis, baby." I stood rooted to the spot in the kitchen, scraping as much as I could get out of the empty peanut butter jar to spread on my piece of bread.

Simone draped herself over me, pushing me so forcefully into the counter the empty peanut butter container tipped, skidded across and hit the floor. Her laughter echoed off the walls as she danced away from me.

"Simone, babe, you've gotta get ahold of yourself," her boyfriend said, his voice slurring almost as much as hers.

With disgust, I swooped down to pick up the container while their laughter echoed down the hallway. They'd better not wake up Ivy, I thought. I should go get her out of the bedroom before anything happens. She shouldn't stay in there while Finn is here, but they were already down the hall when I spun around with the thought. Hopefully, she stayed asleep.

I'd just turned fourteen last month, just before Valentine's Day. Ivy would be two in July. This was getting old. Two more years and I'd be able to get a job and start putting away money to get us the hell out of here. Dealing with Simone's lust for drugs and alcohol, as well as her revolving door drug dealer boyfriends, would have to continue for two or three more years. This one with his long, shoulder-length hair, usually tied back in a man-bun and his sleazy-looking clothes. Two more years of dealing with David, waking me up every couple of nights to go out thieving. Two or three more years of hell.

I turned back to my sandwich, folding the piece of bread in half and pressing it down with my palm. The tremors in my stomach were easy to get used to, but I wished I'd saved the last of the peanut butter for Ivy. She'd need something to eat in the morning. I could only hope David would bring home some groceries when he got home from wherever he was.

I turned, gasping at the sight of Finn leaning against the wall next to the stove with a chip in the front of it. It was chipped from when Simone threw a can of brown beans at a boyfriend in stoned anger.

The curve of Finn's mouth, lifting at the corners, made me back up a step with the sandwich still clutched in my hand. He wore a thin button-up shirt that was unbuttoned almost clear to his navel, revealing a dusting of brown hair. I shuddered in repulsion.

"You're looking pretty fine tonight, Alexis Rose," he drawled. "Your mother didn't last long and is out for the count already. Thought maybe you and I could get to know one another better."

He cocked his head to the side. I made a dash, trying to get around him, but his arm snaked out and caught me in the midsection. The impact stole my breath and knocked the sandwich out of my hand. With the force of catching me, he propelled me back into the kitchen until my back slammed against the refrigerator.

"I don't think you like me much," he said, his breath hot against my neck below my ear. "Why don't you play nice for once? All I want is one kiss. Just one."

I pushed against him, but he wouldn't budge. Turning my

head, I felt his lips against my jaw while my stomach rolled in disgust. The knife block was just within reach, even though there weren't many knives in it. If I could just reach one, I could threaten him away from me. Stretching my arm out, his lips connected with my mouth and I pushed until my fingers brushed the handle of a steak knife and I pulled it out just as he pushed against me again. A gasp ripped out of my throat when he staggered back, clutching his shirt where red was seeping out.

His eyes were wide, blood oozing out from his hand and making the light color of his shirt blossom with bright red. I looked down at the steak knife in my hand, red coating the serrated blade just as he fell down. His eyes were closed. I covered my mouth with my hands, one of them still clutching the weapon while blood trickled down my arm. The front door opened and a whistling David walked in.

He looked at the man on the ground with the chest wound, then looked up at me in shock. "What the hell did you do, Alexis?"

"He ... kissed me."

"Where's Simone?"

"Passed out in her room." I lowered my hands, my heart thumping wildly while David crouched down next to Finn and felt for a pulse in his wrist. "Did I kill him?"

"No, but he's going to have to get to the hospital, so you're going to help me get him into his car." He looked up at me. "NOW!"

I moved to get past him, yelping when he grabbed my wrist and removed the steak knife from my grasp. He wiped the blood off using Finn's shirt and set it on the counter before he grabbed him under the arms, nodding at me to grab his feet. I was surprised at how heavy he was for such a scrawny prick.

Thankful it was dark outside, I let David lead the way to Finn's car and helped fold him into the front seat. The entire way I was afraid Finn would wake and scream bloody murder that I'd attacked him when it was the other way around. He attacked me. I wasn't sure anyone would believe me.

David slid into the driver's seat and yelled at me out the open window. "Get into the house and wash that blood off you. We'll talk when I get home about what happened."

Wasting no time, I sprinted across the lawn while he pulled away. I did more than wash the blood off. I bathed and changed my clothes. There was nothing else to do but wait. I paced the length of the living room over and over until David returned hours later. It was four in the morning. And I was wide awake.

"What happened?" I asked.

David's mouth flattened. "He died on the way to the hospital, Alexis." He looked at me, looked deep into my eyes. "I had to hide the car and body where they won't find it. I had to cover this up for you."

I gasped, shaking my head. "No. No, no, no."

"Why did you stab him, Alexis?"

"He kissed me."

The laugh that came from deep in his throat would haunt me for the rest of my life. "You stabbed a man to death because he kissed you? Jesus."

"What am I going to do, David?" I cried.

He strode over to me, taking me by my arms and giving me a shake. "You're going to calm down and keep quiet. I covered this up for you, but you did it." There was a fiery gleam in his eyes. "You owe me for this, Alexis."

When I completed my story, Cameron's face remained stoic. Was he surprised at what I'd done? Proud of me for standing up for myself or angry for what I'd done when a guy kissed me? I couldn't tell.

"Say something," I whispered. "Please."

His face softened. "It won't stick. That was ten years ago, Riles."

I shook my head. "You don't get it. This is my life. It would mess up everything if it got out. My job, my relationship with

Ty."

"You shouldn't hide it from him. Tell him the truth about you, about your past."

"He'll hate me. He won't want to stay with me."

"Don't you think that's for him to decide?"

Guilt ate at me. Ty deserved to know the truth about me, even if it was unsavory. He deserved to know the complete truth about my past. But it scared me to death to think of telling him.

He pulled away, leaning up against the counter opposite of me. "You know we'll fight it with everything we have. Regan. Me. Reno."

As much as I wanted to continue my conversation with Cameron, my phone vibrated in my pocket. I dragged it out, frowning when I saw it was Ty. It wasn't like him to call me. A text was usually enough.

"What's wrong?" I asked.

"I don't have long," Ty said, quickly. "They're transporting Queenie tonight."

A forceful, very colorful curse ripped from my throat as I threw my fist on top of the counter, though there was not enough force behind it to rattle anything. "Where? To who? Is it the ransom?"

"Riley, leave it alone."

"This is my job!"

"And this is mine," came his soft reply.

We were at an impasse. I couldn't jeopardize my job without endangering his case and his life, and he couldn't set his aside without causing a landslide of risks to him and Jack. As much as it split my heart in two, I couldn't threaten his safety for the sake of my job.

"Are you going with?"

"No."

Even knowing he wasn't going on this mission, I had a bad feeling deep in my gut. The need to know where they were taking

Queenie reared its ugly head, but I bit my tongue. I had to trust him. Trust in him.

For his sake, I had to let this case go. I could only hope Queenie was being returned to Ellie Varro and she was paying the ransom, even if it was a ridiculous amount. She'd have her dog back and be able to meet her tour schedule. If not, I'd have to move on from it. Once Ty's case was wrapped up, I could turn over everything I had on those involved.

"Be safe," I whispered. "Please."

"Promise me, Riley. Promise me you won't do anything about this."

"I promise. I won't risk your life."

"I'll call you as soon as I can."

A tear escaped from the corner of my eye, and Cameron was right there to wipe it away. I tried to push him away, my phone getting jostled in the process so I couldn't answer Ty.

"Are you there?"

"Yes. Sorry . . . my brother . . ."

He paused. "I'll call you later."

This could be the break in his case that he needed. At least, I hoped it was. I set my phone on the counter, looking at Gus and Gatsby, who were laying on the edge of the spacious living room floor. That was enough to send me into a full-blown meltdown.

Cameron's enormous arms came around me while I sobbed my heart out against his chest. Brother or not, I was glad he was the one here for me. I needed someone more than I wanted to admit. I wasn't sure if my meltdown was coming from the fact that I lost this case, or that I had finally admitted to someone what had happened ten years ago.

"Oh, God, what happened?"

I lifted my head at Regan's voice, pulling away from Cameron at the same time. She dumped her bags on the chair he had vacated and came around to us. Cameron looked down at me, and I nodded.

"She couldn't crack her case."

"Oh, Riley," she whispered, bumping Cameron aside and folding me into her embrace. "I'm so sorry. What are you going to do now?"

I shrugged. "I'll need to break the news to my boss. This might be the result of the ransom being paid, and Queenie is being returned to Ellie Varro. I don't know."

Regan pulled back, anger lighting her blue eyes. "But you did what you could! It can't be a simple job, and you said yourself this was more dangerous than any other job you've ever done. She has to understand that!"

"You would think, but it's still my job." I sighed. "I need to talk with Ty as soon as they're done delivering Queenie. And hope he can nail his case since I couldn't mine."

But I needed to know where they were bringing Queenie. It wouldn't hurt to know that, at least. I slid toward the door, trying to hide that I was grabbing my keys.

"What're you doing?" Cameron asked. "Riles?"

"I need to run an errand."

"Don't do this." I moved toward the door, ignoring him. "Riley, don't!"

Chapter Twenty Four

Ty would be angry if he knew I was sitting in my car watching the house again. It was dark now, the sun just having set, so I had to strain my eyes to watch Grady's car in the driveway. I'd been here for a while and had promptly blown out a deep sigh when Ty's motorcycle was absent from the patio.

I'd had every intention of abandoning the mission to protect Ty. I still did. But I needed closure. It wouldn't hurt to see where Grady would take Queenie. If it turned out to be Ellie Varro, the case would be closed. If not, I'd need to take some pictures inconspicuously to turn over later.

Grady, Merrick and Jack strolled out of the house a half hour later, Queenie cradled in Jack's arms while he got into the backseat. Once the car was backing out of the driveway, I could start my car and follow behind at a safe distance. In my training, I knew not to get too close by hanging back when we stopped at stoplights. When we hit the freeway, I set my speed to match his while keeping aware of my surroundings.

Oddly enough, it seemed there was a car following me. If someone was following me, knowing I was following Grady, this could be extremely bad. And dangerous. I switched lanes, watching in my rearview mirror to see if the black Dodge Charger switched lanes. Damn it, I said, watching the car fall into place behind me. I couldn't tell who was behind the wheel of the car.

If the car continued to follow me, I decided I'd bail. But as soon as the thought entered my head, Grady pulled off at the next exit. I followed even when they turned the corner. It was a risk, but I purposely got into a different lane and pulled into a gas station to allow the car following me to proceed before I looped around and followed them both.

By the time the two cars rolled into a stop in a busy parking lot, my heart was thundering and my palms were sweating. I parked a safe distance away, wiping my palms on my thighs while I watched Grady and Jack get out. Queenie still snuggled in Jack's arms, content where she was. I smiled, thinking maybe Jack should get a dog.

The passenger side door of the Charger opened and I froze, my blood pumping through my veins like ice. *David.*

"What.In.The.Hell?" I whispered. "How in the hell are you involved in this?"

I threw the shift into gear and rolled out of the parking lot as quietly as I could, hoping no one had seen me stop nearby to see me slink away. Questions raced through my mind while   I drove away. I could hardly concentrate on the road.

When I got home, Naomi and Hannah were in the kitchen making popcorn. I lingered by the door, watching them move around each other like a dance, giggling and talking. Gus and Gatsby didn't realize I'd snuck in yet, which means Naomi and Hannah didn't either. I could watch them with no one knowing. Cassie perched on the couch with her tablet open, but I didn't see Cameron and Regan.

This was home. The bane of my existence. My family. I would do anything to protect them. Maybe going with David was what I would have to do to save Hannah. It was obvious now that he was involved in this somehow. One thing I knew, I'd be including his name in my reports. And he'd be back in jail. It might buy me the time I needed. But there was something I needed to do first, as much as my heart broke to do it. To save them, I needed to save Ty first. Save him from me.

The drive back to Grady's house was time I needed more than

I could admit. I scrutinized what I did and didn't do, trying to determine what mistakes I might have made. They all led back to the fact that I couldn't endanger Ty. I couldn't endanger Hannah.

By the time I pulled onto the street and parked, I had collected my thoughts enough to be in a better mood. The need to find out what happened to Queenie gnawed at me. And to find out what David was doing there, and how he was involved, was worse.

Grady's car was absent, thankfully.

As soon as I got out of the Jeep, walking around to the other side, I spotted Ty on the patio, crouched next to his bike. I wondered what he was doing tinkering with his bike when it was drizzling.

Today's letdown melted away when Ty stood, noticing me walking up the driveway. Alarm hit his face when he saw me, then he must have realized I was safe.

Ty met me halfway, pulling me swiftly into his arms. The feeling of euphoria swept through me, settling deep into my bones. I sank into him, the security of his embrace erasing all the pain. The sigh that slipped from my lips went unnoticed until he pulled away a bit, his eyes searching mine.

"You okay?"

I nodded, the question poised on my lips. Irritating him wouldn't be good. Other than when we had first met, I had yet to see him truly irritated or angry. I often wondered if he was angry that first time we met, or if it was an act. It might have been a show to get me to go away, although I had knocked over his motorcycle.

"I will be." I sighed again.

He kept his arms firmly around me. Tenderly, he drew his finger down my cheek, his mouth finding mine when this fingertip reached the edge of my jaw. I inhaled deeply, giving in to the feel of him.

Questions could wait until later. The kiss deepened, drawing me in and not letting go. I opened fully to the sweep of his tongue against mine, felt the path of his hand against my jaw until his fingers tangled in my hair.

"You're all I think about," he growled against my mouth, wrapping his fist into my hair and giving it a gentle tug until my head tipped back. "Why is that?"

If I could have found my voice, I would have answered, but my body was tingling in all the right places. My hands on his biceps braced me against tumbling to the concrete driveway beneath our feet. Instead, I could only release a throaty laugh.

"What are you doing to me, Riley?" His lips found an especially sensitive place just below my ear. "I want to keep you with me all the time."

Still, I couldn't find my voice. With a sudden jerk, he swept me off my feet with an arm hooked beneath my legs. Ty wasted no time in bringing me back to his bedroom. Despite not being tucked away safely in his house in the woods, I found security in his arms as his mouth brought about the most delicious re-actions from my body. I wasn't sure I wanted to be apart from him, either.

But reality would hit eventually. As much as I wanted to, I couldn't run from it forever. Eventually, David would find me.

A shudder ripped through me. I wouldn't allow him to invade my thoughts now. I'd deal with that later. Right now, Ty was all that mattered.

It was hours later when we finally emerged from the bedroom to find the living room still vacant. I would have thought Grady and the boys would be back by now. I'd expected to stay and packed an overnight bag but left it in the back of my car.

I stopped at the hallway door. I was about to tell Ty I was going to get my things from the car when he came up behind me. The feel of his arms wrapped around me, his fingers entwined with mine, rendered me unable to speak again. This was safety. Even if it was temporary.

"Marry me," he whispered in my ear.

Those two words immobilized me. The breath couldn't even

fill my lungs completely. Every muscle in my body tensed as my mind raced. We'd only known each other for a couple of months, but I knew without a doubt I would. If it wasn't for my past. To know about it, he would hate me for it. I hated myself for it. How could he not?

Reluctantly, I pulled away from him but couldn't turn to face him yet. I wasn't sure what to tell him. An outright refusal was cruel, and I couldn't do that to him. But I couldn't say yes and give him a false hope.

"Answer me."

At his order, firm but not malicious, I turned slowly. His eyes told me everything I needed to know. There had been nothing about his offer that wasn't serious. I choked, my hand flying to my mouth.

"You don't want to marry me, Ty," I whispered.

A blond eyebrow raised, and he took a step toward me. I stepped back. He took another step. "I don't?" I shook my head. "How do you know what I want?"

"We've only known each other a couple of months."

"And I told you I've met no one else like you. I don't *want* anyone else. I don't want to *think* about *you* with anyone else," he said, and there wasn't anything about his words I didn't believe.

Again, I shook my head. "You hardly know me."

"I know enough."

You know nothing! Everything that he would learn would devastate him. He would have no choice but to arrest me if he knew what I had done.

"You don't." I hadn't meant for it to come out as a snap. "You know absolutely nothing about me, Ty. We knew this was temporary, and it would end as soon as my job was done."

"I never gave you that impression, did I?"

"No, but . . ."

Ty suddenly reached for me, pulling me to him and burying his lips against my neck, whispering: "You didn't give me that impression. Why wouldn't we continue? You'll start another case, and I'll continue this one until I've cracked it." He shrugged. "I'll talk to the captain and see if I can get into another department, so I'm not undercover and away for months at a time."

Shocked rippled through me. He would uproot his career and change everything for me. And he didn't even know me. I couldn't let him do such a thing. Not without knowing who Riley Parker was. Who Alexis Monroe was.

"I can't," I whispered. "I'm sorry."

I pushed out of his arms, feeling the cold air against my body as soon as I lost contact with him.

"Riley, wait!"

It was too late. Despite my lack of decent clothing, I was out the door quickly. I was already in my car before he caught up to me. Ty got to my car door before I could start it to drive away.

He pounded on the window. "Riley, don't."

The tears started despite how hard I tried to keep them at bay. I couldn't look at him, turning the key to start the car. It wasn't all Ty's fault. He couldn't have known.

"Please," he whispered. "Don't do this."

I looked at him. "I need time, Ty. Please. Give me time."

The anguish in his eyes was nearly my undoing, but he stepped away from my car and allowed me to leave. Tears blinded me as I drove down the lane. Smacking the steering wheel a few times did nothing to stop the complete agony coursing through me. Ty was the last person I wanted to hurt. He'd shown me that not all men were bastards like David.

Chapter Twenty Five

"Oh my God," Regan gasped when I walked into the house, the boys winding around me while I fought to get in.

"What the . . ." Cameron jumped off the couch, grabbing a blanket and throwing it around me. "What happened?"

It took a significant amount of determination to suck back the tears while Cameron led me into the living room. I was interrupting their movie night. Cassie paused the movie. Naomi and Hannah moved over, and I sat down like a lump.

"Ty asked me to marry him."

Between the five of them, I couldn't tell who gasped and who cried out. I don't think Cassie, Naomi, or Hannah knew how deep in I was, but they knew I had met someone. But now they would all know that I was irrevocably in love and that no one had cracked my force field ever before. Until now.

"What did you say?" Cassie whispered.

"I told him he didn't know me. And I ran."

Cassie jumped up and came over to me, putting her arm around my shoulders. "You did what you do when you feel threatened." She squeezed. "I don't blame you for that but think for a minute. You haven't been yourself the last couple months. Why?"

I didn't give Cassie enough credit. Maybe she knew how deep in I was. I didn't need to think about it. Or hesitate. I knew why I hadn't been myself. Job aside, I had been happier than I'd been in my entire life. Ty had done that. Cassie wouldn't understand.

None of them would understand.

"You know why," I whispered. "But I can't marry him. He doesn't know me."

"I should have probably told you he came here. Fully thought he was going to kick my ass for putting marks on your neck."

My eyes shot to Cameron, and my mouth fell open. "Ty came here?"

"I denied it, of course. After he left, it made sense that you would tell him David was your brother. There isn't another way to describe that punk. He was your brother for a long time."

"Did you tell him about David?"

"It's not my place to tell him, but we also don't know a hundred percent you're my sister, so I didn't confess that I was your brother. He knows we're friends now, though."

"I didn't know he'd track down where I live. I . . ."

"It's okay," Cameron said. "It just shows me what he's willing to do for you. He cares a great deal for you."

Regan scoffed, smoothing a hand over her rounded belly. "Cares? Oh, please, Cam. There wasn't anything you wouldn't have done for me if you thought I was in danger. Even after knowing me for only a few *days*."

"He loves her," Naomi said.

"But he still doesn't know me," I whispered. "Not the real me."

Cassie's arms remained around me but relaxed. "Don't you want to be happy, Riles? You know you would be happy with him. Why did you run? Why didn't you say yes? Be fucking happy."

I gasped. Cassie, like me, never swore. Not the terrible words, anyway. She smiled, a secret smile like she was trying to show me that people didn't always know everything about someone else. But she didn't know everything about my past.

"I need to get some clothes on," I said. "I'll be right back."

Disengaging myself from Cassie, I left the living room and took the stairs two at a time to get to my room. Gatsby followed me, but Gus stayed behind. I pushed open the door, panic rising into my throat. The scream wrenched from deep within brought Cameron up so fast I thought he'd break the door off the hinges.

My bedroom was trashed. Normally, I wasn't an organized person but my room looked as though a tornado and a hurricane had been through it. My bed was upended, my nightstands tipped over, lamps broken. Every single drawer in my dresser was open and clothes were flung everywhere. My curtains were ripped to shreds, and my closet doors carved with a . . .

My hands slapped over my mouth. In the center of my headboard, holding a white piece of paper much like the one under my windshield wiper at the airport, was a black-handled steak knife. Tremors shook my entire body, even when I felt Regan's arms come around me and pull me out of the room while Cameron went to retrieve the note.

I didn't want to know what it said. I had a feeling I already knew what it said.

Regan guided me back downstairs, helping me to the couch and pulling the blanket back around me as though a blanket would stop me from shaking. This had done it.

"We need to get out of here," Naomi said. "If David did this, we need to go. She needs to go."

The sound of Cameron coming down the stairs wasn't enough to calm me down. Even the sound of him opening his gun to make sure there were bullets in the chamber didn't. He came around to the couch, squatting down in front of me.

"Riles, you know I'd do anything to protect you. To protect all of you. And I will. But now is the time to think about Hannah, Naomi, and Cassie. It's not just you that might need protection."

"What did the note say?"

"You don't want to know what it said."

I gritted my teeth. "Tell me."

He let go of a heavy sigh. "You'll have to promise me something."

I nodded my head.

Taking my hand, he withdrew a crumpled piece of paper and tucked it into my palm. I still shook so badly I almost couldn't uncrumple it. The same black ink was scrawled on the piece of paper except there were only three words on it this time. I cried out, letting it fall from my hand. *Time's up, Alexis.*

"Go see Reno," Regan whispered, laying her cheek against the top of my head. "Please, Riley. Hannah needs his protection as much as you do."

Silence wrapped around us, echoing throughout the room and bouncing off the walls. I stared at Cameron. He nodded. Regan was a force to be reckoned with. And she was right. It was time to face Reno. I needed the answers, and I needed Hannah to have his protection as much as I hated to admit it. At least Hannah was out of school for the summer.

"Yes," I whispered.

"Yes?" Cameron said.

I nodded. "I'll go. It's time to talk with Reno. I've put it off long enough, and I need some distance between me and here. I told Ty I needed some time, but I can't be certain that he's going to be patient enough for it. A few days away won't hurt."

Chapter Twenty Six

Cameron didn't trust not being followed and called in another favor from a friend. We took a private jet, the first time I'd ever been on one in my life, to Las Vegas the next day. Naomi and Cassie insisted on staying in Seattle, but with friends. Naomi swore she'd be safe and Cassie was convinced this didn't have anything to do with her, and she'd be safe with her friend as well. Both of them felt better if Hannah and I were under Reno's protection. There was no talking either of them into coming with.

Regan tried to warn us that Cameron's family home was much bigger than the De Luca family estate in California. Despite my skepticism, my jaw dropped as we drove through the gates. She hadn't been kidding. It had to be at least twice the size, if not more, with a beautiful garden right in the center splitting the driveway in two directions.

Cameron drove to the left, and I watched the center garden until we stopped in front of garages. Arm in arm, Regan led Hannah and me toward the massive front door while Cameron grabbed our overnight bags.

The doors opened automatically for us, and once we stepped into the spacious foyer; I understood why. There was a small, balding butler with a mustache that looked like a square above his lips. Hannah and I managed a quiet laugh, earning us a nasty glare from him.

"Retton, this is Riley and Hannah Parker," she announced. "Where is Mr. Moretti?"

He seemed stunned by Regan's outspokenness, but his eyebrows drew together and he answered, with an air of superiority, "He is in his study."

Regan released Hannah's arm but pulled me to the right, barely giving me a chance to look toward the living room or anywhere else before we were facing another set of doors, one of them open. Hannah, mystified by the house, trailed behind us. I looked up at the two story walls of books around us while we walked in, ignoring the man rising from behind the desk in front of the windows.

"Reno," Regan called out, keeping her arm firmly linked with mine.

"My darling, Regan!" His booming voice carried to us across the room. "Miss Parker, how nice to see you! And who is this?"

"This is Riley's sister, Hannah."

I managed a smile, wondering if he would think it was nice to see me after he found out the reason I was in his office. Nothing and no one had told me otherwise, but I thought he still didn't know I might be his daughter.

"Did you bring my son with you?" he asked as we approached his desk.

Regan wrinkled her nose, waving her hand in front of her at the cigar smoke rising from his ashtray. "Yes, and he won't be happy about you smoking in front of me while I'm carrying your grandchild."

Reno snuffed out his cigar. "Had I known you were coming, I wouldn't have lit it. I thought you had pressing business in Seattle?"

I looked over at Regan to see a smile spread across her face. "We still have a few issues to work through. Isn't that right, Riley?"

She expects me to answer that honestly? "I think I'm fine now."

"Nonsense. Cameron and I will see you back and make sure of it."

"You are going to make an excellent mother," I muttered, to which her smile grew.

"Of course she is," Reno said. "Anyone with Regan's tenacity would make a wonderful mother, and anyone who can handle my son even more so."

"Does she handle me?" came Cameron's rumble as he joined us. "Hey Pop."

"Cameron, wonderful to see you." Reno pressed his hands to his desk. "What brings you four by? Come to show Riley and Hannah the excitement of Las Vegas?"

I've already seen it, and it sucks, I thought silently. And he should know it.

"I grew up here," I said, watching surprise light his warm, brown eyes. "Hannah was pretty young, but I grew up in the seedy parts of town, not the more well-off parts like Lake Las Vegas."

I could have sworn I heard Cameron mumble "ouch" under his breath. Gathering courage, I moved closer to Reno's desk while my eyes swept over the organized papers and the high-end pens. The pens had his initials carved into them, and I purposely didn't look at anything on his papers. Those were none of my business, and not my reason for being here.

"I thought you said you were from Seattle."

"I am. But I grew up here. Until I went to live with my grandmother when I was fourteen." I watched his eyes for any sign of recognition, but I wasn't giving him much to go on. "My mother is Simone Monroe."

Reno stumbled back and sat down in his chair with a thump. His hand passed over his face, and I thought he was going to reach for his cigar to relight it, but he pulled open his left-side drawer. Curious, I watched him rifle through some things and pull out a picture. A picture of Simone, twenty-some years ago, from what I could see. The picture Cameron spoke of, I surmised.

"We'll leave you two alone," Regan whispered.

I didn't watch her and Cameron leave, ushering Hannah out

with them, but I heard the click of the second door to the office. There was a slight shake to his hand when he let it flutter back into his drawer. There was a quiet thud when he closed it, but he said nothing until he raised his eyes back to me.

"I'm not sure what to say," he said.

"Regan will be a great mom." I knew that beyond doubt. "Simone was less than ideal. She preferred drugs and alcohol to being a mother, couldn't hold down a job long enough for us to have anything, and subjected me to a life of stealing money from people in Vegas. Now, do you have anything to say?"

"I made a mistake."

My ears burned, and I was sure my face was red. I couldn't believe he said that. He had the audacity to call me a mistake? So I was a gangster's mistake? As though I were the one to cause him to cheat on his poor wife with my sick excuse of a mother. When I opened my mouth to tell him exactly what I thought about his mistake, I nearly choked. *How could he say that to me?*

He was staring at me. "Alexis."

"Riley." I gritted my teeth. My throat felt like I had taken a drink of acid. *How did he know that name?* "My name is Riley. Alexis died long ago when Naomi saved me from that hell."

"Riley. The mistake is mine. My mistake was that I didn't believe Simone. I didn't believe her when she said she'd gotten pregnant. I thought it was a lie just to get me to stay with her. When she contacted me a year later, said she had a baby girl . . . Alexis, I thought you belonged to someone else. I didn't fight for you. That was my mistake."

Tears were gathering in the corners of his eyes, giving me cause to doubt he was giving me anything but the truth. *I wasn't a mistake to him? He really truly didn't know, or believe, I had existed?*

My eyes widened at the tears sliding down his face. This powerful man with a tremor in his voice, looked at me as though he would break down and weep at any moment.

"I'm not a mistake?"

"No. You are so like your siblings. You are so strong. What you've faced . . . You've got guts, girl. Guts I admire."

I smiled. "I had no choice."

"Whatever I can do to help you, I will. What is mine is yours."

"I've come this far with no help. I can handle the rest on my own. "

Reno pursed his lips. "Stubborn, just like the rest of them. There was something about you when I met you at the wedding. God, you look like . . . Doesn't matter. There is no doubt in my mind that you're my child. Would you like to sit?"

I nodded, sliding into the chair. "Will you tell me what happened?" His jaw tensed, and it reminded me of Cameron. "And just so you know, I don't doubt Simone would have tried to dupe you, but I'm interested in the story."

Reno sighed, then looked at his cigar before looking back at me. I nodded. Fascinated, I watched him light it and take a puff before leaning back in his chair. It was almost as though I could see the flashback enter his mind, etching fine lines into his face. Not wrinkles, not like Simone was already sporting when she was far too young to have them. No. Reno had lines and ridges in his face that were the marks of a well-off, distinguished man.

True, it was his fault he hadn't been in my life, but Simone was likely to take the blame. At least, in his story. I had yet to determine whether I would seek her out while I was here. David was still out there, somewhere.

"I was thirty, down on the strip for business." He paused, taking another puff from his cigar. "She was only eighteen, but she was young, beautiful, and persuasive. Orianna and I were having some problems and I'm not proud of it. Simone and I started an affair."

I tried to keep quiet, but questions were running rampant through my head. Rather than pepper him with them, I waited to see if he answered them. Hearing only his side, I would have to make my own judgements unless I wanted to speak with Simone. I should. As many faults as she had, Simone was still my mother. And above all, I loved her. I cared about what happened to her, regardless of where I was.

"I knew she was trouble, knew she was likely after a man that had money. Still, we clicked. We were good together."

"In bed," slipped out, and I bit my lip.

His eyes were stern. "Yes. It took me almost a year to realize that was all there was to us. My marriage was tumultuous when I met her and it blinded me. It's not an excuse. It's what happened. I will not regret it. I won't regret you, Riley."

I offered him a smile.

"When I tried to end it, she became unreasonable. Threatened to go to Orianna and tell her of our affair. She wanted me to leave my family and be with her, you see. That's when I understood she really just wanted my money. Maybe me, but mostly my money. I refused to leave my family."

"Did she follow through with her threat?"

His eyes dulled with sorrow. "Yes. She contacted Orianna and told her the details of our sordid affair. It nearly broke Orianna. She's never been the same, but she stayed with me for the sake of our family and, well . . . I broke it off and never spoke of it again. We tried to repair our marriage. Stefan was born seven months after you, then Peter, then Zoey. But it's never been the same."

"I can tell," I whispered. "She's haunted."

"Simone contacted me once again and told me she was pregnant, but I thought it was a ruse to get me to stay with her and not end things. I chose not to believe her." He hung his head. "She contacted me one other time about a year later to tell me you were born, Alexis. I still didn't believe her."

"Reno, my mother has many problems. I wouldn't have trusted what she said was true, either. She's had a lot of partners over the years. I could be anyone's daughter."

His gaze held mine. "You are beyond any doubt, my daughter.

Even with seven years between you, Zoey is almost the spitting image of you. I don't need a paternity test to know you are mine."

I didn't know why I was sticking up for him. There were several ways he could have verified the truth. He didn't. *What would my life have been like if he had? Would he have taken me to live here in this mansion?* Or would he have stuck with Orianna and just sent money to Simone so she could shoot it in her arm, or fill up her liquor cabinet? I would never know. Or would I?

"If you did, what would you have done? I don't think she was a junkie then, but she is now. Giving her money would not have made life better for me."

His guarded eyes met mine. "I can't honestly say what I would have done. I chose not to believe her. Part of me didn't want to believe her, and part of me didn't think for a minute it was true. I suppose I would have given her monthly child support, but I don't shirk duty. Although I couldn't marry her, I would have still tried to be a father to you. And if I had seen less than desirable conditions, I would have removed you from them."

I nodded.

"You are my daughter, Riley." He stopped, not releasing my gaze. "Why did you change your name, by the way?"

To divulge that went deep. "Simone had a boy in her care when I was born, abandoned by a former boyfriend. Did you know that?" When he shook his head, it bolstered my nerve. "David is a manipulative, abusive bastard."

"He didn't . . ."

"Naomi got me out in time, but I'm almost certain it would have led to that. For years, he's searched for me and when he found me, we moved. He's tried to stop at nothing to make me his in every way possible. But when we were young, he made me his follower. If I didn't do what he told me to do, there would be consequences."

Red crept up Reno's neck to his face, his fist curling. I

could hear his deep, even breathing as though he was counting his breath as I do to contain myself. Anger, panic, whatever I needed to calm myself.

"I survived."

"And now?"

"I'm handling it."

"Are you?" He controlled his tone, but he was clearly not to be reckoned with. Damn if Cameron wasn't just like him. "I'll not have you involved, running from this man any longer. You will not be in any danger."

"He's threatening Hannah if I don't cooperate."

The look in his eyes unnerved me. They were so serious. "We will take care of him."

"Cameron is trying to locate him. But David is cunning. You won't find him." I took a deep breath. "It's why we're here. He got into our house. Destroyed my room."

"Riley, I'll not have you running. I'll not allow my daughter to deal with any of this sort. I forbid it. You will remain here until-"

"No!" I jumped up from my chair so it toppled backward.

Cameron strolled in a moment later, curiously. He was at my side in an instant, staring at Reno with determination to protect me. I had not lived through everything I had from being weak, and these two men wouldn't maneuver me.

"I won't keep hiding from him."

Reno looked at Cameron. "I'm trying to locate him," Cameron said.

"I want every scrap of detail on him," Reno said. "Where he's been. Who he's been with. Has he done time in prison?" I nodded. "I want everything. We'll find him . . ." His eyes met mine. "And end him."

Murder wasn't something I wanted on my conscious again. Looking at these two men and their determination, it would be impossible to convince them otherwise. I could tell Reno what I had done to Finnegan Caspian. I was surprised Cameron hadn't mentioned it yet.

"When I was fourteen, David . . ." The words were stuck in my throat. Tears prickled my eyes.

Cameron's eyes widened. Reno took on another look of fury. "You said he didn't."

"Not that," I told Cameron before turning back to Reno. "He helped me cover up a murder. I stabbed the guy. He died on the way to the hospital. David hid the car and the body. They've never found them, as far as I know."

Reno was staring at me. I was waiting for him to laugh or judge me. Something other than to stare at me. But he was just staring at me.

"Stop staring," I finally snapped. "I stabbed him and he bled everywhere. And I owe David for covering it up."

"Are you sure you killed him?"

I nodded. "David is going to go to the police with the whereabouts of the car, if he hasn't already, with this. And my life will be over. They'll arrest me."

Reno laughed. My eyes shot to his. *Now he laughs*? "They won't arrest you, my dear. Not my daughter. If this bastard goes to the police, they'll laugh him out of their office. He's a felon. And since he's out of prison, he's got nothing to gain by tipping them off."

"I already told her it won't stick," Cameron said.

The Moretti family probably had connections. It made me feel a little more at ease. Maybe there was a way that I could be with Ty after all. I could confess to him what I had done and tell him that maybe the guy hadn't died. Maybe he would believe me.

"I would like you to stay at least a few days. Would you?" Reno asked.

"Of course we will," Cameron answered. "I'd like Hannah to stay here for the summer, if not Riley, too. And Regan needs to rest."

"Stop babying her, Cam," I shot. "She's a stronger woman than

I am."

His answer was to grin at me. Jerk, I thought, even though I was smiling back at him. "I'll show you around the house and to a room."

"Dinner is at six. Sharp."

Cameron took me by the elbow. "Yeah, yeah," he called behind him as we walked out. "Don't be late. We got it, Pop."

Cameron guided me out of the office, releasing my elbow as soon as we were out in the hallway. Glancing around, I could see a large living room across from us, open to the second floor. It was amazing.

"He's got a thing about being late for dinner. Regan is taking a nap. Hannah is taking a tour on her own."

The edge in his voice wasn't hard to miss, and I suddenly felt bad for giving him shit. Pregnancy was an unknown to me. What Regan was going through, I didn't know and had no right to tell him what he was doing and what he wasn't doing.

"I shouldn't have snapped at you."

"I'm worried about her."

My heart lurched.

"The doctors say she's a little underweight for how far along she is. It seems like she's tired all the time, but they say it's normal. I know nothing about babies and being pregnant. Hell, I know nothing about being a dad."

I stopped when we reached a stairway. "I don't either. But I know that you're going to be a great dad." When he looked sheepish, I touched his arm. "Cameron Armando Moretti, when I tried to take your wallet, you took one look at me and made sure I got a meal. Not only that, but you made sure I had your phone number. You will be a fantastic dad."

In his eyes was hope, and I knew no matter what, he would take care of Regan and she would take care of him. It was never a goal in my life to find someone to take care of me, or to take care of. Not until I met Ty. *Dear God, I love him so much. I need to make it work with him. It's not like I haven't taken risks before. I need to take this risk and tell him about my past.* If he ran for the hills, I would know he wasn't the person I needed in my life. Not the way Cameron had Regan.

"Maybe all of you should stay here instead of going back with me." It was a suggestion I knew he would consider for Regan, which was why I mentioned it. "I can get on a plane. If you're worried, staying put and resting might be the best thing for it. And having Hannah here would help me. She has the entire summer."

He scoffed. "Regan will never go for it. She's about as stubborn as you are."

"Well, I tried."

We continued up the curving staircase to the second level, and I stared in shock at the hallway system. It was open but daunting. The vestibule looked down over the family room below, but the hallways split there. Cameron led me to the left, pointing to the room where Stefan stayed when he was here and the room he shared with Regan when he was here. Hannah was on the total opposite side, near Zoey's room.

The room he led me to seemed like the farthest from civilization, but I was fine with it. Coming to terms with what I needed to do with Ty, I suddenly couldn't wait to get back to him. Reno deserved more of my time, and I would stay, but it wouldn't be for too much longer. I was certain I would be back.

After my talk with Reno, I decided it was worth it to look in on Simone. It was scary to think of what I might find when I went to see her, but I would once again try to convince her to get help with her life. I held onto hope that one of these times, she would take it.

Cameron left me to check in on Regan with strict instructions on dinner. He said he'd be back for me in a little while, but if I wanted to venture out on my own, to feel free. I was family, after all. I smiled a little, pride in my relation to such a remarkable family.

From talking with Stefan at the wedding, he seemed likeable enough, but in a charming, dangerous way. I could understand why he warned me away from Stefan. He was my brother. Ew. I had talked very little with Peter and his wife, and even less with Zoey. What I wanted more than anything was to speak with Orianna. But she had enough to deal with, and recalling her reaction to me at the wedding gave me everything I needed to know.

Chapter Twenty Seven

I watched out the window of the sleek, black Lexus as we pulled into the neighborhood I had spent the first fourteen years of my life in. It still surprised me that Simone had kept this place, and I had wondered how many times it had been close to foreclosure. It had been many years since she worked a job.

Hannah wanted badly to come with me, but I convinced her I needed time alone with Simone first and if I thought it was safe, I would bring her by later. It killed me to lie to her. I knew I wouldn't bring her back here.

When the car stopped, I waited patiently until the driver opened my door and I stepped out into the scorching afternoon sun. Kids playing in a cheap plastic pool stopped to stare while the adults standing around in the shade gawked. *In and out*, I told myself.

"If you want to drive around for a bit, I'll be fine here," I told the driver.

"I'll wait here."

Reno would never allow a driver to leave me somewhere like this unattended, especially when the catcalls from bystanders started. Regan tried to teach me to take a little more care in choosing what I wore, while still being quick, but habits were hard to break and I still wore my Docs with a pair of leggings and an oversized shirt, sliding from my shoulder. Closing my eyes against the onslaught of vulgar language thrown at me wouldn't have done any good.

I looked at the two-level townhome, with its torn window screens and crumbling concrete steps greeting me in return, grateful I no longer lived here. Simone lived on the lower level. I gulped in a few deep breaths and walked to the door, stepping carefully up those crumbling steps to the door. I prayed David wasn't here.

Simone answered the door a moment later, and it took me a minute to recognize her. Her brown hair was duller, liberally spread with gray. *She's only in her early forties. She shouldn't look like this*, I thought. Her eyes were red-rimmed, flecks of old mascara beneath her eyes.

"Baby!" she said. "Why didn't you tell me you were comin'?"

Before I could step to the side, she pulled me into her arms and the smell of cigarettes and cheap whiskey assaulted my senses. When she pulled away, I noticed she was staring at the black Lexus, her mouth ajar.

"Come in, baby."

The place was filthy, littered with overflowing ashtrays, takeout containers stacked on the coffee table, and an overfull garbage bag under the kitchen table. It looked and smelled like it hadn't seen a thorough cleaning for months. The stench was so bad that I had no choice but to breathe through my mouth.

"Are you living here alone?" I asked, stepping carefully.

"No, I have a roommate, kind of," she whispered. "He's been helping me pay the bills and whatnot."

"He?"

"His name's Vic."

"Vic Martin?" I asked.

She looked at me strangely. "How do you know Vic?"

Maybe the bastard knows where his son is. It's about time we have another chat. I'm tired of running. "I'm just here for a quick visit."

"Oh." Her pitch was higher. "Okay."

My eyes caught the same old couch, more cigarette burns

than there were before as we went to the table in the square area just outside the kitchen. Simone tipped the full ashtray into the garbage bag, but half it sprinkled the floor. I sat down, waiting for her to join me when the ashtray was empty.

She leaned back, pulled out a smashed pack of Pall Malls, and lit one up. The smoke billowed up and around us. Coughing, I waved my hand in front of my face to clear the smell away.

"What brings you by, baby? How've you been?"

"I've been fine. Getting by." I shrugged, now all sense of purpose failing me.

If she didn't remember Vic Martin abandoning her and his son, would she remember Reno and what happened before I was born? I studied the deep wrinkles in her face and the sagging skin of her cheeks. Looking down, I saw the years of track marks in her arms.

"Simone, I need you to tell me about my father."

Her eyes lazily met mine. "Why?"

"Because I need to know."

I could make up a lie to tell her, but I was a criminal, not a liar. If she was going to tell me her side, I wanted her to tell me of her own free will, not by coercion. If she could remember the details about it. It was over twenty-four years ago.

"Reno Moretti," she sighed, taking a long drag from her cigarette before tipping her head back to blow out a long string of smoke. "God, he was a good lookin' man. I would have given anything to keep him. Anything."

"What do you mean 'keep him'? Wasn't he married?"

Her head snapped up, eyes narrowing. "Yeah. He was married to some little tart. She wasn't what he needed, though. I was what he needed."

To keep her talking, I softened my tone. "Why do you say that?"

"He wasn't happy. Yeah, they had a little boy, but he could have left them and they would have been just fine."

As much as I tried to imagine Cameron growing into the man he was today without Reno's guidance, I couldn't. Things happened for a reason. I shook my head.

She laughed. "Tell that to your grandmother. Stole you and your sister away from me when you needed me the most."

Screw the sympathy. "That's crap, and you know it. You saw how David was looking at me. And here you are, shacking up with his dad again."

Her eyes widened like she was remembering. "I don't want to fight, angel."

"No," I whispered. "I don't want to fight with you. I came to ask you about Reno and what happened. Did you ask him to leave his family?"

"Yessssss. And he should have, but he wouldn't. Wouldn't listen to me."

"Did you threaten to tell his wife about your affair?"

I had to wait for her to take another couple of puffs from her cigarette. "I thought it was the only way to get him to see. But he didn't."

"So you told her?"

"I did. She was pathetic. Crying and going on. Told her I was pregnant. Told Reno, too, but he didn't believe me. Made me pissed. Told him he was shirking his duty, trying to get out of paying any money for a kid that was his." She shook her head, strands of her hair coming dangerously close to her cigarette. "But he didn't believe me. He left me to raise you on my own."

Reno had told me the truth. As much as I tried to see it from her point of view, I couldn't sympathize with her. She had tried her hardest to extort the best life she could from him, and when he wasn't buying it, she threatened him. Then she tried to ruin his life by telling his poor wife and ruining her life.

"Simone," I whispered.

"I'm Mom," she said, smashing her cigarette into the ashtray. "Why do you never call me that? You always call me Simone, never

Mom."

"You have to earn that to be called it. Moms don't ignore their kids, leaving them to fend for themselves."

She stared at me. I couldn't tell if her eyes were tearing up or if they were just that red. There were no tears falling. "Since when did you get so philosophical?"

"Since I went to college and took those kinds of classes. Remember? Naomi gave me and Hannah a better life than this?" I nudged her leg, dotted with ugly bruises. Those weren't bruises from drugs. "Let me help you. Let me get you out of here."

"This is where I belong. You can't help me."

"I can. There's treatment. There is a better life."

"You don't think Naomi has offered before?" She laughed. "Many times. This is my life, baby. It's too late for me."

"It's never too late. Never." I stood up, thinking I heard a door. "I appreciate the information."

"You're leaving already?"

"Simmy!" came a roar from down the hall.

Damn if my insides didn't tighten up with fear. If Vic was anything like his damned son, I didn't want to be around when he came out here. Judging by the look of the bruises on her legs, I was certain there were more hidden beneath her clothing. There was something about this place that held nothing but chaos and desperation.

"Out here, babe," she called.

"I have to go. Call you soon."

I leaned over to give her a quick kiss before I beat a fast retreat, but it wasn't enough. A shadow filled the end of the hallway just as I passed, and I looked up to see an older version of David with a ratty white tank top and dirty blue jeans.

"Who're you?" he growled.

"That's my daughter, baby. It's Alexis."

I would have corrected her, but I didn't think he needed to know my name. The less he knew about me, the better. I couldn't see track marks in his arms, but his eyes were as red as hers. There was stubble along his jaw and upper lip and his gray-blue eyes were hard as they stared into me. *Holy hell, David looks like him.*

"I was just leaving," I said.

He stared at me, studying me. "Damn, that boy was right. You are pretty. Worth it."

"Excuse me?" I snapped. "Worth what?"

"Davy. Got quite a thing for you, an' I can see why."

David. Would I ever be rid of him? A smile curved my lips. "Would you know where David is? I've been looking for him."

He snickered, folding his arms across his chest. "Haven't seen him."

"What did you mean by worth it?"

"Hang on, girly," he said, moving past me toward the kitchen.

Patience wasn't a virtue I had at the moment, watching him yank open the refrigerator and pull out a can of beer. The same refrigerator Finn had me pinned against. I shook the memory out of my head. Vic took his time in cracking open the beer, shaking off the spray from his hand while he walked to the table and sat down heavily.

He looked up. "You gonna sit down?"

"I'd rather stand. I was just leaving, like I said."

"You wanna know about David or not?"

Resigned, I slid into the chair and clasped my hands together before I leaned closer. "Just so you're aware, I'm a private investigator. You don't want to get on my bad side, Vic. Tell me the truth about David and you'll never see me again."

Simone gasped, but I ignored her. I could be fairly certain I wouldn't see her again after this, as much as I wanted her to get help.

"David came back here after he got let out of the big house. He was antsy, you see. Hadn't been able to find you and wanted to get you back here so you could start new."

My teeth clamped down on my lower lip to keep from scoffing. I'd rather die, but we'll see what happens. I wouldn't put Hannah at risk, but if I could draw David out, it could be enough for Cameron and Reno to handle him. I could move on with my life, and no one would ever know what happened to Finnegan.

"Why would he think we would have a life together? I haven't lived here since I was fourteen."

He shrugged. "Ask him that. I just know he's been saving up those Benjamins, wanting to give you the world. You shaking him off when he found you only made him more determined."

"What's he doing to get money?"

The smile that curled his lips was sinister. Maybe I didn't want to know. But David would have told Vic what he was doing up in Seattle doing business with a kidnapped dog of a popular popstar. I couldn't imagine why David would have a relationship with the man who abandoned him almost three decades ago. David wouldn't have even remembered him unless Vic came back into his life at some point.

"He told me about your thieving days, you and him going out to lift them rich people's wallets."

Simone gasped. I shot her a look. "Don't you dare judge. Not only did David make me do it, we had no money coming in. No food. Nothing. Pretty sure he used some of the money we stole for food until he got a job."

"Wh . . . when did you start stealing?"

"I was eight. David was thirteen when he first showed me what to do. I was small, could easily blend into crowds without being noticed." I shrugged. "Why do you think I went with Naomi? I needed a new life, away from crime. And if I hadn't taken Hannah with me, David would have had her doing it."

"Now, wait a minute," Vic said. "You don't know that."

My eyes blazed anger. "Were you here? Did you watch your son grow up to terrorize me? Even now, when he's just broken into my bedroom in Seattle and destroyed it? He's been stalking me for years."

"Why?" Simone whispered.

"I don't know. He's had this weird thing that he and I are going to be together forever. Don't ask me why. But I'm hoping to find out, which is why I need to know where he is." I aimed my stare at Vic.

He held up his hand, one still clutching the beer can. "I don't know where the boy is. Haven't seen him for a few weeks."

"When?" I demanded. "When did you see him last, Vic?"

"Uh . . . end of last month?" He scratched the patch of hair on his chin. "Middle of last month? I don't know, in the last couple of months. Came back to say he'd finally found you and everything was fallin' into place now."

My eyes widened. Was David the one who kidnapped Queenie? And if so, why? He had no associations with Grady or Merrick that I could find in the system. That didn't help at all. I had nothing to go on. What the hell was David up to? He could have grabbed me on more than one occasion, taken off where no one would find us. Yet he didn't. This cat-and-mouse game was getting old and really getting on my nerves. It needed to end.

"I appreciate the information, Vic. I need to get going, though."

As soon as I stood, the front door swung open with such force it banged against the wall. My eyes widened as Reno and Cameron filed in, followed by the driver. Vic stood up, rushing both of them, but Cameron punched him before he could utter a single word. Vic spun around once and hit the floor, out cold.

I stared at Cameron in question. Then I looked over at Simone, who was staring at Reno in shock. *Shit.* She slumped back into the chair, fumbling for her pack of cigarettes. Emotions were running wild in her eyes. I couldn't imagine what she was thinking seeing Reno after so many years. Cameron's hand was on my shoulder.

"Riles?" he said. "Are you okay?"

"What the hell are you doing here? You didn't have to punch

him. I wasn't in danger. He was giving me information about David."

Reno was behind him, still looking at Simone. I shook my head.

"Simone," I said. "Get help. Please."

"We can help you," Reno said.

She looked up at him, her eyes large. "You could have helped me by staying with me, but you didn't. I don't need help. I need to be left alone."

The tilt of Reno's chin, the pride he had behind the decisions he had made, gave me a sense of exactly the man he was. He would offer help to a woman who had spit on him because he felt a sense of responsibility for the mess my mother had made.

"Simone. Mom." I reached out, pulling her hand into mine while she continued to draw on her cigarette with the other. "Please. Let us take you out of here. You can start a new life. A better one."

Cameron's hand curled around my shoulder a minute before I released her hand and stood up. She could have had help many times through the years, from Naomi and from me. Never once had she taken it, and she wasn't taking it now. Reno could afford to get her enrolled in the best program, would probably foot the bill for her to start her life completely over. And yet she refused.

Numbly, I let Cameron lead me toward the door. I looked down at Vic, still out cold on the floor, then back to Simone.

"Goodbye, Simone," I said, turning to walk away.

At that moment, I wasn't sure I would see her again. Once I was in the Lexus, I looked out the darkened window at them until we pulled away. I was certain I wouldn't see her again.

Chapter Twenty Eight

Parking my Jeep on the street, I waited patiently to get out until my call concluded.

"I'm sorry I couldn't grab Queenie before it was too late," I said. "I'll understand if you continue to have me as a junior investigator."

"Don't be hard on yourself. This was a tough case," Maria offered. "But you're right, and I wouldn't have it any other way. Had you tried to grab her and got caught, you might be dead."

"Did Ellie get her back? Did she pay the ransom?"

"Unfortunately, no."

My back straightened. "What? What do you mean?"

"What you tailed last week was a trade, but it wasn't for ransom. Ellie has received a notification that they are demand-ing more ransom."

Anger shook me, thrumming through my veins. "You mean we have to start back at square one?" I couldn't believe what I was hearing. "Why the hell would they have moved her? No one knew she was here other than me."

"Afraid so. When you say you failed at your assignment, you didn't. You just extended it more. Keep your eye on Grady Allen. He's involved in this still. I know it. In the meantime, did you get the plate number for the other car at the drop site?"

"I ran it. Came back with William Smith," I said. "There's nothing on him other than he's a driver with no record."

"It's a cover for someone else."

"Yes, but who?"

"I'm willing to bet Grady Allen knows," she murmured.

God, I didn't like him. Worse than David, he was the one person I dreaded seeing. I could see his car in the driveway parked near Ty's motorcycle. But the need to see Ty outweighed having to see Grady. I wouldn't back down from Grady. Not like I did David.

"Find out, Riley," she said, gently. "But stay safe."

Minutes later, I walked up to the house with controlled footsteps, even though I wanted to sprint. I didn't know if I should knock on the door or just open it. Usually, Ty greeted me outside or at the door. With a deep breath, I knocked. A few minutes later, Grady answered with his stoic look. He said nothing, just opened the door to let me in. There was no heavy metal music blaring and no sign of Jack or Merrick as I walked through to Ty's room.

We had stayed in Nevada longer than we intended and took the same jet back. When we arrived in Seattle, it was late and I was exhausted. I knew Ty would be at Grady's house, and although I was tired from the trip, I needed to see him. I needed desperately to see him. Texting the last few days wasn't enough. He had given me the space I needed, but our messages were not lengthy and not like a face-to-face conversation.

As I opened the door to his room, my breath caught in my lungs in anticipation of resuming the conversation we had spoken right here only last week. It hadn't been my intention to hurt him by saying no to marrying him. I would marry him if it wasn't for my past, and it was something I would need to tell him. Squaring my shoulders, I opened the door wider to see him sitting on his bed, bare feet planted on the floor, forearms resting on his knees and his head hanging. His head snapped up.

As I neared, I felt something was wrong, and I knew it instantly when I noticed his eyes. They were cold. Hard. Any other time, he would have met me halfway, pulled me into his arms and kissed me. Not now. Was he angry that I hadn't said yes?

Or that I had run away? But we had been texting with each other, and he hadn't led on that he was upset about it. I thought he was giving me time. I had asked for time, and he had given it.

I closed the door and walked toward him, my steps slowing nervously. Ty stood up, and I stopped when I noticed his jaw clench. Suddenly, I wanted to retreat.

"What brings you by . . . Alexis?"

That froze me in place. My heart picked up its beat, thundering erratically in my chest. If he knows that name, he knows everything. Every sordid detail of my past. Of my crime. *Damn David*, I should have known he would find a way to get to Ty. Now, I wondered if Ty was going to let me walk out of here without being arrested. I suppose he'd have to or blow his own cover.

"Surprised?" he continued, staying where he was. "While I was at the coffee shop, your very concerned boyfriend approached me."

My eyes flashed with anger. "He is not my boyfriend. No matter what he told you, Ty, he is not that. He has never been that."

Bile rose in my throat. He would stop at nothing to have me, and he found a way. All he had to do was take me away, maybe somewhere remote where no one would find us. The police wouldn't find me. David had a knack for staying hidden.

"And the rest?"

I flinched like an icicle had stabbed me in the heart. I wasn't sure what to say to him. By the look in his eyes, the coolness in his voice, he had condemned me already. And rightfully so.

"Was any of this real to you?" His voice was low, but the way he was looking at me was killing me just as much as his words. "Or was it just a job?"

The invisible punches kept landing, bruising my heart. I pressed my balled fist to the middle of my chest, hoping to dull the hurt there. Never in my life had I felt this type of pain before.

"I was going to tell you," I whispered, hoping he would believe it. Believe in me. *It wasn't just a job.*

"Was it just a job, Alexis?"

"My name is *Riley*. It has been since I could legally change it." I lifted my chin, despite the tears forming in my eyes, and walked up to him. Looking him in the eyes, despite the hurt deepening in my chest, I felt like my heart was going to plummet to the ground. "But don't ever . . . EVER . . . call me Alexis again. She is gone."

"Is she?" he asked.

"What do you want me to say to you, Ty? Do you want me to admit that I murdered someone when I was fourteen? I did. Do you want me to tell you I was a thief growing up? I was. Turns out, I was a good enough thief to get a job actually doing it."

His jaw clenched again.

"But you've already decided about me, haven't you? There isn't anything I can do to change my past and what I've done. And I won't. It's done. All I can do is move on. But it was real to me. I gave you everything."

"You didn't give me the truth. You could have told me about him."

"There is no *him*, Ty. I've been running from him for ten years."

"And you couldn't trust me enough to tell me about him? Or about your criminal past?" He stared at me. "We never had a chance, did we? You wouldn't let it. You just couldn't trust me to decide for myself."

"Could you live with a criminal? A murderer? Marry her?"

"I might have been able to help you." That wasn't an answer.

"You would have hated me sooner."

When his eyes flashed, I knew I struck a nerve. The last thing I wanted to do was hurt him like he was hurting me, but what we had was over. It was gone. I knew it from the start, we wouldn't be able to continue. Except my heart had to get tangled up in it.

I walked backwards, keeping his eyes locked with mine until

I couldn't take my unruly display of tears any longer. Whirling, I threw open the door and ran out. *Congratulations, Ty Cavanaugh. You're the first one to break my heart. And I swear, you'll be the last one to do it.*

When I reached the living room, Grady was sitting in Jack's usual chair and he was smiling. I'd never seen the man smile since I'd known him, and the way he was smiling chilled me from head to toes. And I fled.

Chapter Twenty Nine

Over ten years later, I still didn't understand it. If I didn't understand it, Ty wouldn't. Even then, I wondered when it would stop. What else would David make me do, or punish me with if I didn't? He would be around eventually. No one had seen him. But I knew David, and he wouldn't go quietly. Not without me.

I screwed things up royally this time. How would I continue to watch Grady when I didn't have an inside presence any longer? If I parked outside the house, I'd be noticed. If not by Ty, by Jack, Merrick or Grady. I'd be no better than my stalker, David. And embarrassingly so, like I couldn't let go of Ty.

I shuddered, my heart twisting painfully. I couldn't let go of him. He haunted my thoughts, my dreams, and with each thought, my heart ached to where I thought I was having medical issues. Was this what being heartbroken was? I'd have asked Regan, but I didn't want to think about it, much less bring it up.

I was waiting in the line for coffee while Cameron and Regan went to a monthly checkup. With less than three months left of her pregnancy, she was being careful. Cameron insisted on it and Regan, being gracious, humored him. He still thought she was small for being six, almost seven, months pregnant. They decided to limit their morning exercise to walking instead of running, and he persuaded her to switch to decaf coffee.

When I stepped up to the counter, I almost smiled. I needed full-fledged black, dark coffee, which is the order I gave the red-headed girl. As I handed over my card, I noticed Merrick come around from the back. And he was avoiding eye contact.

"Hey, Merrick," I said, trying to be casual about it.

"Uh, hey." He scratched behind his ear, barely glancing at me before he started a coffee order.

I wanted desperately to ask him what Ty had told him. What he'd told all of them. Did Merrick know I was a killer? A thief? It wasn't something I could imagine Ty tossing around in casual conversations. But the way Merrick acted seemed weird. Weirder than he normally acted.

Moving aside for the person behind me to order, I leaned over the counter while he poured my cup of coffee. He set it in front of me, raising his eyes to meet mine for the briefest second before turning away.

"Merrick." He turned back. "Are you okay?"

"Yeah." He scratched behind his ear again. "Why?"

"No reason. See you around."

I tried not to give it another thought while I walked to the end to put a lid on it. With one more glance at him, I took my coffee and left. I could dwell on it for a long time and never know the reason for his coolness toward me. No point in doing that.

It didn't surprise me there had been no word from Ty. I sighed. I would have had to tell him, eventually. But it still hurt. When he asked me if what we had was real, it had told me enough. *Shit, I basically gave the man my virginity since I'd only slept with one other person way back in high school.* What else did he want from me to convince him it was real?

Regan suggested going to Cape Haven with them for an extended stay and putting all of this, and David, behind me for a while. Hannah was staying with Reno still, having made fast friends with Zoey, but she'd have to come home eventually for school. And leaving Cassie and Naomi would worry me. Especially with David still lurking, not to be found. Cameron had been unsuccessful in finding his whereabouts. Even Reno had people looking for him with no success. After my failure in rescuing

Queenie, David had gone silent and, to my knowledge, hadn't gone to the police.

As soon as I stepped out into the midday afternoon sun, I noticed Grady leaning against a parked car directly in front of me. He was staring straight at me with his hard eyes. I looked behind me to make sure. The curve of his mouth, the same menacing smile he gave me when I'd left after my reckoning with Ty, appeared. *Shit.* I wanted to tell him to stop smiling. It was creeping me out.

"Someone wants a word with you," he said.

I stopped. "What do you want, Grady?"

"You. To come with me."

"How did you know where I was?" I turned, looking at the door to the coffee shop. It didn't take me but a minute to figure out why Merrick was acting weirder than normal. When I turned back to Grady, his smile had deepened. "Merrick."

"You don't honestly think he wouldn't call me when he saw you?" His voice, the deep tone, was as chilling as his eyes. "I've been trying to find you."

"Why?"

His jaw clenched. *Oh, am I being annoying?* I smirked even though I didn't say it out loud. But Grady was the kind of bastard that wasn't about to give me the reason. Not a second time, anyway.

Judging by the look Grady was giving me, and the absence of anyone around, there was no good way out of this. I pulled my phone out of my pocket, hoping to drop a quick location pin, but he was on me in an instant and my phone was knocked out of my hand, hitting the pavement. *Shit. No one is going to know where I am.*

With his meaty hand around my upper arm, he propelled me toward the car and opened the door with his free hand. Before getting in, I pushed my face up to him. "This has nothing to do with me, Grady." It was a total bluff. I didn't have a clue who wanted to see me and why.

Beneath the golden hair surrounding his mouth, he smiled. I was finding out really fast that I didn't like it when he smiled. "I don't give a fuck. If you know what's good for you, you'll get in."

"What's this all about?"

His eyes narrowed, the smile vanishing from his lips. "You'll get in the car, or you won't be making it to where we're going."

I smirked. "You don't want to mess with me, Grady. You've no idea what I'm capable of." I shouldn't goad him.

He discreetly grabbed a fistful of my shirt and pulled me closer to him. "Get . . . in the god . . . damn . . . car!"

When his fist released its hold, I stumbled back but caught myself against the car. Unfortunately, my coffee didn't make it, ending up in the street. I wouldn't cower. Instead, I shot him a glare and ducked into the backseat. The door slammed behind me and a moment later, it lurched into motion.

Silence engulfed us for the duration of the drive, which was not all that long. We were deep in the city, tall buildings surrounding us. I couldn't tell by looking out the window exactly where downtown we were, but when Grady ushered me out of the car, I looked up at a prominent building that was apartments and condominiums.

The building was secure, and the foyer well-maintained, with a sitting area facing a fireplace off the side and elevators at the back. Grady pushed me toward the elevator. Grady didn't say a word, pushing the button for the thirty-fifth floor. The very top.

Counting my breathing started as we neared our stop, my panic beginning to rise. I had been in countless dangerous situations, most of them I had little knowledge of what I might get myself into. This I had zero knowledge. I was blindly walking in to a situation.

When the elevator doors opened, it was to a spacious living room with a wall of windows looking out over the bay. Dark furniture gave the room an ominous look, despite the afternoon light. I looked around for whatever details I could grab. This wasn't a place I had been to. I would have recognized such a ritzy place. These were circles I didn't run in. Grady pushed me forward, harder than necessary.

Walking further in, around the corner was a cozy kitchen and rooms behind, I assumed, were bedrooms and such. A tiny bark resounded and the pitter-patter of tiny nails danced across the hardwood floors. Around the corner came Queenie, still decked out in her hot pink bejeweled collar.

"Queenie!" I gasped, squatting down as the little dog ran to me.

"I see you've found my dog," came a deep, gravelly voice.

My eyes narrowed at the man, dressed in a pair of loose, gray dress pants and a white button-down shirt that was open a few buttons at the top. His straight, brown hair flowed to his shoulders, but his blueish-hazel eyes stopped me. An odd color. A color I'd only seen once before.

I stumbled back, hands going to my throat. "What the fuck is this?" I snapped, no care in the world for my language. "I killed you."

Finnegan Caspian smiled at me. "You're still looking pretty fine, Alexis Rose."

Chapter Thirty

He stopped in front of me, the curl of his lips disgusting. "You'd like to think you killed me, wouldn't you? But you didn't. I came to in the car while your boyfriend was bringing me to the hospital." He tilted his head to the side. "We've become friends, if you will. I've had him in my pocket since."

Words failed me as I watched him stroll toward a bar and uncork a Waterford decanter. Queenie squirmed, and I set her down, watching her run to jump on the couch and lay down. Finn poured amber liquid into a glass and took a sip, closing his eyes to savor it.

"The interesting thing is his fascination with you. Fortunately for you, he was in your house when he overheard you give him information I very much needed."

Hearing such a thing made me feel colder than if icicles had been drawn down my back. David was in my house, listening to me. Was it when he destroyed my bedroom? I tried to think of who I was talking to then, or if that was even the only time he'd been there listening? I felt more violated than I'd ever felt in my life.

He waved Grady over and I watched, terror growing deep in my stomach, while he crossed the shining floors to the other side of the room and disappeared into a room. This would not be good.

The elevator dinged, announcing the addition of someone else to our party. My eyes remained on where Grady went. My breath lodged in the center of my throat when a minute later his shadow fell through the door opening, except it wasn't his shadow. It was Ty. Grady gave him a solid push, sending him stumbling into the room. Bound with his hands in front of him and a gag in his mouth, one of his eyes was swollen so much it was almost closed and there was a gash on his cheek along with bruises. With a shallow breath, I took in the blood on his shirt and the light blue of his jeans.

I cried out, rushing forward, only to be yanked backwards. But I fought. I fought like a wild she-cat, kicking and clawing, until arms came around me to immobilize me. Ty took one look at me and tried to get to me, too, except Grady drove his fist into his midsection and he fell to the floor with a loud thump.

"Alexis, stop." David's voice filled my ear, his voice unsettling.

I knew he had something to do with this. David, holding me, only made me attempt to be free of him again. I threw my head back, my skull connecting with his face and causing him to loosen his arms enough for me to kick back against his shins.

"Enough!" Finn shouted.

David's arms banded around me again. "You're going to listen to him, baby. And when we're done here, you and I are going to leave here. *Together*."

"Let him go," I shouted. "He's not involved in this."

Finn laughed, thick and dark. Even Grady, who crossed his arms like some badass bodyguard, was smiling again. I would gladly wipe that smile off his face, smear it on the floor, preferably with his blood.

"Oh, but he is," Finn said. "He's involved as much as you. You have no idea just how involved you are, but I know everything about Ty here."

"Stop struggling," David said, tightening his arms around me even more.

Finn prowled the room. "David grabbed the dog while Miss Varro was at a show in Las Vegas. Easy enough. Except, as you can see," he waved his hand around, "this isn't the type of venue one would keep a dog. So the dog stayed with Grady until we could extort more money from Miss Varro. She has quite the connections, you know. Worth a lot of money. Money I can use to grow my empire bigger."

He stopped in front of me, far enough away for me to see the malicious gleam in his eyes, but not close enough for me to kick him. *I should have killed him.*

"Imagine David's surprise to see you there, watching the place. After some digging, we found out exactly who you work for and why you were there." He smiled, turning around to continue to pace. "Well, I couldn't have you interrupting my plan. David needed to keep you occupied, but then he found out a vital piece of information."

"Just let Ty go."

Finn laughed again. "I think you're smarter than that, Alexis."

"It's Riley," I ground out.

Finn casually set his drink down on the bar, pulling open a drawer and withdrawing a gun with a silencer attached. I eyed the gun with caution, hearing Ty's muffled shouts. I drew myself up. At least it would be quick.

"Just tell me what you want," I said, once I composed myself.

While he strolled toward me, I lifted my chin. No amount of courage could stop my body from shaking. He was going to kill me, or Ty. I'd much rather he kill me than Ty. I'd do what it took to keep his attention on me.

"David overheard you talking about sleeping with a cop."

David's arms tightened around me, his mouth close to my ear. "I might forgive you for letting him touch you when you *knew* you were mine."

Apprehension crept down my back while David's hand came around, his palm resting on my stomach. His mouth touched the edge of my jaw while I watched Ty's eyes teeming with anger. I shook with fury, tears burning at the corners of my eyes while I met Ty's gaze. Both of us were powerless to stop this.

"I'll go with David," I whispered. "Please. Just let Ty go."

I watched Finn stroll to the couch, sit down and press his forearms to his knees with the gun dangling between his hands. He was entirely too close to Ty for me to be comfortable.

"Let an undercover cop, who's been involved in my operation for months, go?" he snarled. "Just like that? I should kill him now, just for that."

He aimed the gun at Ty's head and I screamed out, twisting in David's tight hold. "Please!" I begged. "I'll do whatever you want. Please."

"So here's what's going to happen, *Alexis*." He straightened. "You're going to tell me everything you know about our operation. How much did you tell your agency, and how much are they sharing with law enforcement?"

My eyes grew wide.

"If you don't start talking, I'll start with him." He waved the gun toward Ty, laying on his side on the floor staring at him and unable to do a damn thing about it. He waved the gun at me. "You'll be next."

"No!" David said, releasing me and stepping in front of me but keeping his hand on my arm as though to warn me not to move. "You said she'd be free to leave with me after this no matter what went down, Finn. You swore to me."

Finn shrugged. "I lied."

"I'll go," I whispered. "I'll tell you what I know, and I'll go with him. Just don't hurt him anymore. Please."

Seeing Ty hurt on the floor was killing me. I did this. If I hadn't been open about sleeping with him, David wouldn't have overheard it and he wouldn't be in this position. I got us into this mess, and I would get us out of it.

There was only one problem. I didn't know everything the agency knew about Grady and his operation, and I wasn't sure they knew anything about Finn. Maria divulged nothing to me. This was about Queenie, not about anything else. All activities, firearms and drugs, were all law enforcement. That was Ty and

Jack, not me. My job was to get Queenie. But I needed to give him something. Anything.

"Talk!" Finn shouted, making me jump.

"My agency was hired to find Queenie. I reported back to them about the guns and drugs, but nothing more. What they did with that information, I'm not sure," I said. "I'm only a junior-"

"Blah, blah, blah," Finn mocked. "Listen to yourself. You think I'm stupid enough to believe they don't know more about our operations?"

He stood up, striding over to me to grab me by the arm and pull me toward him. David pushed back, trying to protect me against Finn.

"Leave her to me, Finn! She'll talk, just give her a minute!"

"She had her chance. Someone better talk right now, or bullets are going to fly."

The stairwell door flew open, the first person I saw rushing in with his gun drawn was Jack. And with a shirt on. Several others followed him in. I almost breathed a sigh of relief, except Finn still had the gun in his hand.

"Drop it," Jack growled.

Finn turned toward me. It looked like he had other plans. David pushed me back, using his body as a shield. My eyes widened when Grady pulled his gun. I wanted to shout at them not to be stupid. There were too many officers and only two of them, but when Finn raised his gun while Grady raised his, it was all too obvious they didn't care.

"No!" David and I both shouted at the same time, him trying to protect me and me trying to protect Ty.

Shots were fired, making my ears ring. David whirled, his hands on my shoulders as we hit the floor. Almost every part of my body screamed in agony, the impact rattling my bones as I took the brunt of his weight to the floor. The breath pressed out of my lungs at his heaviness.

Frantic, my eyes meeting Ty's. He was staring back at me with terror in his blue eyes while the officers filed in. I watched Jack race toward him, helping to untie him. Just beyond him, Grady was on the floor not moving. Finn was on his knees with his hands in the air, his gun on the floor and away from him.

"David, get off me." I pushed him, realizing there was blood on my hands as I did so, but he was looking at me.

"Alexis," he whispered.

"Riley," I bit out, looking for where the blood was coming from.

Jack was helping to free Ty, but he was looking directly at me. I looked down. There was blood on me, and blood on David. But there were holes in David's shirt. David's chest was bleeding. I didn't understand why my arm hurt so badly. Had he broken my arm? Placing my hand over where it hurt, it came away with sticky blood. *Oh no . . . where else was I shot?*

David's eyes searched mine. "You have to know . . . I've always loved you."

"Funny way of showing it."

His lips curled, but when they did, I noticed the blood trickle from the corner. It was then I knew he wasn't likely going to make it. He grabbed my hand, our hands slick with blood. "I didn't know how else to show you."

"It's over now," I whispered. "Don't talk."

"And you'll be with me?"

I couldn't lie to him. "Yes."

He smiled, his teeth flashing red. "Good."

"You may not have done all the right things, but you gave me the one thing I will always be grateful for." I could feel his breathing slow, his heartbeat beneath our joined hands growing fainter. "You gave me the gift of bravery."

David smiled again. "I'm cold."

"I am, too." And I was telling the truth. I was cold, too, even though David was covering half my body. "Remember when we used to go to the park?"

"Yeah," he breathed, his eyes taking on a glassy look.

I watched him, trying not to panic while he slipped away. Tears couldn't come for him when he had tormented me for all of my life. Other than our times at the park, my earliest memories, there were no other wonderful memories between us.

All of his life, he struggled. His father abandoned him to a woman he barely knew, who ignored him as much as she did me. It would be easy for me to blame him for every injustice to me, but in the end, it wasn't.

Someone pulled me up and away from David's lifeless body, and I could see that paramedics had arrived. They were leading me away. I looked down at the bloody mess of my clothes, my blood and David's blood. I didn't know how much was David's blood and how much was mine.

The questions asked seemed like echoes in my head. I couldn't understand what they were asking. My lips were trying to move to answer, but nothing was coming out. *What is happening?* No one had shot me before.

"She's going into shock," someone said.

My eyes felt heavy. I wanted to go to sleep. My eyelids fluttered once. Twice. And everything around me fell into darkness.

Chapter Thirty One

I woke up in a hospital bed, the bright florescent lights overhead eerie and the rhythmic beep of machines. Flowers lined the windowsill, and the mounted TV in the corner was on, but I wasn't sure who was watching it since I had just woken up.

Someone shouted. Another voice shouted back, following by a thump and another thump. I lifted my head, thinking I heard Cameron. My eyes widened at the two men grappling outside my open door. Ty's eyes met mine an instant before I closed mine. He shouldn't be here. I didn't want him here. His face looked better, his eye fully open but still black.

"Just let me see her," Ty said. "Let me talk to her."

"She needs time. You've got to give her time."

Time stood still while I waited to hear what Ty would say back to him. Maybe he had accepted it and left. Risking it, I opened my eyes again to see Cameron's back and Ty on the other side of him.

"She could have died!"

"But she didn't. Give her time. Please."

I heard an anguished cry and lifted my head while my heart lurched. Ty broke my heart. I should have broken his in return, but I couldn't do that. Cameron told him the truth. I needed time. Almost getting killed, confronting my past and now knowing I didn't kill someone, as I believed for a decade, I was struggling to think. I felt like I was in a cloud.

"You'll tell her?" Ty whispered so softly I almost didn't

hear him.

"I will."

"Please. Tell her."

"I'll tell her. But you need to leave. She has to rest."

I closed my eyes, listening to my breathing for a few minutes while I thought of everything I wanted to say to Cameron. Darkness slipped back around me, holding me close like a hug until I couldn't hear anything else. Dreams flittered in and out, dreams of my past and dreams of a future of what could or could not be.

When I opened my eyes again, Cameron was sitting in the chair next to the bed with his leg crossed over and resting on his knee. I immediately thought about Ty, then I looked around and didn't see him. My heart sank. I almost wished he would have been more persistent, even though I hadn't any idea what I would say to him. What did someone say to someone who had crushed their heart?

"You're awake," he said, standing to pour some water in a cup for me.

I shook my head. "I feel like I'm in a fog. What the hell happened?"

"You took a bullet to the arm," he said. "Clean through."

Shit. "Finnegan?"

"In jail. He'll be In jail for a long time, trust me."

A nurse wearing red, white and blue scrubs breezed through the door, her shock of red hair swept up. She checked a machine next to me before leaning over me to look at my bandage wrapped arm. I tried to look down at my arm, but there wasn't much to see.

"How do you feel?"

"How am I supposed to feel?"

Her laugh was high-pitched. "A bullet to the arm and some painkillers to dull the pain. I should think you're feeling pretty good right now. I'll increase the pain killers now that you're awake."

"I don't want any drugs. Turn them off."

"Honey, are you sure?"

"Absolutely. My mother was a junkie. No drugs."

"Okay."

She looked at Cameron. I assumed for assurance. He nodded.

"How bad is it?"

"You'll mend, just don't move your arm around too much. You'll be in a sling for a while."

A few minutes later and she was extracting the IV from my arm and I breathed a sigh of relief. Without a doubt, I would be in excruciating pain, but I didn't care.

"I'll get you some ibuprofen. You'll take that?"

I nodded.

"I'll order you some food and be back in a little while."

As she left, wheeling the machine out the door, Reno sauntered in with another bunch of flowers. Saying nothing, he set them on the windowsill. They were beautiful red roses.

"Finn will go away for a long time," he said. "I will make damn sure of that."

My lips tilted in a half smile when Reno walked to me, pressing a kiss to my forehead like a doting parent would. For a minute, he just stared down at me. I almost wanted to know what he was thinking. Was he proud of me?

"I'd kill him myself for almost killing you." He sighed. "I'll settle for him living the rest of his life in prison, although I'm not sure it'll be a life sentence."

"You don't have to worry about trying to find David anymore," I whispered.

"And you don't have to worry about him continuing to find *you* anymore."

My mouth quirked up. As much as it was a relief not to continue looking over my shoulder anymore, I felt bad for David and the life he had to live. I was positive he hadn't any friends. No family, no friends. A lonely life. I understood why he was so insistent on having me in it. He had no one else.

"He loved me," I whispered.

"There's someone else who does more," Cameron whispered.

I looked away. "I don't want to hear it."

"Who?" Reno asked.

"Riley should probably explain her relationship to you." I closed my eyes, listening to Cameron's deep voice. "He's a cop."

My eyes opened, just to see Reno's eyes widen. "Oh?"

"Yes, Pop. You heard me right. And that's not a bad thing." I felt Cameron's fingertips on my wrist, where my tattoo was. "He's been asking about you," he continued. "He wants to see you."

"I don't want to see him, Cameron. I can't."

I looked back at him while he was settling into the chair in the corner while Reno insisted on hanging around by my side. Arguing with him was as pointless as arguing with Reno, but it wasn't about him. It was about me. And I didn't want to see Ty. Not yet. And definitely not here.

"He came to the house."

My eyes met his. "If you say another word, you can leave."

Cameron stared back at me, but wisely said nothing. I wasn't certain if he would take my warning or continue on. It wasn't as though I could force him to leave. If he really wanted to, he could bring Ty here and I couldn't say anything about it.

"You win, Riles."

"Don't upset yourself," Reno chided.

"How's Regan? Did her doctor appointment go well?"

He laughed. "Only you would go through what you did, take a bullet to the arm, and ask about my wife's checkup."

"Me? I'm concerned about her, too. I like her. She's like another sister to me. A sister to go along with my brother. Brothers." I frowned, thinking about David again. As much torture as he put me through, I felt sorry for him. He'd been so alone.

Before I was born, he'd had no one. Not even Simone. At least when I was little, I had him, even if it wasn't much. We were just kids. Then he had to grow up a little and get into bad dealings. It didn't seem like his fault.

"I feel bad for David."

"Are you sorry?" Reno asked, surprise in his voice.

"I am, and I'm not. He didn't have anyone. No friends, no family. He only had me. I think that's why he kept coming after me. His dad abandoned him when he was three, and I know it's not an excuse. Only God knows what his upbringing was like before his dad abandoned him. Anyway, I'm glad he's at peace."

Cameron nodded. "Look, I know you don't want to hear this." My eyes narrowed. "Please. Think about Ty. He's been beside himself with worry. Think about how I am about Regan. If anything happened to her, I don't know what I'd do."

I nodded. Cameron's feelings for Regan, I understood. But Ty hurt me and I wasn't sure I could go through again if he walked away a second time. It would take me some time to consider speaking with him, but I would think about it. I remembered seeing him here unless it had been an illusion.

Chapter Thirty Two

Driving with my arm in a sling was something to get used to. I had a feeling I would be out of the sling before I got used to it. Today I was going out driving for the first time, hoping it would be a worthwhile drive. I was only in the hospital for a day, driven home the following day by Cameron and Regan, with Reno sticking close. Being in a sling was hard to get used to for the first few days, and I had nothing else to do but sit and think.

Everyone insisted on doing anything and everything for me when I came home. Reno thought he was going to stay in a hotel, but there was no way Cassie or Naomi would hear of it. As immobile as I was, I asked to be set up in the living room and Reno could stay in my room until he left the next day, satisfied I was safe and on the mend. Naomi and Cassie were gracious enough to fix up my bedroom while we were visiting Reno in Vegas.

Above all else, I missed Ty. I wouldn't allow Cameron to get a word in about Ty, so he sent Regan after me. She didn't get far, though. I showered and was getting dressed when she knocked on my door. Words didn't need to be spoken when she noticed I was taking care of my appearance. She knew.

It was a nice enough day to have the top down on my Jeep as I drove through the familiar grove of trees, thick with bright green leaves. The sun was high in the sky, only hours until it would set on the horizon behind me. I was taking a chance that Ty would be at his house in the woods, figuring that his case had wrapped with his criminal behind bars. Finnigan Caspian was behind it all, and

Ellie Varro got Queenie back before her world tour. And just in time, too.

A little guilt crept in for leaving Gus and Gatsby at home, but I didn't want Ty to give me anything but the truth about what he wanted. The boys had a way with people, and they didn't need to have any pull in his choices. I might go home with my heart broken all over again, and I'd prefer to do that without the boys.

Familiar lights illuminated the house when I pulled off the road and into the clearing, even though there were still a few hours of daylight left. This deep in the woods, he had to have some lights on most of the time. The charm of the house held me captivated when I parked in front of the house.

If things didn't work out between Ty and me, I was determined to have a house like this for myself. A place of peace for Gus, Gatsby, and me to live. Cozy, quiet and mine. Except my job didn't pay squat. I'd have to figure out how to do it. Maybe Reno would give me a loan to start a business, a private investigative company I would run myself.

Movement in the house grabbed my attention, and I turned off my car when Ty appeared in the doorway and opened it. Instead of his usual bare chest, he had a white sleeveless t-shirt on. After not having seen him for so long, my mouth still went dry, but my heart gave a little lurch. I had to suck back the tears, even though a few wet my lashes.

I slid out of the car, hesitating for a minute while we stared at each other. His face had healed except for a bruise near his eye. It only made him more sexy, like he was a badass or something. Uncertainty claimed me. Not having been in this kind of situation before, I wasn't sure what to do.

Ty decided for both of us, coming down the path toward me. He didn't make any move to pull me into his arms or kiss me. Instead, he drew the back of his finger down the strap of my sling. His eyes were sorrowful when they met mine.

"I'm so sorry."

"For what?" I blurted.

"For not being able to prevent this. I was so close."

I shook my head. "It was my fault. You told me not to tell anyone, and I told Cam. I didn't know David was in my house, listening."

It took willpower not to step back when his hand dropped. I so badly wanted him to pull me into his arms and tell me everything would be fine. It wasn't fine. At least now I knew I wasn't a murderer. I had no way of knowing if Ty knew that. It was a freeing feeling to know that I wasn't the hardened criminal I thought I was.

"I came to you."

My eyes wandered away. "I know, but I really couldn't see you yet."

"Yes, in the hospital, but I'm not talking about that." My eyes slowly met his, the familiar flutter in my stomach returning from the intensity of his gaze. "I went to your house. Cameron was there. I thought he was your brother."

"He is my brother. You traced my address?"

That wasn't the question I wanted to ask him. I knew he was a cop. Of course, he had access to all kinds of information to find me if he wanted to. My heart wouldn't hurt so much if he wasn't. I may not have killed Finn like I thought, but I was still a criminal. Had led most of my life stealing from people, while he was squeaky clean.

"I knew where you lived before. After I saw the bruises on your neck, and you told me your brother did it." His eyes searched mine. "Why did you tell me your brother did that?"

I shrugged. "I thought David was my brother for a lot of years. It's only recently I found out Cameron is." A sigh slipped from my lips. "I panicked. No one has ever worried about me like that before. I gave you an easy excuse instead of the truth."

When his hands dropped to his sides, I had a sinking feeling in my stomach that he was giving up. My guard was coming up, anticipating a punch to my heart. Tears gathered in my eyes.

"You have to know David was never my boyfriend. Never anything more than my puppet master." A shaky laugh slipped out. "He lied to me about Finn. Told me he died after I stabbed him. He was . . . hitting on me. Kissing me. I was fourteen."

"I knew you couldn't have killed someone, Riles."

The breath hitched in my throat. Never had he called me by my nickname before. "But I did. Or I thought I did. And I didn't deny it."

He took a step closer to me and I stood still, waiting with my breath held. "Killing someone in cold blood differs from killing someone because you're being threatened. At fourteen." His hand came up, curved around my jaw until my face rested in his palm. "But I wish you would have told me. Trusted me."

"It wasn't that I didn't trust you, Ty. I've always trusted you. I was afraid you'd leave me if you knew."

He was right. Years of blaming myself were over. David was gone. Finn would go away. I hoped for more years than I would live. Reno could pull strings. I knew that. There wasn't a threat to my well-being now. My life was finally mine. I smiled, closing my eyes at the feel of his strength seeping into my soul.

"What now?" I whispered, opening my eyes when I felt his other hand curl around my waist and tug me closer.

"What do you want?"

"I want to live in a house in the middle of the woods, with a yard a half a mile long for the boys to run around in, and a lake to go skinny dipping in any time I want." He laughed, pulling me fully into his arms, careful not to hurt my arm. "If you don't want me . . ."

His mouth captured mine so quickly, my head spun dizzily. Tongues warred, fingers tangled in hair, hearts began beating wildly, and I felt a sudden lift in my heart as his mouth gave me reason to believe things may have changed for us. And in a good way.

"Riley," he whispered, his mouth still on mine. "What am I going to do with you? I want you here with me, and nowhere else. Please. Don't make me beg. Be my wife. Say it."

Looping my arm around his neck, I nipped playfully at his lips. "I will. I would love to become your wife. Actually, the sooner the better."

His eyebrows kicked up. "Vegas?"

I laughed. "How else will you get my father's permission?"

With a groan, he leaned down and carefully lifted me, cradling me in his arms. There were no words while he carried me into the house. I hoped mentioning my father didn't scare him off. Besides, I was only half kidding. Reno didn't get any say in this, and if he tried to, we'd need to come to blows.

"I'm not serious," I whispered in his ear. "But I would rather not go to my old stomping grounds. Brings up old memories. Is there somewhere else we can be married quietly?"

"There are so many places we can get married. We can get married right here. All we need are a couple of witnesses. I'm sure Jack would."

"I'm sure Cassie would."

Without setting me back on my feet, he laid me carefully on the couch and covered me with his body without his lips moving away from me. His fingers deftly plucked at the buttons of my shirt. With the sling, he'd have to try much harder than that.

"What about your job? Are you going on another assignment soon?"

His teeth captured my earlobe, emitting a gasp from me. "I'm retiring."

My hand met the wall of his chest, giving him a feeble push until he was staring at me with wide eyes. *Oh, I dared.* Taking a break from my job was one thing. *Retiring* from his job was another. He wasn't even thirty yet.

"You're quitting?"

Sighing, he pushed my hair behind my ear. "Can we talk

about this later? I want nothing more than to get you naked. We can go through all of this once I've had my way with you."

I giggled, cool air washing over me after he successfully separated the two halves of my shirt and worked it over one of my shoulders. Firm hands pulled my hips until my legs wrapped around his waist.

"Ty?" I murmured.

"Mmmm?" came his reply, his lips pressing a blazing trail down my collarbone.

"I love you."

He lifted his head, eyes shimmering. "God, I love you, Riley."

Chapter Thirty Three

The bump of the ferry against the dock knocked me backwards against Ty, who only tightened his arms around me. We stood on the deck watching the island of Cape Haven draw nearer. Regan said she hadn't seen the island so packed full of people, especially after the island's Labor Day celebration had ended. We were lucky to get a spot on the ferry, people still flocking to resorts on the island for a much needed get away.

"Are you ready?" he murmured against the curve of my ear.

I turned in his arms, my arms firm around his waist. "I'm so excited to see them. It's been too long."

"Not that long."

Dramatically, my eyes rolled as I disengaged and hooked my hand in his to lead him back to our rental car. "Long enough. I got used to having them around, and then they had to go."

Ty released me, only so we could get back into the car. "You were spending almost all of your time at my place anyway," came his reply. "Not that I'm complaining."

"You asked me what I wanted."

He kissed my knuckles, waiting patiently for the ferry to weigh anchor and the gates to open. "Something I'll never regret. These last couple months have been nothing short of amazing."

I grinned. He wasn't wrong by a long shot. Amazing didn't come close to describing it. Gus and Gatsby were ecstatic to run around the yard, and with the lake to take turns leaping off the dock. Everything I said I wanted, he gave. And then some.

Ty had 'retired' from the police force, but only to open his own private investigation firm. Reno, catching wind of what Ty would do for me, insisted on setting me up with an allowance until I got back on my feet and that had set us up considerably well. He told me to consider it everything I was due for the first fourteen years of my life that both he and Simone had robbed me of.

I hadn't returned to the agency, not that Maria hadn't tried hard to get me back. I loved my job, but my arm had to recover. It took a few weeks before I could finally remove the sling. Then weeks of physical therapy to get a full range of movement back until I could return to work. But my heart belonged to something else. Rescuing dogs, yes, but more of a rehoming than a re-stealing. And helping Ty with investigative work.

Ty and I decided once we got home, I would start taking on clients in situations that needed to find homes for animals because of illness, old age, loss of income, any type of situation where they found they could not care for their animals. We had hope that we'd save many animals from being dropped at animal shelters and euthanized.

As soon as Ty drove off the ferry, my eyes widened at the scene unfolding before me. Main street, a row of restaurants, shops and the hotel, all faced south toward the beach. The tallest on the street was the hotel, owned by Regan's mom. The beach looked endless, curving around the southern side of the island to the right of the ferry. I looked out the window at the bodies crowding the beach.

The day was beautiful, the sun still plenty hot enough to take in a nice suntan before winter was on us. Houses lined up behind the beach, and I knew Regan's house was one of them, the one Ty and I would stay at while we were here. Cameron and Regan were living in Cameron's house up the coast, making it their permanent home.

"Regan texted. They're at her house getting things ready for us," I said. "Go right on main street."

He laughed. "You just tell me where to turn."

"Deal." I pressed a hand to my stomach. "Why am I suddenly so nervous?"

Ty slid his hand into mine, keeping one hand firmly on the wheel. "Breathe, Riles. They'll understand. Trust me."

"Regan will. It's Cam that has me worried. He's overbearing and overprotective." I paused, keeping my eyes glued out the window. "Oh, my God. It's beautiful here. Can't we just live here?"

Beach games were abound, kids splashing in the waves. The town was quaint and inviting. Touristy, but welcoming. I loved it.

"There probably isn't a lot of investigative work to be found here. Or animals that need to be rehomed, but I'm sure we can make beaded necklaces to sell on the beach if you really want. We'd make it work."

Giving him a soft punch to the arm, I pursed my lips and continued to gaze longingly out my window while he turned   on main street. Even after his reminder to pay attention, I felt the need to wipe the drool from my chin.

"I'll settle for visiting. Regan said we could anytime."

"She says what she means."

"That she does." I was silently counting each house that we passed, surprised they weren't all crowded together They actually had space enough between so you could still see the house next door but not directly into your neighbor's windows. "Right here!"

He laughed again, and I decided I would never tire of the deep rumble of his laugh. Still holding my hand, he gave it a squeeze while pulling into the circular drive. These houses were stunning. Even after living in Cassie's house for the last few years, I wasn't sure I'd ever get used to staying in these kinds of houses.

When the car stopped, I slid out without waiting for him and he grabbed our bags from the trunk before following me to the door. Knocking would have been useless. The door swung open and Regan pulled me into her arms. Geez, but she was strong.

"I'm so glad you're here!"

"She's been waiting," Cameron drawled, coming around the corner with the baby cradled casually in the crook of his arm like he was holding a football.

To see him, with his enormous arms cradling such a tiny baby, blew my mind. It seemed like yesterday he was worried about being a father. Ty closed the door as I covered my mouth, smothering my screaming gasp at the sight of their baby.

"You won't wake him up," Regan said with a chuckle. "He sleeps like the dead. Such a good little man, already. I'm sure the next one is going to be a terror."

"That she's thinking about having another one after what she just went through makes me doubt my strength," Cameron said, but he was looking directly at Ty.

A tear eased out of the corner of my eye when I stepped closer to Cameron, peering down at the tiny round face with the smallest fist I had ever seen tucked up beneath his chin. Another tear sprung out. *Oh no*, I thought. *Not now. Hold it together.* I hadn't had moments of panic since the day David died, but I was extremely emotional. It took little for me to shed a tear, happy or sad.

"Nicholas," I breathed, reaching out to pull away the baby blanket to see his sweet face better. Perfection greeted me back.

"Nicholas Cameron Moretti," Regan said, the pride thick in her voice.

"Nicco for short," Cameron added.

I couldn't miss the glance Cameron gave Regan, or her sly smile. Nicco was one of Regan's earliest friends, serving as her driver as a young girl, unfortunately caught in the crossfire during her kidnapping by her father's enemy. Even though Gavriel De Luca had tried to make amends for getting rid of the driver for what hadn't been his fault, Regan forgave him but could never forget.

"Riles, are you okay?" Cameron asked.

I swiped at the wetness on my cheeks, surprised at how many tears I had spilled and only shedding more. "Yes. No." I looked at Ty.

He set down the bags, moving toward me quickly. "I told you, they'll understand."

"Understand what?" Cameron said, his voice tight as he passed off Nicco to Regan.

Shit. Regan laid Nicco down in his travel bassinet, coming to stand next to Cameron with equal concern in her eyes. "I'm um, I'm . . . pregnant," I whispered.

Cameron took a step toward Ty, but Regan slid her hand around his arm and he stopped from moving any further. Still, he pointed his finger at him. "Make it right, my friend. If you don't, my father won't allow it. A Moretti doesn't shirk duty, and that goes for his daughters."

Ty smiled. "There's no need for threats."

"There is," Cameron insisted. "You may not understand how important she is."

The feel of his fingers dancing up my spine was warming. "I understand perfectly how important she is, Cam. How can I not?"

I heard Regan laugh under her breath, shooting her a look. "I don't think I've seen Cameron this rattled for a while. When are you due?"

"Not until there's a wedding." Cameron's eyes dancing in animosity.

"Cameron!" I gasped.

"Calm down. Please." Regan slid her hands up his arm, and I thought for a moment he would shuck her off, but he covered her hand with his and took a deep breath.

"That's not all," I said. "We've made arrangements to get married while we're here. Everyone is on their way. Reno, Naomi, Hannah, Ty's family, our friends." I looked back at Ty, who rewarded me with his smile, before I looked back at Cameron. "We would have gotten married at home, but I couldn't do it without you there."

Never in all the years I had known Cameron had I seen him at a loss for words. He looked like he was being strangled but pleased. Regan left his side, hugging me tightly.

"Congratulations on the wedding and the baby. I would imagine you aren't too far along?" A smile curved my lips. "You are?"

"Three months," I whispered. "I think we might have been not careful enough."

"I wasn't, and she didn't make it easy to be," Ty admitted, guilt etched on his face. "But I'll be damned if I regret it. God gave me this woman and is giving me another gift. I can only be thankful."

Cameron finally snapped out of it, stepping toward Ty with his hand extended. "You're lucky. I was about to beat your ass."

"Right," Ty laughed. "You can try."

"Someday . . ."

Cameron pulled me into his arms, resting his chin on the top of my head. "Little sister," he whispered. "I can't begin to tell you how much I appreciate you not getting married without me. I'm not sure I could have forgiven you that. Even you."

Regan and I looked at each other, grinning. "Come in, let me show you around and then you can tell me all about these wedding plans you made in secret."

◆

If I thought the sunrise in Seattle was the best, and the one in Malibu second best, I had never experienced it on Cape Haven. The morning of the wedding, I woke wrapped in Ty's arms with a smile on my face. The house was full, as was the hotel. Reno was due to arrive midmorning but Naomi, Hannah and Cassie had arrived yesterday morning and had grabbed rooms in Regan's beach house while Ty's parents and brothers had arrived and got rooms at the hotel.

Ty and I had been planning this for a while and had secretly booked the rooms before they could fill up for this weekend. Jack came in with Ty's family but he refused to get a hotel room and was bunking on the living room couch, swearing that he wasn't leaving Ty in a house full of women. I think there was more to it than that, the way I saw him watching Cassie but I had known Jack enough to know Cassie would never let him get close enough. She was too smart. She knew a man who chased women when she saw one.

I turned in Ty's arms, burying my head between his shoulder and neck while his arm pulled me closer. "Not sure I can wait," he murmured.

"Cameron's lucky I felt inclined to include him," I admitted. "But you know I would regret it if he and Regan weren't here. And this place is more perfect than I thought it would be."

"As much as I don't want to let you go, I know you have an appointment this morning." His hand traveled up my side, curling around my waist. "Damn it, but I wish we could stay here in bed."

My mouth found his. "Tomorrow," I promised before slipping

out of bed.

As soon as my feet touched the floor, there was a knock at the door. "Riley, we have to go soon or you're going to be late!"

Cassie was nothing if not punctual. She wasn't about to let me run late today, and I was glad for it. Ty was watching me pull on my leggings, throwing a loose-fitting t-shirt over my head before I blew him a kiss and slipped out of the bedroom.

A half hour later, I was sitting in the salon with my hair in large curlers and facing a mirror waiting for the stylist to come back to do my make-up. The wedding wasn't going to be a big affair, but it was going to be on the beach up toward Cameron's house where it was more private with less residential houses. I was sneaky when I called around to make inquiries about the geography of the island.

"Have I told you how proud I am of you?"

I turned to Naomi, smiling. "If you're going to make me cry, do it now before she does my make-up. You know how weepy I've been lately."

She only shook her head. "I won't make you cry. I just wanted you to know that I'm proud of you. I can't even get mad at you for getting pregnant. Ty is perfect for you."

Tears were forming. "He is. And I've always known you were proud of me. If it weren't for you, I wouldn't be where I am today. Neither would Hannah. It's because of you that she's able to miss some of her senior year to be here. You gave us a fighting chance."

Naomi patted my hand and wandered away. When the stylist came back, she did my make-up in record time, pulling the curlers out of my long, dark hair to reveal big bouncing curls that cascaded down my back. My eyes widened at my reflection. This wasn't me. I didn't look like myself. I looked . . . nice. She pinned and wound my hair up, leaving part of it down.

We were to get back to the house to get dressed before heading up to the beach to meet the rest of the party, and my husband-to-be. Warmth spread in my heart when I thought of Ty as my husband. We had waited patiently enough for the   last couple months, and it was nearly time.

Ty and Jack had gone to Cameron's house to get ready while Regan and Nicco were waiting at her house when we got back. But she wasn't alone. When we walked into the door, I saw Reno stand up from the couch with Nicco in his arms, Orianna by his side. Almost the same as Cameron, he looked like a giant next to the little baby in his arms. It was crazy to think he was going to be a grandfather once more in six months.

Orianna looked at me, really looked at me. She inclined her head, an acknowledgement to me. "I hope you'll accept my apology for my behavior toward you, Riley."

"Behavior?"

Her smile was demure. "Let's not mince words. I've not been welcoming of you into my world. But, I hope you know I do welcome you. I accept you're a part of our lives now." She smiled. "And I heard you are pregnant, which pleases me a great deal."

"You like children?"

When she laughed, I was surprised. It was the first time I'd ever heard her laugh though I'd not spent a lot of time in her company. I exchanged a look with Regan, which told me she was experiencing the same.

"My dear, I didn't have four children because I didn't like them. Now, I will be out of your way now and give you congratulations. I'll see you all later."

While Orianna took her leave, Reno passed Nicco back to Regan, walking to me and folding me in his arms without a word. I couldn't help but notice how careful he was not to mess up my hair or make-up. A kind consideration but I fear that my makeup was going to be ruined before the wedding whether I liked it or not. Someone was going to make me cry.

"You look stunning, my daughter," he whispered, pulling away from me and cupping my face in his big hands. "I couldn't be prouder of you."

I smiled, pressing my hands to his. "Are you sure you aren't mad that I'm making you a grandpa again?"

He laughed, deep and melodious. "You should know by now that I adore children. And you should also know that I don't intend on missing out on any more of your life."

"That goes for me, too."

My head snapped up at the familiar voice coming from the deck. I looked around Reno to see Simone stepping in, looking much different in a summery dress. Her hair was swept up, wisps escaping and falling gently away from the clips.

"Simone . . ." I wasn't sure what to say. She looked like a different woman. "Mom."

A slow smile curved her lips when she stopped next to Reno. "Are you surprised?"

"I am. You look so good. I didn't think I would ever see you again."

Her smile deepened when she looked up at Reno. "Reno contacted me again after you left and convinced me to get help. He promised to help get me out of there and into a better life. I went to Arizona to a treatment facility. It's been hard but I'm doing my best."

"How long have you been sober?"

"Only about a month. I left the facility to come here under Reno's careful watch, but I'm going right back to complete my program. Reno is helping me to find a job and get a place of my own, away from Las Vegas." She looked up at him. "If it wasn't for his generosity, I'd be stuck with Vic."

I pulled her into my arms, tears running despite my effort to keep them in. "I am so happy," I whispered. "We will do everything we can to help you."

The feel of her arms coming around me was like nothing I had felt before. Never before had I remembered my mother holding me. That did it. The dam broke, but Regan was quickly coming to the rescue.

"Okay, okay," she said, a tissue in one hand with Nicco cradled in her arm easily. "You have plenty of time for a reunion, and tears, after the wedding. Let's get dressed and head on up before those boys get stupid."

"Cameron wouldn't do that," I said, pulling away from Simone giving her a wink.

"The hell he wouldn't. Same as Ty. You're just too in love to know that."

Laughter burst out of me. "You're one to talk! You're still technically newlyweds."

"Simone and I are heading up the beach with the others, so you can finish getting ready," Reno called out to us.

Regan and I turned, smiling our secret smiles. "We'll be right behind you."

I met Reno's gaze. "I'll meet you in the house. I hope you'll allow me to walk you down the aisle, or er . . . down the beach."

"I hoped you would."

Regan took my arm, but Reno wasn't finished yet and I turned back to him even when I sensed her aggravation that   he was stalling. "You should know that Ty called me."

I half turned. "He did what?"

"He called me. He said he couldn't marry you without my permission."

"And you gave your permission?"

He spread his arms wide. "He doesn't need it, but I respect that he asked. Other than my sons, and Gavriel, I've little respect for many other men. But Ty is different. Other than getting you pregnant before getting married, he has my utmost respect. So I'll forgive him that."

I disengaged from Regan and went to Reno, putting my arms around his neck. My actions might have surprised him. It took him a moment before I felt his arms come around me, holding me tight. All the years we lost, I was determined to make up. I turned back to look at Simone, giving her a smile. God willing, my mother would be a part of my life going forward in addition. Not together, but at least a part of my life. There was only one thing missing, and that was something I wasn't going to wait another minute for.

I withdrew from Reno, motioning for Regan to hurry so I could get changed. The need to be married to the love of my life was pulling me, and I wasn't about to wait any longer.

Chapter Thirty Four

Nervousness wasn't something I typically experienced, but when I was standing in Cameron and Regan's house looking at the people on the beach out the window, nerves started infiltrating my calm demeanor. There weren't many people on the beach and I could see Ty standing next to Cameron. They were both dressed casually, in khaki shorts and loose button-up shirts.

"Don't be nervous," Regan whispered behind me.

I turned with a smile. "How did you know?"

"When you're pregnant, you experience a lot of things you didn't before. Focus on Ty. It's just you and him."

That I could do. "Thank you. For being there for me."

"Anytime. I'm going now. Reno is waiting."

I turned while Regan hurried out the patio doors leading to the deck and beach below, sensing Reno behind me. He was dressed a little more formally in a pair of dress pants with a loose-fitting shirt. He offered his arm to me and I slipped mine through, the nerves easing when he tightened his arm to pull me a little closer.

"Thank you for this," I whispered.

Suddenly, I couldn't believe that Ty and I were going to get married without having anyone with us but a few people. Reno and I were only just getting to know one another, but from the way he looked at me with such pride in his eyes, I knew we would have regretted it. Changing our minds to get married here, surrounded by the people that loved us was the best decision we could have made.

"My dear, it's the least I could do for you."

We glided toward the doors. "Please don't feel guilty about the past. What's done is done, and there isn't anything that either of us could have done. What you're doing now, for me and Ty, and for Simone, is more than I could ever ask."

"None of this would have happened, had I believed her."

I shook my head. "You can't think like that. What you're doing for her now might have saved her life. I can't promise you she'll stay sober, but she's giving it a chance. That's more than she's ever done before."

"The only reason she agreed to go to treatment was because I apologized to her and recognized my mistake. None of it was her fault." A deep sigh slipped from his throat. "She might not have fallen into this life if I had provided for you and her. Enough of this, though. You have an eager man waiting for you."

He patted my hand as we walked across the deck and stopped at the edge of the deck. All eyes were on us. The breeze stirred my dress, the lightest fabric I had ever worn. It was loose-fitting except for the bodice, tickling against my legs. I looked down at my bare feet. No socks. This was me. And this was the perfect way to get married.

When I looked up, my eyes caught Ty and I would have stumbled headlong down the wooden steps if it hadn't been for Reno holding my arm. The look in Ty's eyes was so intense. The feeling that I couldn't wait to get down to him and feel his arms around me rushed against me, flooding me with emotion.

"Calm," Reno whispered. "Don't panic now."

I laughed. "I won't. Not this time."

We stepped down onto the beach, walking carefully across the sand to the makeshift altar set off to the side from the dock. The sound of the waves washing gently against the shore and the feel of sand between my toes calmed me. The local island man we hired to marry us stood next to Ty, but I hardly saw him, or anyone else standing on the beach. I only saw Ty. The breeze was ruffling his blond hair. I could already guess he had been running his hand through it nervously.

I almost laughed when Reno handed me to him, welcoming the feel of Ty's hands clasping mine, strong and confident. Memories of when Cameron and Regan were married flooded my thoughts and how Cameron had started kissing her in the middle of the ceremony. I wondered if Ty was going to do the same thing, the way he was looking at me.

But he didn't. He kept my hands in his while the officiant began the ceremony. Ty's eyes never left mine. I couldn't hear anything but the waves. I couldn't see anything but Ty looking at me. There was nowhere else I wanted to be.

When we exchanged our vows, I needed no encouragement. There was nothing else in the world I wanted more than to be Ty's wife. When the officiant announced us as husband and wife, Ty had only to give me a tug and I fell into his arms with a laugh. It was abruptly cut off with his mouth on mine.

"I love you," he whispered.

His hand curled around my neck, lips meeting mine with persistence until we heard a few throat-clears from our audience. When he pulled back, the blue of his eyes sparkled.

"Happy?"

I nodded. "I couldn't be more. I love you so much."

"Good because now you're stuck with me."

"I think maybe you're stuck with me."

When he pulled our joined hands up and kissed my knuckles, I could see a tear in the corner of his eye. "I won't lose you, Riley."

"No," I said. "We won't lose each other."

Everyone began to clap and whistle, our blissful bubble about to be abruptly interrupted by well-wishes. We'd have a casual evening with our family and friends on the beach with a cook-out, having invited some additional people Regan and Cameron knew on the island, including Regan's mom Isabel. But later . . . that was for us.

I had only one regret. And that was not being able to live closer to Cameron and Regan, and baby Nicco. Maybe one day we would, but for now, I wouldn't give up my life for anything. I was exactly where I wanted to be, and who I wanted to be.

Author's Note

I've mentioned several issues in this book, none of which I take lightly. As a writer, I always strive to make sure facts are accurate but also to be mindful of my audience. But I'm also here to tell you a story and as my copyright page states, "this book is a work of fiction". When it states that characters and incidents are either used as a product of my imagination or used fictitiously, this isn't just words thrown on the page to warn people. It is true. I know people who struggle with mental health issues, myself among them. I know lots of people who struggle with lots of things. I imagine there are probably a lot of us out there struggling in this day and age. When I was growing up, you didn't talk about these things while today they're discussed openly. Know that you are not alone in whatever struggles you face, whether you struggle with panic attacks, alcoholism, depression, anxiety, autism, and a plethora of other issues. There is always help.

Acknowledgements

I would be remiss if I did not thank those who have supported me through this last year. Family, friends, neighbors, acquain-tances, friends of friends, community . . . so many have been there. There are not enough words to express my gratitude to those who have helped me along. There is no turning back now.

My beta readers of this book – Emily, Tonya, Jackie and Jessica – I know none of you would give me anything but your unbiased, honest opinion. For that, I appreciate you more than you will ever know.

To my children, Blake and Brooke, I hope I have taught you determination and to go after your dreams. Life is too short to let it slip by. Go for it. I hardly doubt you will regret it.

Find more books by

Jodie Leigh Murray

by scanning the QR code below

Books are also available through:

Amazon

barnesandnoble.com

Bookshop.org

Tertulia

Select Bookshops

www.ingramcontent.com/pod-product-compliance
Lightning Source LLC
Chambersburg PA
CBHW071411300726
48976CB00006B/2065